# She was black

In the days before the nukecaust, that had made a difference. Being in this community had put her back in touch with that lost part of herself, and that was good. But was it that great when it came to making her doubt J.B.? Besides the relationship they had built, there were more pressing issues: the companions had been through so much together, formed bonds of loyalty forged in fire. There were things that went deeper than age, race and sex: the knowledge that they would pull together without it even being spoken of or thought about.

And she was doubting that, denying it? There was a rift between her and the companions. But perhaps that was a good thing. It made her examine herself, her priorities and loyalties.

In the end, the ideals of the island were pitched against pragmatism and experience of reality in the world outside.

Some wanted nothing less than war. But who would make the sides in a war?

**Other titles in the Deathlands saga:**

# JAMES AXLER

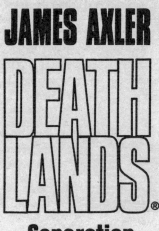

# DEATH LANDS®

## Separation

**A GOLD EAGLE BOOK FROM**

# WORLDWIDE®

TORONTO • NEW YORK • LONDON
AMSTERDAM • PARIS • SYDNEY • HAMBURG
STOCKHOLM • ATHENS • TOKYO • MILAN
MADRID • WARSAW • BUDAPEST • AUCKLAND

First edition June 2004

ISBN 0-373-62576-6

SEPARATION

**Printed in U.S.A.**

Most people are *on* the world, not in it—
have no conscious sympathy or relationship
to anything about them—undiffused,
separate, and rigidly alone like marbles
of polished stone, touching but separate.
                    —John Muir,
                      1838–1912

# THE DEATHLANDS SAGA

This world is their legacy, a world born in the violent nuclear spasm of 2001 that was the bitter outcome of a struggle for global dominance.

There is no real escape from this shockscape where life always hangs in the balance, vulnerable to newly demonic nature, barbarism, lawlessness.

But they are the warrior survivalists, and they endure—in the way of the lion, the hawk and the tiger, true to nature's heart despite its ruination.

**Ryan Cawdor:** The privileged son of an East Coast baron. Acquainted with betrayal from a tender age, he is a master of the hard realities.

**Krysty Wroth:** Harmony ville's own Titian-haired beauty, a woman with the strength of tempered steel. Her premonitions and Gaia powers have been fostered by her Mother Sonja.

**J. B. Dix, the Armorer:** Weapons master and Ryan's close ally, he, too, honed his skills traversing the Deathlands with the legendary Trader.

**Doctor Theophilus Tanner:** Torn from his family and a gentler life in 1896, Doc has been thrown into a future he couldn't have imagined.

**Dr. Mildred Wyeth:** Her father was killed by the Ku Klux Klan, but her fate is not much lighter. Restored from predark cryogenic suspension, she brings twentieth-century healing skills to a nightmare.

**Jak Lauren:** A true child of the wastelands, reared on adversity, loss and danger, the albino teenager is a fierce fighter and loyal friend.

**Dean Cawdor:** Ryan's young son by Sharona accepts the only world he knows, and yet he is the seedling bearing the promise of tomorrow.

In a world where all was lost, they are humanity's last hope....

# Chapter One

Black clouds of pain and despair washed over Dean as he began to surface from the mat-trans jump. Like being lost in a sea of black, brackish water that infested every pore, clogging him with filth and filling his mouth and lungs, it was a complete isolation and a slow death. Every muscle flooding with lactic acid, making any movement painful and difficult beyond imagining, he began to stir, swimming upward to try to strike the surface. There was a patina of light that washed across the thin skin far above, separating the air from the water. He moved toward the light with a determination born of the will to live.

He struck the surface, emerging from the icy thickness below into the weak light of the air above, gasping as the oxygen hit his lungs, the viscous liquid falling away from his skin, dripping off his hair.

That moment between unconscious sleep and awakening, that fraction of a second that seemed to move on into an eternity...that was the time when the hallucinations came, the time when the dreams and nightmares at the back of his brain were called forth to haunt him once more.

It was always this way for Dean Cawdor and, as he floated on the surface of the sea of consciousness, breaking for land, he drifted back to the world of his deepest fears and insecurities, the things that he dare not admit into his conscious mind.

Although not always the same in every respect, often it was always the same in essence. A younger Dean— still the same strong, resilient youth, but still a boy— standing before his mother as she told him of his father, the son of a baron, not the man who was her husband and the powerful baron of his own ville. He could still see her face clearly. Sharona—Rona to him—had once been a beautiful woman. But that was something that lay in her past. She had been ravaged by sickness. Where once she had been slim and graceful, with feminine curves that had drawn the eye of Ryan Cawdor, she was thin and gaunt, her flesh nonexistent with seemingly only skin to cover her skeletal frame. Her once-attractive cheekbones were skull-like, her eyes sunken back into their sockets, resembling burning orbs in which the fire was slowly dimming. Her lank hair hung like hanks of rope tied into bunches to be pulled back from her forehead to stop irritating skin that was beyond pale. Ghostly and gray, her once-smooth complexion had broken out with sores in patches around her hairline and her bloodless lips. Her clothes hung like rags from her body.

"But why can't I stay with you until you buy the farm—why can't I be with you?" he asked, hearing himself as he was before his voice broke, the high pitch sounding alien to his own ears.

"Because it isn't safe," she answered simply. "When I die you'll be all alone. I've taught you how to survive, but a little boy alone in the Deathlands doesn't have much of a chance. Your future lies with your father."

"If he's so great, where's he been when we both needed him?" Dean asked with disgust.

Sharona's ravaged mouth twisted into a wry smile. "He doesn't know about you."

Even though there was a part of him that knew it was only a half memory, maybe a hallucination as the result of the mat-trans jump, he still felt that same heart-tearing burst of emotions he'd felt when he had been separated from her.

It had happened exactly like that, and it didn't happen the same way every time the memory haunted his dreams, but it was still the same in essence. A woman came out of the shadows and took him by the hand, gently but firmly guiding him away from his mother, who stood and watched. As he was pulled farther away from Sharona, he could see that she was no longer the tall, graceful figure that she had once been: she was bowed over by her illness, the sudden stabs of light illuminating the paleness of her face and hands, reflecting the moonlight with an equal deathly glow. Walking backward, he could feel the pull taking him away from his mother, could see her recede into the background, her eyes seeming to follow him, intense even as the distance between them increased.

And then the scenes changed, rapidly passing in front of his eyes. He was reunited with his father who had saved his life. He was in the Nicolas Brody school, then kidnapped, forced to fight for his very life in the ruins of Las Vegas as part of a gladiatorial contest for the entertainment of warring barons. He'd been rescued by his father and the group that had become his friends and family.

Since he had joined the companions, he had forged

strong bonds with all of them, particularly with Ryan, his father. But there was something within him that was still empty, still missing. Sharona had taught him to survive. She was always with him; he could never forget. Yet time had pushed her to the back of his mind. She came to him in his jump dreams, and he remembered her fierce love, a mother's comforting touch.

The light was closing in on him, the brightness hurting his eyes, burning into his retinas, becoming almost a physical force that made the blood pound in his ears as his eardrums threatened to blow. He felt his sense of balance lose any equilibrium it may otherwise have contained. His guts turned, the bile rising as he felt the wave of nausea about to crest.

Dean screwed his eyes tight, trying to block the light and failing as he opened his mouth and felt the contents of his stomach spill out in front of him, everything forgotten in the wrenching pain.

The pain of regaining consciousness.

"CAREFUL THERE, my boy, or you may tread softly on my dreams…or at least, vomit upon them, which is perhaps no more than they deserve."

The soft voice drifted into a high-pitched giggle that faded like a last breath, indicating that the speaker may have little or no energy of his own.

Dean's eyes hurt, the muscles around the sockets cramping. It was only then he realized that he was holding them tightly shut. He relaxed and opened his eyes slowly, slit-peering at the area around him as the outside light burned into him. As his eyes adjusted to the brightness, he could see that he was in the mat-trans chamber, face to the floor. The disks beneath still held the faintest of glow of the activity of the jump, giving the floor a depth that made the nausea return. It wasn't helped by the stench of his own vomit pooled around his head.

Shutting his eyes to stem the nausea and turning onto his back, away from the vomit, Dean slowly opened his eyes again, adjusting more quickly this time to the light. The armaglass walls that enclosed the companions were white, shot through with the faintest tinge of blue. Doc Tanner was the nearest to him, which explained why he had responded to the projectile vomit that had splashed near his legs, speeding his awakening. Doc's lion's-head swordstick and LeMat percussion pistol were by his side. Dean instinctively reached out to grasp his own Browning Hi-Power, which he had placed by his side before the jump.

As he grasped the blaster, a head appeared above him, framed by plaits secured at the ends by beads that draped down over him and partly obscured the face. However, there was no mistaking the warmth in the brown eyes that ran over him with an expertise to assess his condition without hesitation.

"How're you doing, Dean?" Dr. Mildred Wyeth asked, the traces of hardship etched into her skin breaking into laugh lines as she smiled.

"Terrible," he managed to croak.

Mildred's hand moved over his face, her thumb gently lifting his eyelid to expose more of the eyeball. "That's very yellow there," she said half to herself, "and you're sweating badly. By the look of what you've puked, I'd say you were dehydrated, which sure as hell isn't going to help you get over a jump that easily."

Dean raised himself up onto one elbow, then grimaced as the chamber spun around him. "It doesn't usually hurt this bad," he whispered hoarsely.

Mildred turned away from him for a second. "John, have you got any water?" she asked.

"Sure." J. B. Dix came into view. Like Mildred, he was in full control of his faculties and was walking easily, suggesting that they had both recovered from the jump sometime earlier. The Armorer handed a canteen of water to Mildred and she proffered it to Dean.

"Drink, but take it easy or you'll just bring it back up," she told him.

Dean took the canteen from her and took several small sips, feeling the water slide down his throat. He didn't feel any better immediately, but he knew he would after a short while.

Mildred took the canteen. "Take it easy. Just let your balance come back before you move too much. I've got to see how Doc and Jak are doing. The old buzzard's getting as near to normal as he ever does, but Jak's still out."

Dean nodded and watched her move toward the prone old man. Because of the immense stresses that his body had been put through during his two trawls through time, which had seen him dragged from the nineteenth to the twentieth century and then beyond into the world of the Deathlands, Doc Tanner looked far older than his actual years. At times his mind was as fragile as his body appeared to be. He had regained consciousness, but his words and laughter toward Dean were an indication that he was still severely disoriented.

Dean felt his head begin to steady as he looked around the chamber. His father was in conversation with Krysty. Their voices were low and he couldn't make out their words, but he felt a surge of relief through his veins that they weren't only conscious but once more unaffected by the jump. Because, despite the fact that they had so far made many mat-trans jumps with no casualties, the old technology was erratic and its residual and cumulative effect on the human body was still an unknown.

Ryan Cawdor had already shouldered his Steyr rifle, and stood erect, his muscular frame topped by the tumbling curls that were so like his son's, the handsome face distorted by the scar that ran down his cheek to his jaw from the empty socket hidden beneath his eyepatch. Next to him, Krysty seemed small, although the woman was tall and carried her curves on a muscular frame. Her mane of Titian-red hair curled around her head protectively when her mutie sense told her of danger. At the moment her hair hung loose and free, suggesting that they were, for the moment, safe.

To one side of them, J.B. hovered near Mildred and Doc, waiting to see if there was anything he could do to assist as she gently nursed Doc back to reality. She was talking to him in a mixture of soothing tones and insulting words, cajoling him in the manner that he would expect from her as she tried to root him into his everyday reality.

Dean could see that Jak Lauren was still curled into a fetal ball. Despite the strange jump dreams he usually endured, Dean often snapped out of unconsciousness fairly easily and was very rarely as ill as he had been this time around. Jak, on the other hand, always seemed to suffer badly; his thin and wiry frame ill-equipped for the specific rigors of a mat-trans jump. Although in the outside world he was a strong and resourceful hunter, he was always one of the last to come around, and nearly always vomited heavily in the same way that Dean had a short while before. The youth allowed himself a rueful grin; he figured that at least he had an insight into how Jak suffered.

"Yes, yes, it all becomes clear now. Once more unto the breach, my dear friend, once more unto the breach."

"Yeah, still a crazy old coot, but at least crazy like normal," Mildred said with satisfaction as she stood and moved away from Doc to close in on the still-prone Jak, who was twitching as the first vestiges of consciousness began to stir within him.

Doc's eyes, surprisingly clear and piercing considering his state a few moments before, met Dean's.

"A strange world, is it not?" he asked simply.

"Sure is, Doc," the young Cawdor replied.

He moved his gaze to watch Mildred bend over Jak, with J.B. waiting patiently near. Continuing on, his eyes rested once more on his father and Krysty.

He had the strangest feeling. Something had been eating at him from the back of his brain. Something that had to do with family and the feeling that he had to search for something—or someone. It had been there before the sudden breaking of light and the wave of nausea had washed over him to wipe out everything.

But it was gnawing away, trying to make itself known again.

THE REDOUBT WAS EMPTY. The companions adopted standard tactics for exiting the chamber and securing the immediate area. Because of the opacity of the armaglass and the function making soundproofing thickness a necessity, it was always hard to tell if the area immediately outside the chamber door held any threat. So it was a matter of course to adopt triple-red status until safety was revealed.

From that point it was simply a matter of sweeping through the corridors to ascertain their status. A simple task in this instance, it seemed that the redoubt had been unoccupied for some time and the entrance had either never been discovered or breached by anyone from the outside. Because of that, the redoubt was still as fully stocked as it had been before the nukecaust. The companions were able to sleep easily and comfortably for the first time in ages, and also to shower and change their clothes. For Mildred, it was an opportunity to restock pharmacy supplies. For J.B., the chance to replenish stocks of ammo, grens and plas ex. The kitchens allowed them to plunder some self-heats. The canned food, which combusted with enough heat to warm the food on opening, was far from ideal. But when it was difficult to find any kind of game to hunt, self-heats came into their own and kept the companions fed until they were able to find something more palatable.

"ARE WE READY TO HEAD OFF?" Ryan asked as he shouldered the backpack containing supplies plundered from the redoubt, one of several such bags they had filled from the well-stocked base.

He was greeted with assent from the companions, who hoisted their own loaded backpacks and shouldered their newly cleaned and refilled weapons.

"Let's hope that the reason we've found this undisturbed isn't because the entrance is under a ton of rocks," Doc commented dryly.

"You don't even want to go down that road, my friend," Mildred said before adding, "Not that you could, if it was under a ton of rock."

Her good humor reflected how the companions felt. After two days' rest in perfect peace, and the added bonus of a shower and a change of clothing, they felt more than ready to face what may lay ahead.

"Okay, let's get going," Ryan stated.

They made their way in line through the echoing and empty corridors of the lower level to the elevator. Having already tested the car during their brief stay, they knew it could carry them to the top level. They entered the elevator and traveled up in silence. Leaving the car as it came to rest, they walked briskly along the winding corridor until they arrived at the final set of sec doors, which was all that separated them from the outside world and whatever it may hold.

Ryan, at the head of the line, paused before initiating the procedure that would open the door. As did the rest of the companions, he scanned the walls and ceiling of the tunnel, searching for any sign of stress that may have resulted from earth movement, indicating that the door could be in any way impeded.

It was Mildred who voiced the general opinion. "Doesn't look like there's any problem so far—this tunnel looks as smooth as the day it was built," she said softly.

The sec door began to rise, a cool breeze wafting in through the widening gap. As the viewing space in-

creased with the ascent of the door, they could see that
the redoubt was positioned at the summit of a small
hill. A road twisted its way down the incline of the
slope until it reached the edge of a beach, then veered
off to the left behind the circumference of the hill. The
beach was short, leading into a stretch of water that was
about two miles long before hitting an island that
looked to be only a few square miles in size. Beyond
the island, the sea stretched toward the horizon.

"They didn't exactly try to hide this one, did they?"
Doc commented.

"I don't know," J.B. mused. "Facing away from the
mainland, would anyone have come around this side
of the hill? There's only that island and not a lot else."

"Yeah, I can figure that before skydark, but what
about after? How come no one coming down the peninsula has searched this out, especially as it's so open?"
Mildred asked.

Krysty shrugged. "Could be—if there are no villes
near—that no one wants to come down the peninsula,
even if they're in search of shelter. After all," she added,
looking out to the sea on either side of the hill, with
only the distant coastline to break the view, "it's not as
if this is even much of a peninsula."

"Best to wait to see what it's like when we get
around the other side," Ryan said. "Keep on triple-red,
and string out. We'll follow the road." He looked
around. "There isn't much cover for us or for anyone
wanting to attack us, so I guess we should be okay as
long as we keep alert."

The one-eyed man signaled them to move with a
wave of the Steyr rifle that he held in his right hand,

and began to walk down the road that curved along the slope of the hill. Following him down, it was easy for the rest of them to see that he was accurate in his assessment of the territory. The hill was a verdant green, with only small rocks and pebbles poking through the covering of topsoil. There was little in the way of vegetation to provide any sort of cover on the hillside, and Krysty's hair flowed free down her back, indicating that there was little in the way of hidden danger to alert her mutie sense.

The road had a rough shale-and-gravel surface that crunched under their marching feet, the loose rock shooting across onto the grass and down the slope of the hill toward the beach.

As they descended, Mildred looked at the island that lay only a couple of miles out across the narrow channel. It was fairly flat and seemed to be well covered by vegetation and trees. The environment on the small piece of land seemed to be better equipped for supporting life than the barren hillside of the peninsula.

They reached the bottom of the hill and followed the road, most of them glancing out at the channel. It seemed calm as the waves lapped gently along the shallow beach, but as their glances strayed farther out, they could see patches of white water that pointed to a crosscurrent that could be deadly to the unsuspecting. It was likely the island was isolated and uninhabited because of it. Despite the proximity to land, negotiating the narrow channel would be a dangerous task.

Looking up, the entrance to the redoubt could be quite plainly seen and once more it crossed Mildred's mind to wonder why the predark base had been left so completely undisturbed over the past century.

Rounding the hill, the companions found that they were immediately ascending once more, the land on the reverse of the hill narrowing to a band of rock that formed a sharp slope that led upward to form a bridge between the hill and the mainland. The tides around the coast had to have eaten away at the rocks over centuries, chipping away the land until it formed little more that a narrow causeway. The topsoil that covered the hill became more sparse, slabs of rock showing through and coloring the landscape a slate gray.

"I've got a feeling I know why the redoubt has been left alone," Mildred said as they climbed, the incline becoming steeper with each footfall.

It was a rhetorical statement. They could all quite clearly see what had happened. The centuries of tide had worn the rock to a narrow bridge, the shift in the landscape fashioned by the post-nukecaust nuclear winter rendering a causeway at its narrowest point. Jagged shards of rock fell abruptly away to the razor-sharp granite below, which was consistently being lashed by the current as the tides forced water into the narrow channel. Across the divide, which seemed to be about ten yards in length, the causeway reappeared with the same jagged disruption in the pattern of the dark rock face. It was as though the tide and the earth movement beneath had caused a great chunk of the natural bridge to be ripped wholesale from the causeway and just tossed away, isolating the hill completely from the mainland. Beyond the divide, the causeway widened to join the rest of the coastline, where the greenery was lush and the land looked fertile and verdant.

"Fireblast," Ryan whispered softly. He knew that if there was some way to bridge the divide, they would reach a landscape that offered the promise of good living and perhaps a friendly ville. To their back lay only an island and the barren hill, with the possibility of a quick mat-trans jump to another place—always assuming their constitutions could take another jump so quickly. Knowing how Doc and Jak were always affected, and from the way in which Dean had suffered with this particular jump, it didn't seem a viable option this soon.

Jak joined the one-eyed man at the head of the divide and looked down onto the razor-sharp rocks. The albino looked across toward the far side of the gap, screwing up his red eyes to get a better view in the wind that whipped through the hole left by the missing rock.

"If bit shorter, would say try climb down, mebbe get across, then make rope across."

Ryan nodded briefly. "String some across, then hand-over-hand. Half, mebbe three-quarters, of the distance and we could all make it. But this is a bit much for Doc, mebbe for Mildred and Dean, as well. Anyway, who could get down this side, across and then up the other?"

Jak shrugged. "Mebbe me, if water not run strong down there."

Ryan cast his eye down to the cross-tide as it crashed on the razored rocks. He grimaced. "Yeah, try to get across those rocks with no tide and you could probably just about make it. But if one of those waves catches you, you're fucked."

Jak nodded once. "Cut you up like the sharpest knife."

"Nothing to do except go back, then," Ryan stated.

The other companions moved to the edge of the rock for a better view of the channel. Looking along the coastline that lay behind the hill and peninsula, they could see that the drop from the top of the land to the sea below was sheer for as far as the eye could see. Small strips of sand here and there ended in a sheet of rock that would impede any progress, even assuming they had a craft on which to sail around the hill and the causeway. The rock bridge, so violently severed, was their only practical hope of reaching the mainland.

"I fear this may turn out to be something of an anticlimax," Doc said woefully.

"Mebbe not," J.B. told them. "We've got two choices—go back to the redoubt and get the hell out…"

"Or?" Dean asked.

"Or we try to get to that island, see what it's like there. Mebbe there's some life of some kind, or mebbe just a place we could rest up for some time."

"Life?" Mildred questioned. "John, how the hell could anyone live on there, cut off from anywhere else?"

The Armorer gave her a rare grin. "I only said mebbe, Millie," he countered.

They turned and walked back down the incline of the road to the base of the hill.

"What do you think, Dad?" Dean asked. "Reckon we could get out to the island?"

"Not keen on making another jump so soon?" Ryan queried.

Dean tried to keep the darkness out of his voice, but couldn't stop it crossing his brow as he spoke. "I can't say as I'd be too happy about having to do that," he said simply.

"That is something on which I think many, if not all, of us would agree," Doc muttered.

"Rather chance water than go back to mat-trans so soon," Jak added.

"I figured you'd mebbe all feel that way," the one-eyed man said as they hit the road base and rounded the circumference of the hill. They came to the thin strip of beach that petered out into nothing at the bend of the land.

Ryan looked toward the island, judging not so much the distance or the terrain as the state of the water that lay between. For about half a mile or so the water was quite calm. It also seemed to be calm as it neared the shore of the island. However, there was about a mile of rough sea between these two points, the white water pointing to a boiling rage of current beneath the almost-calm surface.

"Do you think we can make it across that, especially with no raft of any kind—and nothing that I can see around here to build one?" J.B. asked.

Ryan shook his head. "It's a hard call," he mused. "I figure we're all strong enough to make the distance. The only problem is just how much of a bastard that current in the middle is going to be." He continued, pointing to the white water that speckled the surface, "And how deep is this channel? Are there rocks under the current like the ones we've just seen, waiting to rip us to shreds if we get pushed onto them?"

"That's an awful lot of maybes," Mildred mused before a grin creased her features. "I'll tell you something, though. We should go back to the redoubt and have a look around. There may just be something we can use in there."

"I doubt that," Ryan said with a resigned tone. "I can't remember ever seeing anything like a raft or boat in any redoubt we've ever been in."

"Yeah, but when was the last time we landed up in a redoubt so close to the ocean?" Mildred countered.

Ryan paused and thought about that. "Not any time I can recall," he said finally.

"Exactly," Mildred said. "The way I see it, there's a chance that whoever used that redoubt before skydark might have had something, even if only for their off-duty hours."

Ryan's face broke into a grin. "Now that's something that I hadn't thought of."

The group turned and made its way back up the shale-and-gravel road that led to the sec door. They moved freely and quickly, knowing that they were safe from attack, and with a sense of purpose engendered by the search for a craft of some kind to take them across the channel to the island.

As they reached the crest of the hill and the small recess where the sec door lay, Mildred paused to look over her shoulder and across to the island. For just a second she felt a cold shiver run up and down her spine, rippling the muscles and causing a pool of cold sweat to gather in the small of her back. She frowned, wondering why she should have such a portent.

"That's usually Krysty's department," she muttered.

"Did you say something, Mildred?" the red-haired woman asked, moving back to where Mildred was staring across the channel.

"Oh, nothing..." Mildred replied, turning from the sea to walk through the now-open sec door and into the redoubt tunnel with Krysty. They walked in silence, Krysty puzzled as to what Mildred had really meant, and Mildred pondering why she had suddenly felt as if something of significance was about to happen.

By the time Krysty and Mildred had caught up with the rest of the companions, they were already in the elevator.

"Hurry up," Dean said urgently. "We need to scour the dorms and the storage areas."

"Why hurry?" Krysty questioned. "The island's not exactly going anywhere, is it?"

Dean shrugged. "I know, but I just don't like being stuck on a lump of rock in the middle of nowhere."

"Fair enough. I guess I know what you mean."

The elevator doors closed and they descended to the lower level of the redoubt, where the living quarters of the long-since-deceased-and-deserted inhabitants had been situated. It was here they were to begin their search.

It was thorough and systematic. Grouping into pairs—Ryan and Krysty, J.B. and Mildred, Dean and Doc, with Jak operating on his own—they searched the storage and dorm areas looking for a boat or for something that they might be able to use to construct a raft.

It was Jak who hit paydirt. Joining him in response to his shout, the companions found the albino teen in a storage room that contained a lot of sports equipment, as well as three inflatable rafts, two canoes and some paddles. It was obvious from their design that they weren't of military origin, and had more than likely been used by long-gone soldiers for recreational trips onto the sea during off-duty hours.

"What you reckon?" the albino asked, smiling as he dragged the two canoes from under a mass of equipment and separated the rafts from a tennis net and two basketball nets.

"I reckon those are a no-go," Dean said, pointing to the canoes. "You can only get two of us in each, and there's no way we could keep any of the supplies balanced."

Ryan agreed. "Those, on the other hand," he added, indicating the rafts, "could probably take three or four apiece when they're inflated, as well as being able to ballast the supplies."

"Only thing we have to do is find something to inflate them with," J.B. commented.

Mildred shrugged. "If they were used here, then the odds are there are some gas canisters somewhere. Guess we just need to look."

Jak rooted around, and located canisters of gas that had been used to inflate the rafts in predark days.

"Hope there's enough in there to still do it," he commented as he dragged the canisters from beneath some boxes.

"Only one way to find out," Ryan said. "Let's get these bastard things down to the channel and try to inflate them."

# Chapter Two

They carried the rafts and canisters to the strip of beach, not knowing if the containers held enough gas to inflate the rafts. What they would do if the inflatable craft remained uninflated was a problem. They had the two canoes, which they had left in the redoubt, and Dean wondered if it would be possible for them to travel in relays across to the island. As the canoes took two people, two would set off, then one would return to pick up another person. With two canoes and only seven companions, it would take a couple of journeys.

Ryan, however, was unsure about the relays. However it was organized, one person on each canoe would have to make the trip twice. Looking out at the choppy sea where the white-water currents ran, with who knew what lying beneath the surface, he thought it would be too much to ask of any of them—even himself or J.B.—to make the trip for a second time in rapid succession.

"Then what do we do if these rafts stay this flat?" Mildred asked, taking the yellow plastic of a raft in one hand and holding it, noting how fragile the material was for the task it was about to face.

"We think of something else," Ryan replied. "But it looks good so far."

J.B. linked the canisters to the valves on the sides of each raft and released the tap that allowed the pressurized gas to pass into the raft.

The yellow plastic gradually began to unfold and to spread out across the sand as the hollows within ingested the light gas. The rafts began to increase in size and strength, the tubular sides becoming harder to the touch.

Ryan and J.B. stood back to let the craft inflate. Jak, Krysty and Doc joined them.

"It would seem that there may well be enough of the mixture within to give us some hope," Doc commented.

"Looks like," Krysty added. "It'd be worse to see the rafts half inflated and then the gas run out. More of a disappointment."

"An understatement if ever there was one," Doc murmured wryly.

However, there was little cause for such disappointment as, both rafts now fully inflated, Ryan and J.B. moved forward to disconnect the canisters from the valves.

J.B. cursed as he wrestled with the aged valve, creaking and stiff from lack of use. "Dark night, if this all leaks out while I try to seal it…" The canister came away easily but he could hear the gas escaping through the valve opening. Closing the valve with a minimum of delay, the Armorer tested the tubular sides of the raft to see if they had lost any of their tautness. The plastic was still hard to the touch, almost like a solid block of wood.

Ryan, having similar trouble, swore to himself as he

secured the valve on his raft. As had the Armorer, he
found the valve to be stiff from age and lack of use, but,
thankfully, the gas had leaked at such a low rate the raft
was still solid to the touch.

"Okay, people," he said, standing back, "guess we're
ready to go for this. J.B., you take that raft with Jak,
Doc and Dean. I'll take this one with Krysty and Mildred. We'll divide the baggage so that we get slightly
more in this one,' he continued, prodding the raft with
the toe of his combat boot.

"Sounds about right," the Armorer replied, casting
an eye over the assembled companions before polish-
ing his spectacles in readiness for the journey ahead.

The division of personnel and supplies was based
on the size and weight of the individuals concerned.
With seven people and two rafts, one would have to
take four and one three. The problem was how to divide the personnel so that the weights would be roughly
equal in each craft. Given that Ryan would pilot one
craft and J.B. the other, it made sense to put the three
lighter people in with the Armorer—who was himself
wiry rather than muscular like Ryan—and to take the
two heavier individuals with himself. Krysty and Mildred were both muscular for women, whereas Jak and
Doc were very light for men. Dean was still—in this
sense—a child. This arrangement would leave the
weight distribution a little uneven, with the emphasis
on the Armorer having the heavier boat. But by taking
more of the supplies on with Mildred and Krysty, the
one-eyed man would be able to balance the weights
more successfully.

The two parties divided and loaded the rafts before

carrying them to where the waves gently lapped at the shore.

"Take it out some way before launching," Ryan yelled to J.B.

The Armorer agreed. "Figure that this tide is deceptive—could push us back easier than we think. Go up to the waist?"

"Yeah, that'll make getting aboard real easy," Mildred said to Ryan.

The one-eyed man grimaced. "I know, I know. You figure how we can get past the wave limit, and I'll go along with it."

Mildred chuckled. "Yeah, okay, boss. I know we don't have a choice, I was just moaning some."

Krysty raised an eyebrow. "Oh, that? Yeah, I think you're speaking for me, as well."

The good-natured banter helped take their minds off the fact that the seawater was icy cold on their legs as they moved deeper into the tide. The current tugged at the sodden clothing around their limbs, flooding the boots on their feet. It had been a conscious decision to not shed these, in case they became separated at some point from the rafts and thus lost their invaluable footwear. It was just that right now it felt as though that very same footwear was weighing them down as the waves washed over them, trying to tug the raft into shore as they pushed out.

J.B.'s estimate had proved correct. By the time the water washed around the waist of even the tallest of them, they had passed the point where the gathering waves tried to take the raft back to shore. Now they could mount the crafts to begin the short journey in earnest.

As the raft bobbed on the water, Ryan held it steady as Krysty and Mildred climbed in. They found it hard to get purchase on the slippery plastic, which gave too easily beneath them, allowing seawater to pour into the shallow basin. Both cursed heavily but managed to balance the raft as Ryan heaved himself over the lip and into the main body.

"Fireblast, I hope this island is worth it," he breathed heavily. "You wouldn't reckon on something this simple being so damn hard."

"Gets harder, lover. You take first pull at the oars," Krysty said slyly, handing him the paddles and pointing in the direction of the island. "Shouldn't take too long."

Ryan took the oars from her without comment and began to pull toward the island.

Meanwhile the other raft had proved to be less problematic for Dean and Jak, who were light enough to mount the raft without much trouble. But Doc had more of a problem, slipping in the water as he tried to thrust himself over the lip, nearly turning it over. It was only J.B.'s hand at his back, pushing him up, that stopped him from slipping back into the water.

"My apologies," Doc gasped as he settled himself and lay back to help balance the raft for J.B.'s entry. "I fear that the sea is an environment I find all too alien."

"Not the only one," Jak commented, barely suppressing a shiver as the icy cold of the water still chilled his bones.

J.B. took the oars and began to row, with some distance to make up on Ryan. His muscles knotted as the sea gave hard resistance to his strokes, making the tendons stand out as he gritted his teeth and gave more effort.

Both Ryan and the Armorer discovered that, despite the seemingly calm exterior, the tidal currents beneath the surface were strong and pulled in different directions, countering each other and attempting to shift the rafts first one way and then the other. Progress toward the island wasn't as swift as they would have liked, every stroke forward also taking two from side to side. If the sea was to prove this difficult when it appeared calm, how would it be when they hit the white water, the area where the turmoil beneath the waves was actually visible on the surface?

"Here it comes—better hold on tight," Ryan warned as he looked over his shoulder to see the first rearing horses of white water approach.

In the other raft, it was Jak who sounded the alarm. "Real bad sea coming…."

If anyone had had the time to reflect, it might have been obvious that the patch of choppy sea was caused by a tidal stream that ran through the middle of the channel. A tidal stream with a current so strong that it cut through other crosscurrents as they pulled the direction of the water every which way— This tidal stream was stronger than any force that any of the companions could exert on the oars.

"Bastard!" Ryan yelled suddenly, his voice whipped away on the wind that now blew hard and harsh across the channel.

As the raft reached the white water, the first blow of the erratic and dangerous tide took him by surprise. He had been ready for something, but not this. The water moved beneath the raft like a solid floor, suddenly shifting direction and lifting it onto the crest, pulling the oars from the water and tugging them almost out of the one-eyed man's grip. It took all Ryan's strength to hold on to the oars, although they were next to useless as they paddled thin air. The raft was thrown up by the white water and spun in a semicircle before hitting the sea again with bone-jarring force. It was all that he, Krysty and Mildred could do to hold on to the ropes ringed around the tubular structure, curling them around their wrists as much as possible to gain a better purchase.

No sooner had the raft hit the water than it was pitched sideways by another conflicting current. It spun across the surface, almost hitting the raft piloted by the Armorer.

Not that J.B. was having any better luck in his attempt to control his craft. The first patch of choppy water had pitched the raft from underneath, upsetting the balance of the raft and almost overturning it. Water washed over the sides and filled the bottom, making it difficult for J.B. to pull on the oars. Dean and Jak immediately started to bail, but were stopped by the next buffet that lifted them up and propelled them forward. At least it was in the right direction. It did, however, bring them into direct collision with the other raft.

"Dark night! If I ever get off this crappy sea I'm never getting wet again," J.B. muttered as the water forced the two crafts together, the hard, inflated plastic tubes crunching together and forcing his craft into a strange angle from which it was all the occupants could do to keep hold. For the briefest of moments the

Armorer caught a glimpse of Mildred, their eyes meeting across the spray of water that washed into the bottom of each raft. He could see primal fear—the fear of buying the farm—in hers, and he was damned sure that she could see the same in his.

And then they were apart again.

"Fuck it! There's more than just water underneath us!" Ryan exclaimed as the bottom of the raft hit the sea once more and bulged in a shape that was gone before they could even attempt to identify it. The shape appeared again at the side of the raft, where it slammed into the side and sent it spinning once more.

"Oh my Lord, what's that?" Mildred whispered as a lithe, black shape moved out of the water and reared up before falling once more into the waves with an impact that sent a huge wall of water washing into the raft. The water hit them in the face like a rock, forcing its way up nostrils and into mouths, making it hard for any of them to breathe.

"Hold tight. If it hits us, we're over," Ryan gasped, securing his wrists to the ropes along the sides of the craft, any thought of saving the oars long gone.

No sooner had he spoken than the creature reared up in front of them. Whatever it was, it was obviously annoyed they had crossed its path and impeded its progress, and it was now going to make them pay for it.

Whether by accident or design, the creature faced the raft, its black, empty eyes staring. It was blue-black, the sea glistening off its skin and scales to give it a smooth look. The eyes were like black marbles. There was no glimmer of any anger, pain, desire. Unlike any predatory animals they might have encountered on land, this creature of the sea showed nothing of whatever it felt inside…even if this was anything other than merely the mildest irritation.

"Oh, shit, this is going to be bad," Mildred whispered to herself.

Ryan gritted his teeth and tensed his muscles, expectant of an imminent impact.

Krysty pushed back into the side of the raft, her arms entwined with the ropes in the same way her hair entwined her neck, the sentient red tresses coiled close to her scalp and around her neck, reflecting the severity of the danger they all faced.

The creature seemed to hang in the air for an eternity, surveying them with an almost dispassionate and detached air of calm. It seemed as though the sea was suddenly as calm, the tides slipping away. There was no sound, no spray, no movement of any kind. It was one second stretching out forever. The moment of anticipation. The moment for which they were prepared, but which they hoped would never come.

And then it did. Even though their consciousness had slowed to let them absorb and prepare for the situation, there was still nothing they could do.

With a screech that may have come from the creature itself, or may just have been a trick of the winds and their imaginations, the creature rose, pulled back and then crashed down on the raft.

Even though it had seemed that the moment preceding had lasted forever, the impact was still unexpected. There had been no time to prepare. Mildred felt the thundering impact drive the air from her lungs as the raft was plunged beneath the water for a moment, the creature's downward motion driving them into the swirling currents that plucked at their clothes, pulled at their limbs in opposing directions and tried to force the freezing salt water into their mouths and nostrils.

Krysty and Ryan clung to the ropes securing them to the body of the raft, muscles aching and on fire from the effort of holding on grimly, the nylon ropes burning into their flesh, the salt water stinging the torn skin.

And then the raft raced to the surface as buoyancy carried it upward, the giant eel continuing downward as the slippery raft slid from beneath its body, the flesh of the creature sweeping across Mildred and crushing her into the plastic as she passed. The raft broke the surface on a white water crest, the force of the tide adding to its momentum, throwing it up and out of the water.

The fragile plastic shell flew up, the canvas bags stored on the floor long since gone, the three companions secured only by the ropes they had used to tie themselves to the tubular body. The ropes holding Krysty and Ryan held firm, scoring their flesh but keeping them secured to the plastic shell as they hungrily gasped in air, unable to take in their situation but thankful for the ability to breathe once more.

Mildred wasn't as lucky. The ropes on one side of the raft had been scored through at some point in the distant past and, although nylon didn't fray or rot, she knew that the fibers twisted for the rope had been weakened. The weight of her body being flung back and forth had weakened those fibers that still connected. The upward thrust of the raft as it was thrown out of the water, combined with the momentum of her own body, was too much of a strain for the fibers. As she gulped air into her lungs, she was dimly aware of the rope suddenly giving way. Before she truly had a chance to register what was happening, she was flung from the craft and sent spinning through the air. Ryan and Krysty, barely conscious, were unable to see or to comprehend what was occurring. They were only aware of the jarring impact as the raft hit the water once more.

The occupants of the other raft had been bewildered spectators.

The whole process had taken only a matter of seconds and there was nothing that J.B., Jak, Dean or Doc were able to do about the events unfolding in front of them. They watched in helpless horror as the creature drove the raft beneath the waves, and in dismay as the tide tossed it back into the air, flinging Mildred out and away from them.

"Shit, we've got to do something," J.B. whispered.

Jak was more than equal to the challenge. "Ryan, Krysty, okay. You tired, let me and Dean row," he snapped, shifting easily in the raft, his balance sure despite the current tossing the raft around like a toy. Dean, not wasting his breath on speech, also moved around so that he and Jak were side by side.

The albino youth took the oars from the Armorer and handed one to Dean. "Take this. On count three, start pull. Count three each time," he ordered.

"Okay," Dean replied.

J.B. snapped out of his awe at seeing Mildred thrown up in the air like a rag doll and moved across the floor of the raft to counterbalance Doc, making it easier for the two rowers to pull through the water.

Jak counted, and the two young men began to pull at the oars, feeling the water struggle against them before yielding. Not only were they fresher than J.B., who had brought them this far, but they were two pulling where only one had pulled before. Their progress was swifter and more sure. The raft moved through the water across the current, heading for the drifting raft and the unseen figure of Mildred Wyeth, who lay somewhere beyond.

J.B. continuously scanned the water in front of them. There was no movement from within the raft, although he could see the arms of Ryan and Krysty entangled in the ropes. They were either unconscious or too stunned to move, but they were as safe as anyone could be on this sea while they were in the raft. He cursed as he tried to look beyond, his vision obscured by the spray that splattered on his spectacles, making the whole vista seem blurred.

He couldn't see Mildred anywhere.

At that moment the woman lay on her back in the ocean, tossed lifelessly by the current. She had barely been able to take in what was happening as she had flown through the air, knowing only that she was able to breathe again after her immersion. Idly, somewhere at the back of her mind, it had occurred to her that she was weightless and could no longer feel the ropes around her arms and wrists. But before she had a chance, in her dazed condition, to assimilate what that could mean, she found herself hitting the surface of the ocean with an impact that knocked all consciousness from her mind and body. Now limp and seemingly lifeless, she was at the mercy of the currents.

It was Doc who spotted her. Mildred's light-colored jacket contrasting with the black of her braids spread out around her on the water.

"John Barrymore, I see her! Over to the nor'west," the old man yelled above the sound of the crashing waves.

J.B. scanned the area Doc had indicated. They knew the island lay northwest of the coast, and there was land in view to the left. Desperately, hope lifting in him, J.B. ran his eyes over the surface of the ocean.

He saw her. Her jacket had spread beneath her and the air that had been trapped beneath the folds of the fabric was keeping her buoyant. It was imperative that they reach her quickly.

"Steer to the right," the Armorer yelled at Jak and Dean, knowing that would take them to the left as the two rowers were in a reversed position. Jak and Dean didn't waste breath on a reply, instead putting a stronger effort into their attempts to reach Mildred.

In the other raft, Ryan and Krysty were recovering sufficiently to realize what had happened.

"Fireblast and dammit," Ryan said huskily, his throat blocked still by the unwanted onrush of salt water. He struggled into a more upright position, trying to unscramble his brain and to get a better view of what was happening. All he knew for sure was that Mildred wasn't where she should be, two hanks of frayed and broken rope evidence of what had occurred.

Krysty struggled around. It was impossible to tell how her mutie sense felt about the situation and the imminent danger to Mildred, as her hair was plastered to her head thanks to the buffeting it had taken from the sea. But she didn't need a doomie to see that unless Mildred was recovered from the water soon, it would be too late.

Particularly as an ominous black shape was bucking and rising from the water. The giant mutie eel, still not satisfied with the damage it had wrought, and perhaps in some way able to sense the danger and vulnerability of its enemy, was ready to return for the kill.

Ryan tried to disentangle himself from the ropes; but those that had served so well to keep him secure were now working against him, tangling and knotting as his still-weakened muscles couldn't summon enough strength to pull his arms free. He wanted to wrestle the Steyr rifle and to fire at the creature. Perhaps its scaly hide would be too thick for the creature to be chilled, or even severely injured, but at least it would distract the creature from its intended target.

And that target was obviously Mildred.

The eel was moving purposefully across the water, its slithering motion taking it beneath then over the surface of the water. It was moving with a greater speed than Jak and Dean could muster between them, certainly a speed too great for the frustrated Ryan to take aim and fire at such a range, even if he had been able to reach the rifle. With no oars to row, no strength to row with and unable to even reach his blaster, he watched in frustration as the creature moved out of his range and toward Mildred's prone figure.

"Someone blast the fucker," he croaked.

Jak and Dean's raft had passed the drifting raft occupied by Ryan and Krysty, and although it was gaining on Mildred with enough speed to save her before she lost buoyancy, there was no way they would reach her before the eel. It was moving too fast and its diagonal course would take it to her long before them.

J.B. was on the far side of the raft. Although he had untangled one arm from the ropes and pulled free his M-4000, which with its charge of barbed metal fléchettes would be sure to at least cause the beast enough damage to slow and distract it, there was no way he could get a clear shot at the creature without the risk of clipping one of the other occupants of the raft, particularly as the waves continued to toss the raft from crest to crest, making a steady aim almost impossible.

Doc seeing the frustration in the Armorer's face, and realizing what lay in his way, decided to take action of his own.

"Have no fear, dear John Barrymore, I have a clear view," he yelled, untangling his arms so that he was able to move freely. Changing position with a speed born of urgency, he moved around on his knees, swaying wildly as the floor of the raft moved beneath him, but determined to follow through his avowed course of action. Pulling the LeMat percussion pistol from its secure place in his belt, where he had also secured his silver lion's-head swordstick, he spread his knees and rooted himself as firmly to the floor of the raft as was possible. Holding the LeMat in both hands to try to attain a steady aim in such hostile conditions, he fixed his eye on the eel as it moved swiftly and smoothly through the water. With each stroke of the oars they were closing on Mildred and the eel, but the creature was closing in on her with more speed.

"By the Three Kennedys, you shall not have her you foul creature of eldritch imaginings," he yelled before letting loose with the shot charge. The recoil, in such unsteady conditions, threw him back on his haunches. He pushed forward and let fly with the ball-charge barrel before having a chance to aim properly, knowing that there wasn't enough time and that he couldn't guarantee another moment of steady aim in these conditions.

Doc's trust in his instinct was justified, although he couldn't have foreseen the consequences. The shot scored the creature on its side, up near the point where its head almost seamlessly joined with the sinuous length of its body. The smooth blue-black scale was ripped apart by the shot, tatters of skin exploding to show white flesh and blood that began to pour into the sea as the creature suddenly changed direction, blind fury and pain causing it to twist in the water as it tried to locate the source of its pain.

Turning was the worst thing it could have done. As its head shifted, the ball charge sped toward it, hitting the marbled black eyeball with a force that exploded the dark, expressionless orb, the viscous contents splattering out to mix with the spume from the waves as the ball shot continued through into the creature's brain. All functions ceased other than the purely motor, which took a little while longer before the eel's nervous system finally lost the last spark of life. This was barely more than a few seconds, but long enough for the creature to wreak one last piece of havoc.

As the raft powered by Jak and Dean came closer both to the creature and to Mildred's prone body, so it came within range of the falling body of the eel. As the creature twisted in its death throes, its downward trajectory brought it in line with the craft.

"Oh my sweet Lord," Doc breathed as the creature hung for one moment in the air before lifelessly plunging toward them as he jammed the LeMat back into his belt.

J.B., at the rear of the raft, had time to yell, "Take cover, it's coming down!"

The Armorer secured himself to the ropes as Jak and Dean dived for handholds. But Doc seemed transfixed, still on his knees.

"Doc!" J.B. shouted helplessly as the sun was blotted out by the falling creature. Then all sense was lost as the corpse of the eel fell heavily on the raft, thrusting it beneath the waves and throwing Doc from the interior as the other three occupants held on for dear life.

Ryan and Krysty watched in despair, unable to do anything to help, and yet there was a chance consequence that was of some benefit, at least. As the corpse of the creature drove the other raft under the sea, the impact combined with the conflicting tidal currents to lift the raft with the one-eyed man and the red-haired woman onto a wave that swept them onto a collision course with Mildred, herself lifted up on the current and pushed in a random direction.

"Grab her, quick," Krysty said through salt-crusted lips, her voice a hoarse bark. Ryan moved as quickly as he could and joined her at the side of the raft, reaching for Mildred as she was swept past. She was still unconscious, but between them they were able to grab her coat and then get a grip on her body. As the woman was weighed down by the water in her clothes, and the deadweight of her senseless state, it wasn't easy for Ryan and Krysty to haul her into the raft, particularly as their muscles were battered, bruised and weakened by the assault that had taken Mildred from them initially. However, with much cursing and no little effort, they were able to haul her into the raft.

Sinking back, Krysty sighed. "Thank Gaia for that—but what about the others?"

Ryan, still gasping for breath after the last effort and scanning the ocean surface as he clung grimly to the ropes around the raft, could see no sign of the other raft. Then, just as he was about to speak, his breath was taken away by a sight that defied belief. The raft with Jak, Dean and J.B. shot up from the depths, having squirmed free from beneath the falling chilled flesh of the creature by its natural buoyancy. It cleared the surface of the water, and, having avoided being caught by a wave, righted itself with less of a bone-jarring crunch than Ryan and Krysty had experienced.

"Dark night, what was that?" the Armorer spluttered, trying to clear his mouth and lungs of salt water, coughing heavily.

"Fucker chilled now," Jak rasped. "Look for Doc more important."

"Over there," Dean retched, pointing to where Doc was visible as he bobbed up above the waves.

The oars had gone from the raft, but the current was pushing them roughly in the right direction. Doc had hit the water from less of a height than Mildred and had been able to keep conscious. He was weakly striking out toward them with as much energy as he could put into the breaststroke. Jak leaned over as Doc got within range and took hold of one of the older man's hands, using all the strength in his wiry frame to pull the old man toward the raft. Dean leaned back to counterbalance as J.B. joined Jak in helping pull Doc into the raft.

Both rafts were now adrift without oars, at the mercy of the tidal currents. Waves brought the two rafts close enough for the occupants to be able to shout across to each other.

"What the hell do we do now?" Ryan yelled. "No fireblasted paddles."

"What can we do except hope?" J.B. shrugged. "Is Millie okay?"

Ryan shook his head. "Still out cold. I'd feel happier if we could get her on dry land, warm and dry. But how the hell do we get past this bastard current?"

"Sea take us over this," Jak pointed out, indicating the fact that the waves had now swept them across the bulk of the choppy waters. "Mebbe we hit tide, take us into island," he added.

"He's right, lover," Krysty whispered hoarsely to Ryan. "Look."

The white water was now behind them. The tidal current that swept toward the shore of the island had now gripped them and, slowly but inexorably, the sandy strip of beach was moving closer.

# Chapter Three

Twilight's last gleamings faded into the darkness of night as the two rafts were gently wafted toward the shore. Once free of the crosscurrents, the tidal flow around the island was gentle, the waves small and slow, lapping at the sands. Each flow took them in toward shore, each ebb, back out a little, making progress without the oars to assist a painful and slow task.

But for the inhabitants of the rafts, there was little inclination to hurry in any way. In one, Jak, Dean and Doc were lying in a state of half wakefulness, their attention drifting in and out with the ebb and flow of the tide. J.B. was more watchful. He was concerned that Doc had taken more of a buffeting than he could stand, and if the older man didn't get warm and dry soon, there was risk of pneumonia. Even with Mildred's skills, there was no guarantee that he could be saved if that occurred. And on a more communal level, it would make matters difficult to carry a sick Doc if the environment on the island were to prove in some manner hostile. And then there was Mildred herself. With little communication between the rafts, even shouting precluded by the weariness and salt-sore throats of the companions, there was no way for him to judge Mildred's condition or its seriousness. He was worried about her.

So, while the others dozed, the Armorer stayed awake, unable to rest as his aching limbs commanded, his brain racing. What if it was a hostile environment? What if Doc got ill? What if Mildred bought the farm? What if… He knew that it was an extreme weariness and hurt that caused his brain to race feverishly in such a way, but he felt unable to stop it. He looked toward the shore. It seemed to be farther away than ever.

In the other raft, Ryan and Krysty had disentangled themselves from the ropes around the sides of the craft and had moved into the middle. Bailing as much of the loose water as they could from the slightly concaved floor of the raft, they had stripped off Mildred's jacket, which was soaked with seawater, keeping her cold and wet. Krysty checked Mildred over. She was breathing regularly, although her eyes were still rolled up into her skull; it was likely the impact of the sea had concussed her. Her pulse was regular and strong. The important thing was to try to keep her warm until they reached shore. The only way they could do this, marooned in this manner, and soaking wet themselves, was to huddle next to her to try to impart some of their own body heat to her.

"Thank Gaia, Doc was able to chill that thing!" Krysty husked the words out through a hacking cough, choking on more seawater that came up from her lungs.

Ryan nodded, almost imperceptibly. It hurt his aching neck muscles to even move his head. "Wanted to blast that son of a gaudy myself," he croaked, "but it didn't occur to me until just now that I couldn't have."

Krysty gave him a puzzled look that he could barely see in the half light of the moon and stars above.

A grin cracked his salt-caked lips. "We'd already been under…blasters are fucked by the sea. They hadn't been under—they were the only ones who could do it. Now they can't."

The full implication of his words hit Krysty. The seawater had jammed the mechanisms of the blasters they carried and the other raft had been immersed. So chances were that their blasters were now also next to useless until such time they had been dried out, oiled and cleaned. Which left them, apart from the knives carried by Ryan, J.B. and Jak, next to helpless…even assuming that they were fit enough to defend themselves against any threat that may arise when they hit the shore.

"I know," Ryan said simply as he caught her eye and was able to read what ran through her mind. "Shit happens. We'll just have to trust to luck."

It took the rafts a couple of long, cold hours to finally reach shore, one last wave taking them far enough in for the weighted bottoms of the craft to hit the sand beneath the water. In their respective crafts, they felt the increased drag of the plastic on sand as the tide ebbed but failed, this time, to pull them backward.

Half asleep, the muted impact nonetheless made Ryan shoot wide awake, his eye opening and adjusting to the night-time light.

"Krysty, we hit shore," he whispered.

The woman grunted sleepily and moved, her eyes slit-peering at her companion.

"Land?" she asked, her voice fogged with sleep.

"Yeah…yeah!" he croaked in louder tones. "Fireblast! We've got to get out and get this ashore before it starts to drag back."

"Uh…" Krysty could do little more than grunt, but through her weariness her brain was working to kick her into gear and to force her tired and aching limbs to respond to what they had to do. She automatically checked Mildred, who was either still unconscious or merely sleeping, and then began to struggle to her feet, joining Ryan. The one-eyed man was already standing, shakily but with a growing strength as adrenaline pumped through his system, clambering over the side of the raft and falling into the shallow tide, cursing as loudly as his sore voice would allow, regardless of anyone or anything that his cries may alert.

His sodden feet splashed in the shallows as he leaned over and grabbed the ropes on the side of the raft, pulling it toward the dry sand. He slipped and fell backward into the surf, but could only laugh hoarsely in relief at hitting land at last. As he picked himself up, Krysty hauled herself out of the raft, and as Ryan scrambled to his feet, she joined him in pulling the craft out of the foaming shallows that lapped around their ankles and onto the safety of land.

"Get it clear, then get Mildred out. We have to try to get her warm soon as possible," Ryan muttered in hoarse and urgent tones.

Krysty saved her sore throat and nodded, pulling hard on the ropes lining the raft as her feet sought purchase in the soft sand, dragging her silver-tipped Western boots from the water-and-sand mixture as each footfall sunk into the surface.

Each inch seemed to pull and strain on muscles that protested with each exertion, but before too long they had the raft on dry sand. Paradoxically, the last few feet were the hardest, as there was no water to give the heavy plastic, with Mildred's deadweight, even the slightest of buoyancy.

"Bastard sea," Ryan spit as he leaned into the raft and tried to lift Mildred off the floor. His muscles protested once too often, the lactic acid forcing him into a spasm of weakness.

"Come on, lover, it'll take two of us right now," Krysty said, coming to his aid.

"Sure we can manage with just the two of us?" Ryan questioned wryly as the woman joined him. They heaved at Mildred's inert body with a pitiful weakness that would have been embarrassing if it weren't so potentially dangerous.

Krysty allowed herself a short, bitter laugh and looked around to see if the other raft had landed yet. "Figure we're going to have to," she rasped.

The other raft was still adrift. It hadn't caught the wave that had carried Ryan and Krysty onto the sands and was awaiting a crest forceful enough to carry that slight difference in weight onto the shore. Without the supplies that had been lost during the short but eventful voyage, the fact that the other raft carried four people was enough to make it just that much heavier, its progress just that much slower.

From the raft, J.B. watched Ryan and Krysty land their craft and scanned eagerly for any sign of Mildred. He was frustrated that his raft was still adrift and waited for each breaking wave with a growing impatience. Looking at his fellow travelers, he knew that Dean and Jak could be woken in a moment to help him pull the raft in to shore, but he was worried about Doc. There was a rattle in the older man's breathing as he slept that could be the start of something dangerous. The sooner they were ashore, the better—for everybody's sake.

Just when the Armorer felt that his patience had reached its limit, and that he would have to jump over the side to try to pull the raft over the tide himself, the craft hit a crest that carried it over the tide and he felt the weighted bottom of the raft bump against sand.

"Jak, Dean, get moving. We've hit land!" J.B. exclaimed, shaking the albino youth by the shoulder and prodding the younger Cawdor—a little farther away—with the toe of his boot.

Both stirred and opened eyes still fogged by their nameless dreams.

"Dammit, let's get this bastard pulled in," J.B. croaked, the words falling awkwardly from his salt-swollen tongue.

He was over the side and splashing in the shallows before either of them were fully conscious or aware. But they were alert enough to realize that the end of their voyage was in sight.

Leaving Doc asleep in the bottom of the raft, realizing that he was in no condition to assist, Jak and Dean scrambled over the side of the raft, the icy cold of the water barely registering as it swirled around limbs already numbed by their soaking and subsequent drift.

"The other raft's already in—now pull," J.B. implored, grabbing the rope and digging his feet into the soft, yielding sand that lay beneath them.

The Armorer was on one side of the raft. Dean took the other and Jak moved to the front, which faced the shore, and both grabbed a handful of the nylon rope that was threaded around the inflated tubular structure and that had already served them so well. Ignoring the burn of the fiber on their skin, softened and wrinkled by contact with the water, all three began to pull, fighting for footing on the treacherous sand beneath them.

Struggling to get enough air into lungs that were already hurting, they used all the strength they could muster between them. With three people to pull, they made swifter progress than Ryan and Krysty had managed, but it was still some time before they bumped the plastic bottom of the raft onto dry sand.

Dean collapsed onto his back, hungrily gasping in great mouthfuls of air and yet still feeling that he was empty, with no oxygen in his system. Jak sank to his haunches, then onto his knees, coughing heavily in great paroxysms that turned into retching as he puked bile and salt water onto the dry sand.

J.B. straightened, every muscle in his back, thighs and calves protesting at being stretched in such a manner when he was so weary, and yet feeling better for the burn of such a stretch.

Ryan and Krysty had managed to maneuver Mildred from the bottom of the craft, but she was still unconscious. Stumbling with unsure footing on the loose sand, and their own weariness, they carried her up the beach and toward the shelter of trees that fringed the edges of the sand. J.B. watched them go and figured that that was the best thing that he and the others could do with Doc.

"Come on," he rasped painfully, "let's get Doc and follow." He pointed toward Ryan and Krysty.

"Yeah, okay," Dean gasped between breaths. He was whooping slightly, in danger of hyperventilating, and was trying hard to control the level of his breathing. Leaning over, hands on thighs, he held his breath for a few moments, trying to quell the desire to gulp lungfuls that would only make him pass out. Nodding to himself, he straightened and joined J.B. at the raft, where the Armorer was leaning over to take hold of the still-sleeping or semiconscious Doc.

Jak spit the last of the bile and salt from his mouth, wiping it across the sleeve of his jacket. He stood without a word and turned to the raft. Taking Doc's feet, he left the older man's torso and arms to the other two.

Doc was tall, but skinny. Although he had enough wiry strength to surprise many a foe, he weighed very little. It was easy for the three of them to lift him out of the raft to follow Ryan and Krysty's path to shelter.

The moonlight was bright enough on the clear sands to cast the faintest of shadows as the three men carried the prone Doc, and it occurred to Jak that they would be easy prey for anyone or anything that may be lurking in the trees lining the shore. They were tired, their hands were occupied for the first crucial moments in any confrontations and their blasters were currently useless. Okay, all three had knives, but they'd be useless against coldhearts with blasters. Looking ahead as they tramped through the sand that crumbled beneath their feet, the albino youth was acutely aware that Ryan and Krysty were in an even more vulnerable state. Their only weapon was Ryan's panga, and the fact that there was only the two of them to carry Mildred would make them more tired, increase their reaction time by vital fractions of a second.

The sooner they found a dry area for Mildred and Doc and secured their position, the better. Because, although his instincts were muted by fatigue and the disorientation engendered by the voyage, Jak had a niggling feeling that they weren't alone along the shore.

Ryan and Krysty had reached the firmer footing of the trees, where sparse vegetation and tree roots made for a more sure, if uneven, surface. The surrounding area grew darker as the canopy of the trees blotted out the moonlight.

"Find a clearing if possible—anything where we can lay her down," Ryan whispered, unable to raise his voice above an almost inaudible volume.

"Sure," Krysty replied, unwilling to risk her voice, but knowing that he would be unable to see any gesture of assent.

Following behind, J.B., Jak and Dean were able to move more swiftly, and were gaining ground on those in front. They were close enough to see where Ryan and Krysty had entered the cover of the trees and so had been able to follow their path.

As they half walked, half stumbled into the dark and cover, Jak felt all his instincts begin to kick in. They were telling him things that were far from good.

"J.B., need be careful here," he said in a low voice.

"Yeah, we could break an ankle on this," Dean complained as he turned an ankle for the second time in a few paces.

"Not what mean," Jak rasped. "Be triple-red."

"Okay," J.B. said simply. He glanced around him as they made their way through the trees. He could see or hear nothing, but he knew that Jak's hunting instincts were honed to an almost preternatural level and he trusted them implicitly.

If Jak could sense a threat, it was there. It was just a question of when it would show itself.

Now only a few yards ahead of the Armorer and his party, Ryan and Krysty had come upon a small clearing in the trees, no more than a few square feet. It was, however, enough to lay Mildred down and for Doc to be placed beside her. The canopy of trees overhead gave them shelter, and despite the cold of night, it was still warm compared to conditions in the raft or on the beach. The one-eyed man became aware that he was shivering, his muscles locked into an almost continual spasm. They needed to stop, to build a fire, to mount a guard and to get themselves warm and dry. Maybe even some proper sleep. That was a thought that wrapped itself around his mind like a warm blanket.

"Stop here," he rasped to Krysty, who nodded agreement. They placed Mildred on the soft floor of the woods and began to strip her.

"Pity we don't have anything dry to cover her with," Krysty huffed.

"Get some leaves, any bracken…just something to keep the warmth in," Ryan replied, beginning to search the immediate area.

The others reached the clearing, J.B. signaling their arrival with a brief and sore-throated "Us, Ryan…"

The one-eyed man barely had the energy to acknowledge their arrival as the second group laid Doc down by Mildred. Taking a deep breath that rasped in his aching rib cage, he spoke in barely more than a whisper.

"Need to get a fire going, try to get warm, dry. Gather some wood. Blasters are useless, so need knives."

Jak nodded, understanding immediately what Ryan meant. Hands dipping into the hidden recesses of his camou jacket, he produced two leaf-bladed throwing knives. One of these he kept in his own palm, the other he gave to Krysty. Now all of the companions that were conscious had a weapon of some sort that could work. And in the close quarters of the woodland, the knives and the panga sported by Ryan would be much more effective than any blaster that could alert an enemy of their position.

"Dean, Krysty, stay here and keep guard over Mildred and Doc. The rest of us will gather wood for the fire."

And as the younger Cawdor and the red-haired woman took up defensive positions, the remaining three companions moved into the darkness to gather small wood and kindling for a fire. Even if it was kept small, it would still give away their position when lit, but at least they would be able to establish a solid line of defense.

Jak, despite the battering his wiry frame had taken, was recovering more quickly than the others and he moved with speed to gather firewood, his blazing red eyes scanning the darkness as his nose and ears tried to pick out the slightest sound to identify it. He was sure that there was something—someone—out there, but he couldn't be sure what it may be. Whoever or whatever it was, it had a gift for concealment and disguise that made it a match for him. The albino youth gritted his teeth and judged the amount of wood he held—enough for a small fire on its own. He nodded briefly to himself. It was enough for him to get back to the clearing. There was safety in numbers, and it wasn't through any kind of cowardice that he wanted to seek that. Rather, it was the knowledge that J.B. and Ryan were tired and may be carrying more injuries than himself.

For Jak had been able to tell that the Armorer had been limping, the legacy of a long-ago injury thanks to a mutie flying squirrel that had taken a chunk from his leg. It had torn into the muscle of his calf, making it a weak spot that would always succumb first in rough conditions. As for Ryan, the one-eyed man had moved in a way to suggest that movement from the waist up—even from breathing—was painful. Jak suspected that their leader had cracked at least a couple of ribs, and the pain and stiffness would make him much more vulnerable than usual.

While Jak ghosted his way back to the clearing, Ryan and J.B. were both struggling.

As the Armorer collected wood he grit his teeth, his calf muscle feeling as if it were on fire. It had begun as a dull ache and had increased as they had carried Doc through the woods. So much so that he had felt himself begin to drag the leg as he walked, the calf stiffening and refusing to respond before a dull ache began to suffuse it. When they had stopped, instead of a cessation of pain, it had begun to grow in intensity to the point where it now felt as if a red-hot knife had been pushed vertically through it. Sweat spangled his forehead, running salt into his eyes as he continued with his task as quickly as he could manage. He, too, was in a hurry to get back to the safety of numbers and an established camp, being only too aware of the vulnerable state in which he found himself.

Ryan, on the other hand, couldn't have hurried if he tried. Like the Armorer, he wanted to return to camp quickly, but the notion of rapid movement was, at the moment, quite alien. Every breath, every step, sent pains around his ribs and chest, shooting back and forth like snakes in long grass, never letting him know exactly where they would appear next. Bending to gather wood was an almost impossible task, and although he gathered some pieces, he soon gave up on that. It would be all he could do to get back to the others. Breathing as shallowly as possible to cut down on the pain of muscle movement around his ribs, he began to hobble back, taking small, quick steps to make as rapid a progress as possible with as little effort and pain.

Unlike Jak, both Ryan and J.B.—although keeping triple-red—were unaware of any presence around them, their own pain and difficulty misting their usually razor-sharp faculties.

It made the group relatively defenseless, especially as Mildred was still unconscious when Jak—the first back—reached the clearing.

"Me," he said simply as he emerged from cover to join Krysty and Dean, dropping his load of firewood on the woodland floor. "Where others?"

"Not back yet," Krysty replied.

Jak grimaced. "You notice?" he asked.

"Notice what?" Krysty countered.

"Ryan and J.B. both carrying injury—one leg, one ribs. Try to cover, carry on—but must hurt like fuck."

Krysty trusted Jak's judgment implicitly. It was typical of both men to try to work through their pain; but given the conditions under which the companions were trying to survive, it was better that Jak had made them aware of this. They would have to pull together more then ever.

Doc began to moan.

"He's coming around," Dean said, leaning over Doc as his eyes flickered open. They were unseeing, as though the old man was viewing a different world.

"Heavens to Betsy, is there no one who will rid me of this troublesome priest?" he asked in feeble tones. Then, surprising them, he shot bolt upright and spoke in loud, declamatory tones. "Are we not men? Do we seek to hide in the shadows and not to come into the open and declare ourselves? What is this that makes us skulk in the shadows? When they came, then came again, I said nothing. When they came for me, there was nobody left to save me. Oh, who will save the poor widow's son? I do not wish to be split from breast to breast and have my entrails spilled across my shoulder, and yet…and yet…" As he repeated the phrase, his voice suddenly quietened and he sank back, eyes still open. "Oh my sweet Lord," he continued softly, "what has happened to me?"

"It'd take too long to explain, Doc," Krysty said softly, mopping his brow. "Just know that you're pretty safe right now, and we're about to build a fire and get warm. Do you remember being in the raft?"

"I think so," he said gently, nodding with wide-eyed

wonder like a child frightened of the dark and sensing a friendly hand in the blackness.

"Well, that was a rough ride, but we're out of it now. Just got to dry off and get warm."

Doc struggled up onto one elbow. "But the good Dr. Wyeth? What has happened to her? I know something must have, for she is always there when I am troubled in the soul and awaken from a nightmare." He looked around, catching sight of the prone Mildred. "Is she…?"

"She's alive, Doc, but unconscious," Krysty answered, holding on to the hand with which he clung to her, tightly and as though his life were dependent upon it. "It's important that we get this fire built."

"What? Oh, yes, of course," he said, suddenly snapping into reality and letting go her hand. "What must I do?"

"You stay there, Doc, while we do this," Dean answered. "You're still not a hundred percent and that was a hell of a trip. Just rest a moment."

Doc nodded sagely. "You are a wise man, like your father, young master Cawdor." He fell silent as he watched them.

The fire was soon built and Jak began to use a stick rubbed onto dry leaves in a channel cut into a larger branch by his knife. In the dark, the first sparks of fire and the smoldering of the leaves glowed dimly in the dark, brightening as Jak blew gently to fan the flame before transferring it to the pile they had constructed ready for burning.

As the fire took, all four of them suddenly became aware of the fact that J.B. and Ryan hadn't yet appeared.

"Hot pipe, where are they?" Dean asked, a note of concern and worry creeping into his voice. "Mebbe we should try to search for them."

Jak shook his head, his eyes like the embers in the center of the now-burning fire. "They not call for help, and not quick as usual. Wait for while. Light of fire guide them if they lose bearing."

The albino youth was right. After a few tense minutes when no one dared to break the silence, first the Armorer and then the one-eyed man came into view. J.B. was limping heavily, and Ryan moved slowly, the pain of each step, each breath, showing on the lines etched on his face. The two men stopped and looked at each other as they entered the small clearing, wry grins appearing despite the pain.

"And I thought I had something to tell you," J.B. said softly.

They made their way to the fire and settled uncomfortably.

"I'm going to see if there's any painkillers in Mildred's pockets," Krysty said, rising to move over to the sodden jacket and rifling through the pockets to see what was left. To her surprise, many of the medical supplies were still within the capacious pockets, having stayed there despite the turbulence and immersion of the short voyage. As they were all vacuum-packed or shrink-wrapped to keep them sterile, it was only the outer coverings of the medical supplies that were wet. Some pills and dressings that had already been opened were ruined, but these were in the minority as Mildred had filled her pockets as much as possible before leaving the redoubt. Although the supplies she had carried in her satchel were forever lost, the supplies she'd stashed in her jacket pockets would do for the time being.

So Krysty was able to give J.B. and Ryan painkillers. She checked the Armorer's calf, but there was no outward sign of injury. And as Ryan gritted his teeth and swore at the pain, she took a roll of sealed bandage, broke it open and began to bind his ribs. Like the one-eyed man himself, she and the rest of the group were only too well aware that he would be slowed up for some time, leaving him vulnerable. But at least his ribs would be secured as much as possible and they could begin to mend.

All the while Jak kept his attention divided between the group around the fire and the darkness beyond the clearing, trying to discern any movement and to identify the danger he knew was there.

"What is it?" Ryan asked simply.

Jak shook his head distractedly. "Dunno. Something, but good at keeping cover."

Ryan sucked on his hollow tooth. "Okay, we're not in any shape to go to it, so we have to let it come to us. I figure if nothing else, if it gets too close, at least Jak'll be able to hear it coming, if not all of us. Stay triple-red. Meantime, we need to see what we can do about Mildred."

The painkillers had begun to kick in and both Ryan and J.B. were able to move a little more freely without the harsh reminder of pain to bring their injuries to mind. The companions gathered around Mildred.

Krysty pulled back the doctor's eyelid. The eyeball was still rolled back into her head, the pupil lost to view. She had no fever, and there was no cut anywhere on her head, just an egglike lump near the top of her skull, where she had hit the ocean with force. She was breathing regularly and easily now.

"Why won't she come around?" J.B. asked of no one in particular.

"It is nothing more than a manifestation of concussion," Doc said quietly. "There is nothing we can do, no matter how frustrating it may be, other than sit and wait."

"Yeah, but how much time do we have?" Ryan countered.

Doc fixed him with a stare. "How much time does she need?"

"I don't know," Krysty said, "but I figure now is the time to risk something she once told me about—she's been out too long."

"What?" J.B. asked worriedly.

"Adrenaline. Just a little shot. It may just jolt her out of this."

"And if it doesn't?"

Krysty shrugged. "We sit back and wait. Just the one shot, no more. That's what she said." Krysty opened Mildred's shirt and pulled out one arm, the muscle still taut despite her state. The veins in the crook of her elbow stood out like a relief map.

Krysty wet her lips, dry with nerves. "Dean, look through Mildred's pockets and try to find a shot of adrenaline. She must have some, otherwise she wouldn't have told me about it or how to inject it. And let's hope it wasn't in her satchel."

THE WARRIORS WERE SWIFT, silent and sure. This was their land and they knew every last inch of it. They picked their way across the foliage and roots in pitch black, using the darkness of their skins as extra camouflage. Their clothes were blacks, browns and muted shades of green, perfect camou for the woods in both light and dark. They carried their blasters across their backs and holstered, sure of themselves not to need them in hand at this time. The blasters were a motley collection of Glocks, Heckler & Kochs, and Colt handblasters that had been looted and garnered over the year before skydark by their ancestors, who had bargained and bartered for a stockpile of ammo that was still extant.

They didn't often encounter outsiders on the island. It was a difficult place to get to or to get away from. So their community had been insular, aware of the outside and yet protected from it. Their ancestors had soon become wise to the problems of inbreeding, so the community was kept small, the breeding between them strictly monitored to keep any such problems to a minimum. It could be done if a people had discipline, and a cause.

They had such.

Yet despite the lack of outsiders to test them, they were a disciplined and slick community. Much of their meat was farmed, but some came from the wildlife on the island. And that wildlife was as likely to be predator as prey. The outsiders had been lucky to arrive on that stretch of beach at that time of day.

Perhaps not so lucky.

The warriors usually hunted with knives or bow and arrow. Rarely did they use the precious ammo, except in their practice, kept to a carefully worked minimum. They were sharp with both forms of chilling.

So when word had reached the ville that there were strangers landed on the south shore, the warriors had soon been ready and had tracked the strangers, keeping their distance.

The outsiders hadn't spotted them, although the albino had seemed aware of something out of the ordinary. The others seemed to pose little threat. Two of them seemed hurt, two were either young or female and two were unconscious. One of these had since come around, but the other was a sister, and was still out.

Why did they have her? What could they want with her?

The strangers had moved away from the fire they had built and were clustering around her. The woman was leaning over the sister, tearing at her clothing. She had already handled her in a way that was undignified, and they talked of her in coarse terms—their whole language and mode of speech coarse.

Barbarians. They could only mean the sister harm.

They ripped her clothing, and now one of them— the young one with curly hair, not the older curly haired, one-eyed stranger—was rummaging through a jacket, looking for something. He produced a package, which he unwrapped to reveal a needle.

They were going to use it on the sister.

The warriors exchanged hand signals, their eyes attuned to the darkness by long nights on patrol. They moved around to circle the clearing, their progress swift and silent. At a signal from their leader, repeated rapidly from man to man, they moved forward, blasters ready.

"WAIT!" JAK BARKED, suddenly turning as Krysty was about to plunge the needle into Mildred.

"What?" she snapped, feeling her hair tighten as danger suddenly signaled itself near.

"Men closing," Jak returned, palming another knife so that he had one in each hand. "All around."

"Fireblast," Ryan cursed as he moved stiffly. His reactions were slowed, but then, so were the reactions of the others.

Before any of them had a chance to adopt a fighting stance, they were surrounded by warriors who emerged stealthily from cover. They were holding blasters. One of them stepped forward. More than six feet, broad and muscular, and with an air of authority, he was obviously the leader. When he spoke, it was in a rich, dark voice of deep timbre that carried that authority like a prize in front of him.

"Though the night is dark it seems that your purpose is like the day. You will leave the sister alone and move away from her. Any of a wish to linger too long will be like the pig who lingers too long near the butcher's knife, and so does not live a life for long. Be aware and learn, my friends."

# Chapter Four

"No choice, I guess... We'll have to let them take us," Ryan said with weary resignation, dropping his panga.

The other companions acknowledged that, moving away from Mildred slowly. J.B. dropped his Tekna, but Jak was able to palm his knives into the hidden recesses of his camou jacket, so that he kept himself well-armed. He did, however, lose a knife as the one given to Krysty was taken from her by the opposing force as they moved in, as was Dean's bowie. The warrior who took Krysty's knife also dashed the syringe from her hand, stamping on it so that the adrenaline leaked uselessly into the earth.

"That was a really stupe thing to do," Krysty said with deceptive calm, straining to keep her temper. "I only wanted to help Mildred."

"So the sister's name is Mildred...unusual," the warrior leader said with a raised eyebrow. "As to your other point, truly it is as the winds that blow the clouds before the storm. They seek to deceive and it is only the harsh experience of time that teaches otherwise."

"Please yourself, but wrapping it up in fancy talk isn't going to change the fact that she's been unconscious for some time and she needs help," Krysty hissed vehemently.

"Indeed, and you were seeking to aid her purely from the milk of kindness that runs like that of the dark fruits during the summers. It is unknown for those of your kind to help a brother or a sister. The reverse, if the texts of history are to be believed. Your purpose is swathed in mystery like the darkness that enfolds us now. But that is of no matter." He gestured with the H&K that he held across his chest, barrel down but with flexing biceps revealing a readiness to raise and fire. He continued. "Now we go. You will carry the sister between you. That will keep your hands occupied and accord her the respect she deserves."

Looking around at the warriors, all of whom had blasters poised, and taking stock of their lack of weapons and the depleted physical condition in which at least half the group found themselves in, Ryan saw no reason to revise his original opinion.

"Let's do it," he said simply. "We're in no state to take them on, and at least Mildred might get some kind of medical attention."

"But—" Krysty began before casting her eye at the surrounding group of dark-skinned warriors. "Yeah, mebbe you're right. We can sort this out later," she said finally.

Under the direction of the warrior leader, the companions made a makeshift stretcher from their outer clothing and Mildred's discarded jacket. It served a dual purpose: not only did they have something on which to carry the still-unconscious woman, but the lack of covering in the chill night left them shivering and cold to the bone. Now they were in even less of a condition to offer resistance.

The warrior leader nodded his approval at their efforts, eyeing Jak in a curious manner. As the companions moved Mildred onto the stretcher, he reached out to stop the albino.

"Wait, my friend. Tell me, why do you allow yourself to be a part of these people—you have difference and should not allow them to rule you."

Jak flashed him a red-eyed glare that bespoke of a wish to do far more than just reply verbally, whilst being all the while aware that he could not endanger his comrades by so doing.

"No one rules me—they're friends." He spit. "All of them," he added significantly.

The warrior leader shrugged. "Truly, we live in interesting times when such things can occur. The lamb and the lion lay down together, it can only result in bloodshed like the seas that surround us. A perplexing problem, one I gladly leave to others. My only concern is to see that the sister Mildred is attended to without further delay. Now move," he added, gesturing with the H&K.

Jak returned to his comrades and they lifted Mildred. With an indication from the leader, they followed part of the warrior pack into the darkness of the woods, keeping close to see where their captors led them. The remainder of the pack followed. The companions knew that any attempt to break into the cover of the woods would be futile. Their blasters—useless though they were at that moment—were in the custody of the opposition. Any attempt to use the darkened woods as cover would mean leaving Mildred behind. Added to this, half of their group was in no state to make a break and the warriors knew the woodlands inside out where the companions would be moving blind. The familiarity of the warriors with the terrain was born out by the fact that the group in front of them moved through the densely packed terrain with a surefootedness that made it hard for the companions, made clumsy by the unconscious Mildred strung between them, to even follow, let alone think about escape. Besides which, they knew that the warriors had their blasters ready to punish any deviation from the route set by those in front.

The trek through the woods seemed to take forever. There was no light by which to see the path or to take landmarks by which to judge the passing of time and distance. There was only the painful stumble through the pitch-black to a destination that was, as yet, unknown to them. For Ryan and J.B. the trip was made less painful thanks to the narcotic effects of the painkillers they had taken earlier, yet still the long journey would be marked by a gradual return of the pain that cursed them earlier. And for Doc, the disorientation of such a journey in the darkness wasn't helping him to retain the delicate hold on reality that he had attained since recovering consciousness.

In truth, it was only Dean, Jak and Krysty who were able to try to assess what was occurring around them and to try to work out where they were being taken. They had neither pain nor disorientation to fog their ability to analyze the situation. This much was clear— they had to be traveling into the island, as they had walked a greater distance from the clearing than that which they had traversed from the shore to reach their campsite. And, despite the amount of time it seemed to take, they hadn't covered that great a distance. From their estimates earlier in the day, they knew that the island was no more than a few square miles in total. So it seemed that they weren't traveling straight, which course may have been dictated by the growth of the woodland.

It had also been an uneventful march, which suggested that the wildlife to which the warrior leader had alluded was either in another part of the island or knew well enough by instinct to avoid the group of warriors as it made its way through the terrain.

"Is that light ahead, or is it dawn?" Krysty asked softly as a glow of illumination appeared ahead of them.

"Ville," Jak replied. "Hear noises…most probably asleep, but a few up. Mebbe sec."

The light grew as the woodland thinned out and they found themselves walking past a clearing where fenced-in livestock watched them idly. Ahead they could see a collection of adobe buildings, immaculately maintained and freshly whitewashed, some decorated with paintings and others left bare. All were illuminated by oil lanterns that hung on the sides of the buildings and were strung across the beaten earth paths that ran between the buildings.

It was difficult to judge how large the ville could be, only that it was a thriving area that was kept hygienically and with a sense of pride in the surroundings. As the companions were led through the streets, sec guards acknowledged the passing patrol and its captives in silence, as though unwilling to disturb the sleeping inhabitants of the adobe buildings. They were eventually stopped in front of a building that was smaller than many of the others. It had barred metal windows where the others were open or covered with wooden shutters or cloth curtaining.

One of the warriors—obviously a sec patrol, or this ville's equivalent—opened the door, and from the dim illumination of the light on the outside of the building, they could see that the interior consisted of a beaten-earth floor with no furniture. There was a latrine dug into one corner.

"I fear it will not be as luxurious as the fruits of exploitation with which your people have always surrounded themselves, and it will be cramped—we do not usually have as many offenders as yourself at one time—but it will suffice. You will leave the sister and enter, if you please."

The words were polite, but the icy tone of the last sentence belied them, as did the manner in which the warrior leader hefted his H&K. The companions reluctantly laid Mildred down and entered the cell. J.B. lingered and was rewarded with an unfriendly prod from the barrel of an H&K wielded by another of the sec men.

"You'd better take good care of her," the Armorer said quietly as he acquiesced, following his companions into the cell.

Once more the warrior leader raised a quizzical eyebrow. "Strange. It's almost as if you genuinely care about the sister. But that would be absurd."

Upon which he indicated to a couple of his men to close and bar the door and turned on his heel to walk away in the lead of the remainder of the pack, who lifted Mildred and carried her off down another alley-way and out of sight.

"Shit," J.B. swore softly as he watched through the barred window until the unconscious Mildred was out of sight. "Where are they taking her?"

"I don't know," Krysty replied, "but one thing's for sure, she'll be safe."

"I hope so," J.B. said softly. "They seem to have this thing about us being white, but—"

"But what they think of Mildred being with us?" Jak finished.

The Armorer nodded.

Dean, pacing the floor, suddenly spoke. "But what I don't get is how come they're against us."

Ryan shrugged. "I figure it's 'cause we're not the same as them. Put it this way—every one of them we've seen so far has been black. Odds are that every-one else in the ville is, as well."

"How did you work that out?" Dean frowned.

"Think about it," the one-eyed man said as he winced and tried to get comfortable on the hard earth floor. "When was the last time you saw a sec patrol that was all the same? Wherever I've been, I'm damn sure I've worked beside black, brown, yellow, all kinds of skin."

"I don't know. What about when we were on that oil well? They kept apart then," Dean countered.

"True enough, but they'd still work together, and know there were other colors, remnants of predark races. And there's still shit about one being better than another, but this is different. Can't explain how, just a feeling I got off the big man."

"There will always be pernicious and specious ideas about skin pigmentation," Doc said sadly.

"Say again?" Jak furrowed his brow.

"People hating you because you're black, or white, or an albino," Ryan said pointedly. "Like he was giving you back when they captured us."

"That's an interesting point," Krysty mused. She walked over to the barred window and looked through, mindful of the fact that the guards were close. She didn't speak again until she had moved away from the window. "When I was a little girl, back in Harmonyville, there were stories. I figured they were old myths to teach us about the shit we'd get for being mutie in some way, but one of them was about a place called the Carolinas, and an island there. Years before skydark, they used to bring black people across the seas just to use as slaves. Only some of them didn't take too well to this and they managed to escape. There was an island in the Carolinas where they settled. A whole community of none but black people, with no other skin. They lived in seclusion and kept away from everyone else, even after the days of slavery were over."

"And you think this may be that island? That they still exist, and made it past skydark and prospered?" J.B. queried.

Krysty shrugged. "I'm not saying that this is that island…but mebbe it's one just like it."

MILDRED OPENED her eyes. Slowly she had emerged from the fog of unconsciousness, driven onward by the throbbing of pain at the back of her skull. A wave of nausea swept through her with each throb and she wondered in some part of her mind that had started to function why it was that she hadn't already vomited and choked as a result.

There was little noise around her, apart from the rustling of fabric and the soft footfalls of one person, moving quietly. The clink of a bowl or cup against a jug and the sound of pouring liquid indicated that she was somewhere with a degree of civilization. She was apart from her companions. She could tell by the lack of ambient sound, with no breathing, speech or movement apart from the single person in the room with her. Yes, she was sure that she was in a building or shelter of some kind, as it was warm and dry, with no discernible breeze. Other feelings: she was aching all over, that much was for sure. Muscles felt torn in her stomach and in her left leg and arm. Then there was that lump on her head that was causing so much pain. Lying on it, she could feel it was about the size of an egg. No concussion as far as she could tell, though, as she was thinking clearly, wasn't delirious, and despite the waves of nausea she wasn't actually vomiting continuously. An ominous ache in her ribs on the right side increasing in intensity when she took breath. Muscles torn or bones cracked? She couldn't be sure.

One thing that she could be sure of was that she was lying on a bed of some kind. It had a hard base, but there was softness laid on top, as though the board was covered with blankets. And she could also feel the weight of blankets on her, itching her skin.

Where were her clothes? It suddenly occurred to her that she had to have been undressed and her clothes removed somewhere. She should be wet through, but instead she was dry.

What the hell was going on?

The room was delicately perfumed with herbs and there was the scent of burning sandalwood. So she was lying naked in a bed, separated from her companions and in the company of an unknown person.

Dammit, this she had to get straight, and soon. But she would have to open her eyes. And in truth, Mildred was a little scared to do that. Not because of where she may be, or who she may be with. Rather, because she knew that the light, however dim, would hurt while her head throbbed like this, and the room may spin and add the finishing touches to her nausea, making her vomit and strain muscles that already ached.

But she knew it had to be faced, so she opened her eyes.

Slowly…

Yeah, it hurt. The light was like an incredible volley of tiny needles that pierced the membrane, making her wince, despite the fact that it was low level. Probably a lamp of some kind and not located directly over where she lay. All she could see was a whitewashed ceiling, decorated with paintings of huntsmen and dancing women. There was something about it that she knew should mean something to her, yet she couldn't quite grasp it. The women were dancing a little too vigorously at present, and she closed her eyes again to try to gain respite from the spinning. No good, even the lights that danced behind her closed eyelids spun in a way that made her want to—

Opening her eyes wide regardless of the pain and

dizziness, and moving swiftly despite the pain from her protesting stomach and ribs, Mildred turned onto her side and leaned over the bed. Rush matting lay at the side, on a packed earth floor that was remarkably flat and dry…though dry for not much longer, as the spasm in her gut reached its conclusion and she retched heavily, vomiting bile and seawater that splattered onto the matting.

Feeling a sweat break out at the effort, she reached down into her guts and willed herself to vomit again. If she expelled it all in one spasm, then she may be able to settle and regain her equilibrium. Once more, she splattered the rush matting, but this time with less force. Feeling the aching muscles begin to lose the force of the spasm, she spit the sour taste from her mouth and returned to her position on her back, breathing heavily. She had closed her eyes to stop the room spinning as she moved once more, and was surprised— but too weakened to protest—when she felt her head gently lifted and a wooden cup pressed to her lips. The water in the cup felt cool and sweet as she sipped it. Her throat cried for more and she tried to gulp, realizing how dehydrated she had become. But the cup was taken away.

Mildred opened her eyes once more, holding her breath as the room spun then slowed so that she could see who had given her the water. The woman leaning over her was, she figured, about the same age as herself, with lines at the corners of her large, hazel-brown eyes that creased the skin deeply. Her skin was darker than Mildred's, almost mahogany in the dim light of the lamp. Her full mouth was also lined at the corners, the lines being up rather than down, laughter rather than frown lines. Her nose was pierced with a single diamond stud on the right side. Despite the darkness of her skin, she was finer boned than Mildred would have expected, with high cheekbones that came to a logical point in a chin that, on any other face, would have seemed pointed. She reminded Mildred of the Abyssinian women she had met when a child, exiled from Ethiopia in the early 1970s when Emperor Haile Selassie had died, leaving the country in the grip of a military junta and a continuing famine. Certainly she didn't resemble the central and western Africans from whom the majority of African-Americans Mildred had ever known were descended.

And when she spoke, she had the gentlest, softest voice, like the tinkling of a brook over smooth, worn stones.

"So, you will feel better for that. Nature is like this. That which does not belong under the skin must eventually find a route from which to emerge, like the burrowing of mammals that need to come into the light to feed and live."

Mildred tried to speak. At first a dry croak was all that emerged, but as she swallowed, she regained the power to articulate and express herself.

"Is that how you'd put it? I don't think I would, frankly. How I'd put it is, Where am I? Who are you? Where are the rest of my people? And not necessarily in that order."

The woman looking over her laughed, a mellifluous sound that echoed her speech. "You have the spirit of a fisherman in a storm. I think I would be more inclined to thank my benefactor and then rest before asking any more questions."

Mildred raised herself up on an elbow, ignoring the sharp pains in her ribs and the insistent throb at the back of her skull as she rose.

"Lady, I am not you. And I've been in too many positions where the only reason I've been kept alive is for the benefit of those who are doing it—not for me—that I'm not inclined to give anyone the benefit of the doubt."

As she spoke Mildred scanned the room. It seemed to be the living quarters of the woman who sat on the bed. It was sparsely furnished, but what there was bespoke of comparative riches. The furniture was well made, the hangings on the wall of silk and the finest dyed cottons, and on a table stood sculptures and ornaments, mostly of animals, that were made of what appeared to be gold and silver. This was no poor woman's abode, but rather the home of someone with taste and jack to spare. It also seemed that she lived alone, as there were no signs of anyone else sharing. And there was no one actually in the room, no sec guard of any kind. As her benefactor appeared unarmed, she was either taking a risk and had somehow rescued Mildred alone, or she was of such a high rank that she could dictate her own terms. The presence of the precious metals made this the likely bet.

The finely boned woman watched Mildred with an amused expression on her face. Mildred was so preoccupied that it took her a moment to realize it.

"What?" Mildred asked sharply. She knew she should be triple-red, but she still felt shaky, and this woman gave no air of threat to which she could respond.

The woman's full lips broke into a smile that showed strong teeth, stained by herbs and betel nuts.

"You are suspicious, and perhaps a little scared. This is no bad thing, and perhaps in your position I would feel the same. But, truly, you have nothing to fear. You are among your own people now, and need no longer talk of those who would wish to keep you alive for your own benefit. They have been dealt with."

Mildred felt a lurch of panic deep in her guts. "Dealt with... What do you mean?"

The woman shrugged. "I mean what I say. Markos's patrol found you before they were about to chill you as the wolf chills the rabbit. You had all been washed ashore, and they had carried you with them until such time as they were ready to do as their will. Fortunately, we were able to prevent your chilling and bring you back to the fold like the stray that seeks shelter."

Mildred hoisted herself up into a sitting position, the pain in her ribs and the intensity of her headache drowned in the wave of panic and concern that threatened to engulf her.

"Let's back up here for a minute, lady," she began, trying to keep calm and to keep her voice level. "When I asked you about my friends, I meant the people I was traveling with. The last thing I remember was being in the raft and... Shit, some kind of big mutie fish turning the damn thing over. We were tied to the raft, but the rope must have broken." She shook her head gently, as if to clear it, being careful not to aggravate her headache. "I don't know anything about anyone trying to chill me when I was out, but the people I was with were friends, and whatever this Markos thinks he saw, they were trying to help me, okay? Anyway," she added almost as an afterthought, "who is this guy Markos?"

A strange expression crossed the woman's face. It was hard to work out exactly what was running through her mind at that point, but the question seemed to stir up a greater answer than she was prepared to give.

She contented herself with saying, "He is our chief of security and law. Answerable only to my father or myself. He was told of a sighting of boats at sea, falling prey to the sea devils and the turning of the tides. It was observed that the boats were washed ashore and that the ones with the shining skin carried a sister into the woods, with an albino in their wake—"

"That'll be Jak," Mildred affirmed.

"Another slave like yourself," she said, continuing before Mildred had a chance to interject. "You were lost to view, and the darkness was falling. It is easy for our security to move after dark, for the beasts are quiet and they know the island well. Markos decided that they would look for you then. And so they found you, and overpowered your oppressors with ease, bringing you here to recover."

"And where the hell are they?"

"They are safe." The woman shrugged. "Markos has imprisoned them awaiting their trial." She was silent for a moment, a thoughtful expression crossing her face, before she spoke again. "Strange that you should call them friends, as that is just what the albino said, choosing to be imprisoned with them."

"Yeah, and I'll tell you what, lady," Mildred said

coldly, ignoring the pain in her head, "you can lock me up there with them. Because they're not my captors, you are."

The woman looked genuinely perplexed at this. "I do not understand. We are your brothers and sisters. We do not seek to oppress you, only to bring you to us in the spirit of harmony."

"Harmony be damned," Mildred snapped. "I think there's a few things we need to get straight. It's like I said—the people I landed with are my friends. We've been through more shit than you're ever likely to see on this island, isolated from anywhere. You say they were trying to kill me? How?" she demanded.

"Markos and the others saw the red-haired woman try to inject you with a needle as you lay unconscious," the fine-boned woman replied, although in a tone that suggested she was confused and unsure when confronted with Mildred's authoritative tone.

Mildred frowned, her mind racing. Krysty trying to inject her? Why would she do that? Her keen doctor's brain, sharpened by the need to focus, raced through the possibilities.

"Where did the needle come from? Inside the jacket I was wearing?"

"You were wearing no jacket. Markos told me it came from a jacket that was full of pills, bandages and other needles."

"I hope to hell that you haven't done anything to that jacket or what was in it," Mildred said in low voice. "I need those medical supplies."

"You are a medicine woman?"

It was Mildred's turn for an enigmatic expression to

cross her face. "I guess you could say that. Yeah, I guess you could. I was the medicine woman for the group. I taught Krysty—the redhead—to give that injection in extreme circumstances. Guess they must have been worried, and I must've been out for a long time."

"But how can that be? They treat you as an equal?"

Mildred furrowed her brow. "Yeah, why shouldn't they?"

"Because it has never been that way. That is why we are here. That is how we came to be here. And why we continue to be here."

Mildred sank back onto the bed. It seemed to her that there were two different stories being played out, and until both she and her benefactor—why not call her that?—knew each other and understood their circumstances, they couldn't understand each other and would continue to go in circles. If the others were imprisoned, at least they were alive and safe. Rather than try to rush matters, it would be as well to take the time to attempt to explain and understand. For this woman who sat by her feet seemed to hold high position in this ville.

"Look," Mildred began, "this is ridiculous. How about we play a little game of truth or dare? Give me some of that water, and I'll tell you about myself and the people I travel with, and then you can tell me about where the hell I am and who you are. At least that way we may start to understand each other. Sound reasonable?"

The fine-boned woman nodded. Filling the wooden cup and handing it to Mildred as she propped herself on one elbow to drink, the woman said, "Your language is coarse and strange in some ways. It lacks the manner of our ways, and so is sometimes hard to grasp. It seems like the promise of rain on the breeze after a drought. It offers a release, and yet frustrates by being forever just out of reach. And yet you speak sense. Tell me of yourself, and then I will endeavor to reveal to you the history of myself and my land."

Mildred handed her the cup and began to speak. She told the woman her name and about her meeting with the companions—omitting the fact that she was a freezie, as this would only complicate matters unnecessarily—before detailing some of the things they had been through together. She talked of Ryan, J.B., Doc, Krysty, Jak and Dean as individuals, so that the woman would get a fuller picture of the people she traveled with. She told the woman about herself, and what she felt for her companions. And she told her how they had found themselves on the peninsula—changing the mat-trans for a smashed boat to simplify matters and stall unnecessary questions—before deciding to explore the island.

"So you did not wish to come here to join us, and they were not trying to stop you?" the woman asked when Mildred had finished.

Mildred shook her head. "We didn't even know the island was inhabited. And I don't know who you are yet, let alone why I should be looking for you."

The fine-boned woman nodded to herself, before saying, "You have been most illuminating. I will endeavor to be the same."

"THE STORY OF OUR LAND is one that goes back through the mists of time, to a place where legends begin and there is nothing that can be taken for an absolute truth. But there are some things that we know to have occurred and men of legend who we know to have existed.

"Mandrake was the name of he who founded our land. He called it Pilatu after the place from where he came. The lands over the distant seas, where many of our forefathers were plucked in their prime to be brought to the whitelands, where they were used as slaves and treated as lower than the beasts. There were many who sought to escape such places, but where could they go where the paler skins did not single them out and seek to return them to those who would claim to lay ownership upon them? For many, the route to freedom lay at end only with the peace of being chilled.

"But Mandrake was different. He stood apart because he had intelligence beyond any pale skin, intelligence beyond many of us. He traveled far and wide, staying out of the reach of oppression by his wits, until he found this island. As you know from your own experience, the strange waters make it hard to reach, even though the mainland is but a short distance as the birds fly. When he found this place, he knew that it could provide a haven for his fellows and make for a land where we could live in peace. As time went on, knowledge of this place spread to those brothers and sisters who also sought peace, and so they began to make their way here. Not all were lucky. There were many who perished and bought the farm in an attempt to attain that peace.

"However, there were many who landed here. And we made our own way of living, and our own speech, using the common language we had been taught by our oppressors, but keeping the rhythm and tone that was unique to our shared heritage, though the tribes had different tongues. It is said that there were many terrible things that occurred. Children who were shameful because of their parents. But Mandrake had sense and learning, and he passed this on. There were others like him who followed, and so we evolved the methods we have of making sure such abominations before the Lord are not conceived. We make sure that blood does not mix and taint wherever possible, and we keep a strict watch on ourselves. There is always new blood coming in, but in the several generations since the nukecaust, this has lessened. We know from the newcomers that there are less people out there in the world, but still word spreads, and still we get people arriving to join us.

"I know that one of the things you are wondering is why we have not ventured forth since the nukecaust. This is because we are divided. There is a deep schism between us, and there has been since the years before the nukecaust.

"We are told that there was a war called Nam, and in that war the young of our people were sent by those of the pale skins to go and be chilled for their glory. There was talk among those who arrived here that we could never live in their midst as they would not allow us to be ourselves. More, there were those who believed that the only way to stop them harming us was to chill them first. They believed that we should stay apart.

"It was a time of bitter debate, but all this was halted

by the nukecaust. For more than a generation, it was a hard time to be alive. The seasons were wrong, there was little to be made from the land and livestock perished easily. There was rad sickness and many chilled.

"But many survived, and others managed to find their way through the darkness of the world to join us. Pilatu survived, and we have since grown strong. And now the debate rages again. There are those who wish to go out into the world to explore and to see what the lands beyond these shores have to offer, and there are those who wish to stay here, to stay separate from the pale ones. The only thing they would wish to do on the mainland is eradicate those who are not as us—partly as revenge for the past, and partly to neutralize any threat the pale ones may pose. Indeed, there are some among us who would wish to pursue such a fight at any cost.

"The problem we face is that what has been before nothing but a matter for idle, if heated, debate is now a necessity. It was always predicted that one day we would mine the depths of what this island has to offer. There is little left. And now, with the calming of the earth, we find that our population is growing again—we have people living longer, more arriving and more children. It is growing at a time when we can no longer support it. We must move, and it will not be easy.

"For me, the matter is made worse as it comes at a time when our leadership is in the balance. My father, Barras, is the baron, and he has been a good and wise baron. Yet he is old now, and he is tired and ailing. He has not long left to live and is past the peak of his powers. I do not say this to disrespect him, as he is my father and I love him. But the truth cannot be denied. When we need strong leadership, we have a man who is in the twilight of his powers.

"Matters are made worse because I am his heir, and I am a woman. There have been no woman barons in the history of Pilatu. It is strange, is it not, that a community based on escaping oppression should still harbor this? I would wish to take my own responsibility, but the weight of tradition says otherwise, and I find myself at the center of a private battle that would mirror the greater.

"There are two who wish my hand…and my power. One is Markos, who has a distaste for the pale ones and would not wish to leave the island at all. The other is Elias, who believes we must move on and out to the mainland in order to survive. He is not a bad man, neither is Markos, who is a fine security boss, despite his views that I do not agree with…but neither of them wish for my hand because of me. They do not see me as Sineta, a woman who needs a partner. Nor do they see me as Sineta, a woman who will need a partner for her own spirit. No, they see me as Sineta, the daughter of the baron. In matter of truth, they do not even see me as that. They see me as lever with which they can take power and rule over Pilatu, forcing their own point of view upon me and upon the people.

"I would not take either of them if the choice were solely in my hands, but it is not. My father is courted by both of them as though he were to be their wife, not me, for it is on his word that I must act. Tradition dictates that I marry the husband he chooses for me, for the good of the island, as though I am not capable of making any decisions myself, either about my own life or about the future of the people—my people, by lineage.

"And now, Mildred Wyeth, you know all about myself and the island of Pilatu. You have arrived at a time of great upheaval and heartache for our ville, but that is something that truly does not concern you. Neither, right now, does the fate of your friends. All that matters now is that you are a sister who has been hurt by the seas, and you must take the time to recover. Sleep, and we will see what the morrow may bring."

# Chapter Five

The companions were awakened the next morning after only a few hours' sleep. None had any idea what time they had been thrown into the jail cell, as it was impossible for J.B. or Ryan to read their wrist chrons in the darkness. One thing was for sure, though—dawn broke far too quickly. And it brought with it an unwelcome visit from the sec patrol leader.

The wan light was filtering through the small window as Jak sprung awake. His acute hearing and sense of danger picked up the approach of two men, muttering to each other. He also heard the shuffling of feet from the guard on the door, as though he were straightening and wanting to appear alert. Jak allowed himself a humorless grin, little more than his pale lip pulling back from the vulpine teeth.

Must be main man, he thought. Why else guard stand tall?

As the two men came nearer, the sound of their approach woke all the companions except Doc. Exhausted by what had happened, the old man merely stirred in his sleep and turned over.

"Wonder what they want with us?" Ryan mused through gritted teeth, the pain of sitting up immense, despite the strapping on his ribs.

"Well, they've got it over us. We're not in any fit state to break for it," J.B. said wryly as he gingerly felt his sore leg.

"Mebbe they've come to let us know our fate," Krysty said blandly, although her hair told a different story as it moved close to her neck, hugging her.

There was a brief exchange outside and the lock on the door was turned, the thick wooden barrier being flung open so that it swung back on its hinges to the fullest extent, banging against the wall.

Ryan shook his head. "Do you really think any of us would be that stupe?" he asked, squinting at the figures in the doorway. Although the light of day wasn't yet strong, after the blackness of the jail it was enough to hurt his eye. The two men framed in the doorway appeared as little more than silhouettes. If they had blasters, they were holding them across their bodies as there was no silhouette of such weapons by their sides.

One of the men in the doorway laughed. From the sound of his voice, it wasn't the sec patrol leader of the night before. The voice had the same raw-throated richness, but there was a note in there that was almost effete, verging on the hysterical. It was buried so deep that it was inaudible, but the resonance struck something within Krysty's mutie sense and made her shiver.

He spoke. "The whitelands produce nothing but the stupe. It would have been a natural justice if one of your pathetic heads was cracked like a ripe watermelon."

"What a terribly nice man," Doc mumbled, the noise of the slamming door having wakened him. "Such a kind regard for humanity."

"Humanity, you pale old fool?" the speaker snapped. "What do your people know of humanity?"

"You would be surprised...or mayhap not interested." Doc yawned, rubbing his eyes. "Now would you mind not making so much noise, and be so kind as to tell us why you have interrupted our much-needed rest?"

There was a moment's silence. As their eyes adjusted to the light, so the two men in the doorway became more than just shadow. One of them was the sec chief who had led the capture the night before. The other was of the same height and build, but stooped slightly where the other stood erect. He wore spectacles and had a slight squint, even in the dim light. But the most striking thing about him was that he was, like Jak, an albino.

The longer the silence, the more tense Ryan grew. Doc had spoken without thinking, not even properly awake. In so doing, had he annoyed the sec chief?

With no warning or indication, the sec chief burst into loud laughter.

"You may be whiteland scum, but you have the courage of the cornered animal, I will grant you that. Now, let us speak no more of such things. I have come to see the albino, and I have brought my brother to speak with him."

"Why think I want talk?" Jak asked quietly.

The albino in the doorway stepped forward and hunkered down on his haunches so that he was level with Jak, who remained seated on the ground. He looked Jak over with a curiosity that was akin to viewing insects under glass.

"Fascinating," he whispered, possibly speaking more to himself than to anyone around him or to Jak. "I had heard legend that the whitelanders could also produce albinos, and that they were treated in the same manner as we. But I had never seen one, nor had I ever expected such a sight…" His voice then increased in volume as he spoke directly to Jak. "How long have you been their slave, my friend, and why do you wish to stay with them when you could be free in our ville— free of their oppression?"

Jak fixed him with a glare, his ruby-red eyes burning into the pinker orbs of the albino facing him.

"Say it before, say it now—last time. These people my friends, we stand and fall together. Fuck you."

The African-American albino stood and shook his head sadly. "My Lord, they really have you under their thumb, do they not? I offer you freedom, and you are so scared that you yet stand in thrall."

Jak glanced around at Ryan. His expression was impenetrable, but the very fact that he had turned meant that he wanted a sign. And the one-eyed man knew exactly why—even as the island albino had spoken, the same thought had flashed through Ryan's mind. They were treating Jak as one of their own— that much had been obvious the night before. But to be offered freedom would mean a man on the outside of the jail, a chance to work for escape, and perhaps even an opportunity to find what had happened to Mildred.

"You are free to go if you want," Ryan said slowly, trying to implore Jak to read the hidden meaning in his words. "You no longer have to pretend, and you are no longer our slave."

As he spoke, Ryan stared at Jak very closely, and was relieved when he saw the briefest of understanding nods before the albino said, "Okay, you free me now. I join brothers."

The island albino gave Ryan a suspicious look, as though he couldn't trust whitelanders to be so magnanimous. Ryan shrugged.

"We're not in a position to argue, right?" he said.

The island albino didn't answer, although his still-hostile glare was more than eloquent enough. Without speaking, he rose to his feet in one graceful motion. "Come with us," he said to Jak, holding out his hand. Even though it was unnecessary, Jak grasped it and allowed the man to assist him in rising from the floor.

The sec chief, who they could now plainly see was holding his H&K across his body, raised it in salutation.

"I would suppose that you are not as stubborn and stupe as you at first appeared. We shall see. Perhaps you will be set to work as our forefathers were. Perhaps we have learned from their errors and are more charitable. We shall see."

He covered them while the island albino led Jak out of the jail. Once they were clear, he backed out, closing the door behind him. They heard the lock click as they were secured once more.

"Well?" J.B. asked.

"Just wait," Ryan replied. "It's all that we can do. If Jak can do anything, he will. In the meantime, I figure we should try to get some more rest, hope our injuries heal up before we get some action."

JAK RESISTED THE TEMPTATION to look back over his shoulder as he was led away from the jail. Despite being about a foot taller than the wiry hunter, the island albino put his arm around Jak's shoulders.

"You don't know how good it is to have another albino in the ville," he said in a confidential tone. "The brothers and sisters are good people, but there is always the sense that I am different from them. And so I am, in a sense. But to have someone else who lacks all color, rather than being white or black, is good. It gives someone to share identity with."

"Not thought of it that way," Jak answered. "Where the fuck are we?"

The island albino threw back his head and laughed. "My friend, you do not bandy words. I shall tell you."

As they walked to the living quarters of the albino, he told Jak about the history of the island and also of the way in which the people worked, either farming, hunting or mining and scavenging for fuels. By the time he had finished, they had reached the albino's adobe homestead where he led Jak into a one-room hut with two beds on opposite sides of the room, one of which had a table beside it piled high with books and papers. Beside the other bed was a Spartan arrangement of belongings, most of a practical nature.

The albino laughed. Indicating each side, he said, "There you have, in a nutshell, the dichotomy of my brother and myself. I, Chan, I weave the legends and history of the ville, indeed of the world as we know it, into something that can help and guide us through the darkness of the future and into the light of destiny. I work with this," he added, tapping his head, "whereas my brother Markos works with this." He flexed his biceps and hit his chest. "He is a good man, but he believes in actions above words. As I am the opposite, then we are complementary to each other."

"Markos, head of sec?" Jak queried.

Chan looked at him quizzically. "Sec? Ah, you mean security, I would assume. Yes, he is the boss of security on Pilatu. But come, I know nothing about you as of yet, and we will have to decide what you can do to be a part of this land."

"Name is Jak Lauren. And I hunt…" Jak began.

IF THE ALBINO HUNTER had wondered where Markos had disappeared to—for he had parted company with them before they had reached the homestead—he would have been interested to know that the sec boss was walking across the awakening ville to the home of Sineta, with an intention to find out more about the woman he had discovered the night before.

Mildred was still asleep when he knocked softly on the door to Sineta's homestead. The baron's daughter was awakened by the insistent sound, and rose to answer the call. "Markos, what are you doing so early?"

"I have come to see the newcomer. It is important that we find out more about her. Chan has spoken to the albino who was with them, and has taken him away.

The whitelanders freed him when they realized the position in which they found themselves."

Sineta frowned, then looked back at the sleeping Mildred. "Freed?" she repeated. "I would not…"

"Would not what?" Markos questioned, sensing that Sineta was on the verge of a revelation.

The fine-boned baron's daughter returned her gaze to him, and a look of bland indifference masked the curiosity she had felt. "I would not talk to Mildred now. She has only just fallen to sleeping, and she will need rest."

Markos bit hard on his lip. There seemed to be some ambiguity surrounding the outsiders, and it would be best to find out the truth as soon as possible. However, it would not be appropriate to contradict the baron's daughter. He contented himself for now with a brief nod.

"Very well. I shall return later."

Sineta watched him walk away, then closed the door behind her and walked over to the sleeping Mildred.

"What games are being played here?" she asked rhetorically.

THE COMPANIONS SPENT the next couple of days under armed guard, locked up in the jail, only the sound of everyday life outside the barred window and the feeble illumination it offered as markers of the passing of time. They were fed every day, at around sundown. A tray of food, enough for all, was brought in by a woman, while a sec guard stood by with an H&K at the ready for any trouble.

There was no indication that the prisoners wished

to offer any resistance. They allowed the food to be left without the slightest sign of giving any trouble. Mostly because of the five that were left in the jail, only two were fit enough to consider any kind of breakout. Doc was weary and battered by his experiences at sea, and although he had incurred no serious damage, his bruised body and even more bruised mind sought the solace of an enforced peace to gather its resources once more. J.B.'s leg was improving, and he exercised it as much as possible within the confines of the cell, making sure that the damaged muscle in his calf didn't stiffen and seize up. As for Ryan, he still ached all over, but it no longer hurt him to breathe and the pain was lessening with each day. His ribs could do with a longer resting period if they were to heal properly, but as long as he was able to function, Ryan figured that they may not have the time for him to make a full recovery. Each hour, each minute, he hoped to hear news of Mildred, or for Jak to return to facilitate an escape.

But with each hour that Jak did not, he was aware that he was healing more and would be better equipped for when the time came.

For Krysty and Dean, it was frustrating. All the more so for the young Cawdor as he had dreamed of his mother once more. This time, not being in the state of unconsciousness induced by a mat-trans jump, he was better able to remember the dream when he awakened. And it disturbed him. Where the mat-trans dream had been a fantasy of his parting from his mother, this was more the reality of the situation. They were living in a hovel, on the run from who knew what. His mother had been earning what little money they possessed as a gaudy, but her sickness was making it more and more difficult for her to attract clients. She had taught Dean the arts of stealing from trash and from stallholders and merchants, wherever possible, to try to obtain enough food to keep them alive.

They were living in one room, still on the run from ville to ville, and as he watched, a racking cough seized his mother.

"Got to send you away soon," she gasped between coughs. "I'm on my way to buying the farm, and I want to make sure you're okay."

"I'm not going anywhere," Dean replied defiantly. "Who's going to go and get food when you need it if you're too sick?"

Sharona smiled at him. "You're strong, my sweet Dean, but I've made plans, to make sure you get away, to make sure you're safe. I'll go happy if I know that."

"I don't want you to go," he replied simply.

"Mebbe we'll be together again some day, who knows?" she said. "I love you, Dean. Always remember that."

Who knows… The words had grown into a deafening echo around his head, jolting him awake in the middle of the night.

Stuck in jail, there was nothing for him to do but to brood on the dreams. And wonder why he was missing his mother.

"HE GOES THROUGH THE TREES. Swift as he is, the need to thread through them will slow him. Jak, you and Moses take the left-hand path. I and Kanu will take the right."

Without pausing to answer, Jak and the thick-set,

stocky man known as Moses set off to the left, skirting around the edge of the dense clump of trees in which the boar had sought to hide itself. The heavy beast could be heard, squealing in fear as it flung itself through the trees, crashing into the trunks, stumbling on the roots. It didn't have the awareness to realize that his pursuers could predict its path and would take an easier route to cut it off as it emerged.

Jak easily outdistanced the heavier, lumbering Moses, his legs pumping as he covered the ground with ease. The scent of the boar's fear was in his nostrils and the light of bloodlust was in his eyes. While he was about this task, Jak forgot all about his companions, left to rot in jail. When the beast was chilled, then they would return to his mind.

The albino hunter pulled up as he reached the point where the cluster of trees began to thin, gesturing behind him for Moses to slow.

"Still in there," the stocky man panted as he halted next to Jak. "You're lighter, more nimble. You go up into the treetops and get ready to drop. I'll take the animal from the side."

"Okay. Careful, boar triple scared and triple pissed off," Jak said as he began to scale the nearest tree.

"Don't worry, I've been doing this far too long to take unnecessary chances. I'm more likely to thrust my hand into a pit of snakes than take an angry boar head-on," Moses replied, breathlessly but with good humor.

Jak didn't reply, but allowed himself a grim smile as he attained the full height of the tree. Trying to fight wild boar in this way was probably more dangerous than a pit of snakes. The albino youth couldn't believe that a four-man hunting team was assigned to bring down the one creature—and at that by chasing and agitating it so that it was scared, furious and fighting mad. Left to his own devices, the albino hunter would have stalked his prey and waited until it was at its weakest before striking. A beast such as a boar was too strong and unpredictable to be taken in full flight. But he had said nothing of this. In the past few days he had soon learned that the islanders of Pilatu had ways of doing things that had been fixed over the generations, and were now immutable. As an outlander—and one who was biding his time until he could help the rest of his companions to escape—he felt it was best to keep his head down and to not make waves…and mebbe try not to get chilled in the process.

"Here comes," he called down to his hunting partner, his attention suddenly snapped back by the sudden approach of the creature. It had been audible the whole while, but from his vantage point he could now see the boar as it crashed through the foliage and slalomed around the root structures. Even from high up and at a distance he could see the manic gleam of fear in the beast's eyes.

Kanu and Jules, the hunt leader, had arrived at the opposite side of the outcrop. Shaped roughly like an oval, it came to a point where they had met. Each pair had skirted the outside to cover the possibility of the boar taking an early exit from the undergrowth, but the odds had always been weighted in favor of it making the distance in an attempt to lose what it believed to be its pursuers—the four men who waited now for it to emerge. Kanu hunkered at the base of a tree, covered like Moses, while Jules scaled a neighboring tree so that he overhung the narrow path made by the confluence of tree roots that the creature was sure to take. As he edged along the branch to gain the optimum position, he was within touching distance of Jak, and the albino studied the man who led all the hunting expeditions. He was tall and rangy, with a heavily etched face. Streaks of gray ran through his close-cropped head. His hairline was bisected by the weal of an old and badly healed scar, which ran back across his skull to a point beyond the crown. His eyes were watery and bloodshot, and there was tension written in them as they met Jak's.

"Ready, son?" he asked.

Jak nodded.

Both men were armed with short hunting spears, the light shafts made of whittled balsa that were only just heavy enough to carry the finely honed and razor-sharp heads. Double-edged, the heads were barbed so that they would go in easily but resist any attempts by their prey to be removed and, in fact, would cause more damage as the attempts to remove them tore into the flesh.

There was a window of a fraction of a second. The beast, squealing with fear, moved beneath them. For the briefest moment its back would be directly under their aim. In that moment, they would strike.

There was no word of command. There was no necessity. Both hunters knew by instinct sharpened by experience the optimum moment to strike. As one, they plunged their spears downward. The balsa shafts were light, but the heads of the spears were of a heavy pig-iron metal; and the weight used the light balsa as a flight.

One spear struck the boar where the skull joined the spine, the needle-sharp point of the head slicing through the thick layers of muscle that rippled on the creature's massive neck and shoulders. Simultaneously the second spear arrived at an angle, cutting into the animal's flanks, a throw designed to slice through the layers flesh, fat and muscle to rip into internal organs, causing massive hemorrhaging.

The boar simultaneously reared and twisted, the twin points of agony searing into its brain, confusion adding to the pain as it tried to work out where its enemy was and how best it could defend itself. It almost doubled over, flipping around to face the direction it had run, squeals of agony and fear increasing. While it was facing away from Kanu and Moses, the two hunters made their move.

Darting from their hiding places, the men moved in on the creature, pulling back their arms to strike. They needed lightning reflexes at this stage, as the creature was erratic and unpredictable. It thrashed wildly, its awareness now clouded with a red mist of pain as blood flooded its guts and the barbed spearhead in the neck began to work its way down into the spinal cord each time it moved, cutting off motor neurone action.

Moses struck first. The creature turned wildly so that its head was toward him. The eyes were glittering and sightless, lost in some private hell of pain. Knowing it could still smell him and strike on reflex, Moses wasted no time in chucking his spear. It shot straight and true, taking the creature through one eye, the heavy metal head of the weapon driving forward to rip into the soft tissue of the boar's brain.

The result was almost instantaneous. The creature gave one terrible cry that ended in a rattling cough as it flipped over once more. Blind, buying the farm and now almost completely defenseless, its legs waved wildly as it rolled, leaving the soft, white underbelly open and undefended.

Kanu needed no second chance. His spear flew straight and true, taking the creature in the gut and ripping the remaining life from it. It flipped once more, snapping the balsa shaft of the spear, as it had done with all the others, and leaving the head embedded in its flesh. Gouts of blood gushed from the open wound in time with the fading pulse, spilling onto the ground and darkening the soil and vegetation, steaming in the cool morning air.

The creature thrashed feebly a few times and was then still. It was an enormous size, and needed the four-pronged attack to take it in flight. Jak was still of the opinion that this matter could have been settled much more easily if left to his methods, but said nothing as Jules stepped forward to prod the now-still beast with his foot.

"Big bastard. Should feed a lot of people, and the hide'll come in useful," he said simply.

Moses eyed the corpse speculatively. "I'm thinking that mebbe this is the shadow that comes in the night, spiriting away other creatures to join him," he said, referring to a mysterious attacker that had been decimating their livestock supplies over the past couple of weeks. It was a hot topic of conversation among the hunters in the ville, and Jak had heard plenty about it during his few days with them.

"Boar not usually meat eater." Jak spoke up.

"Mebbe not," Moses agreed, "but it could be a mutie of some sort. The long-ago wars have long fingers of fear and hate that stretch through the generations."

Kanu shrugged. "Whatever it is, it'll keep Markos happy, and he is like the gathering storm if he is not."

Jules agreed. "That is never a bad thing. Let's get this back to the ville."

The four-man team cut two strong branches from the surrounding trees and, using the vines that curled around them, made ropes to secure the front and back legs of the chilled beast. Running a branch between both sets of legs, they each took one branch end and hefted the creature. The branches creaked and they could feel the vine ropes give under the weight of the muscle-bound boar. To have tried one long branch running the length of the body with all four legs secured would have snapped a branch without a doubt.

The hunters shouldered the weight and began to move. The boar was a good catch, and would make the journey back to the ville seem much longer than it was. Jak pondered as they walked that it was a simple way of life, but as everything on the island was so close to the ville, it would be hard for the companions to escape without being hunted down like the boar he was now helping to carry.

He wondered if Mildred had any ideas. He had seen her briefly, but she was showing little sign of hurry.

Jak was curious—as much as he ever allowed himself—as to why.

MILDRED HAD FOUND HERSELF faced with a barrage of questions from Sineta as soon as she had awakened.

The baron's daughter had been vexed by the information from Markos that the albino had been "freed" by the pale ones, as this contradicted what Mildred had told her about the companions being friends and equals. However, when Mildred had cross-questioned her about the attitudes of Markos and Chan, she had explained to Sineta that it was perhaps a ploy to allow Jak to go free, and then she did something that she wouldn't have believed possible. She told a possible enemy that Jak would be free to plan an escape.

"I don't even know why I'm telling you this," Mildred said, rubbing her eyes and forehead as if to alleviate the raging cross-current of feelings that built up in her head. "For God's sake, you could tell Markos and have Jak chilled. But I trust you not to." Her eyes met Sineta's, and in them Mildred could see that the baron's daughter was willing her to explain. She continued. "Look, you see my friends as the enemy because of the color of their skin, and they see you as the enemy because you overpowered us and locked them up. So they'll use any method to work a means of escape. Isn't that exactly what Markos would do in such circumstances?"

"I can understand this, but Markos will not, and if your albino friend attempts to free the pale ones, then he will be chilled. They all will."

"Then let me speak to him, try to explain. Let me see the others," Mildred implored.

Sineta shook her head. "Would that it was that simple. Markos will not allow it."

"But you're the baron's daughter, for God's sake," Mildred exclaimed, "surely you outrank him!"

Sineta smiled slowly, sadly. "You forget, I am also

a woman. I have no authority while my father lives and I am unmarried. Nor will I have any when I am married and the wife of the next baron."

Mildred sighed. "Well, this is just stupid. It'll end in a firefight where people will get hurt unnecessarily. Why waste life and ammo when it's not needed?"

"You speak almost as if you do not know which end of the burning stick to grasp," Sineta said.

Mildred frowned. The baron's daughter was right. Normally she would have no hesitation in saying or doing anything that would help her companions. She would go to any lengths to get them out of that jail. And yet this time it was different. Mildred remained silent, and Sineta left her to her thoughts.

The next couple of days went by quickly, all too quickly for Mildred. On the advice of the baron's daughter, she said nothing about their discussion, and didn't pursue the matter of gaining release for her companions. Instead she immersed herself in the life of Pilatu, learning about the society into which she had found herself.

She learned that she liked it. It had occurred to her that she had started to use the phrase "for God's sake" more than the occasional profanity that spilled from her lips. And she wondered why this should be. It took only a day of wandering around the ville for her to realize what was happening to her.

The people of Pilatu were pleased to see her up and about. For the first day, Sineta went with her. That was more, Mildred felt, to prevent her making contact with the companions than to show her around. The people she met were pleased to show her their part of the ville and to talk with her about their island and the place from whence she had come. It had been some time since there had been new arrivals on the island—particularly a sister and an albino accompanied by whitelanders—so there was much curiosity about her history. Mildred skirted this wherever possible. She couldn't betray her friends by describing them as her captors, but neither could she follow Sineta's advice to describe them thus until the initial flurry of interest had died down. Instead she turned the attention back on the islanders by asking them about the ville.

The actual settlement was about half a mile from the sea, built on higher ground on the side of the island that faced the vast ocean. The ville had been located here to secure optimum shelter from the elements. There was a path that led to the inlet where Mildred could see the fishermen's boats. The inlet below appeared to be the only safe place for them to launch, information that Mildred stored in her memory as more than useful.

But her immediate thoughts weren't of escape. Many of the stories she heard about the island echoed what Sineta had told her. However, she also learned through these exchanges that the people of the island had a strong sense of identity. They were linked by their skin color, and although they were all different—indeed there had been many who had differences between themselves that spilled into bloodshed—still at the end of a day they would band together at a threat from the whitelands. They knew that they and their ancestors had existed as a minority within the whitelands and had been treated as little more than animals during their history. They lived on the island because their ancestors had refused this way of existence and had chosen to live on their own, free terms. Petty personal differences counted for little when ranged against the fate of their people.

And it was then that Mildred realized that it struck echoes of her own childhood within her, the days when her father had been a Baptist minister, always fighting against those who wanted his daughter, his family, his friends, his flock to use separate schools, restaurants, buses, washrooms…all because they were seen as somehow lesser. She had been using God's name because it was the strongest curse and the mightiest invocation she could use as a child, and the society in which she found herself reminded her of the one she had wished for when yet another drive-by shooting or attack had stove in the windows of a neighbor's house, when yet another gasoline bomb had razed a church. As she had grown up and become a doctor, moving to places where things seemed much more laid-back, as the sixties had given way to the seventies and eighties, it had seemed that things had changed, that there was equality.

Yet the fact that she was black and the majority wasn't had never been that far from the surface. Some small incident would bring up comments. "You people would say that," "You wouldn't understand, being different…" Never outright insults or condemnation on color, but always the implication.

Here, she found none of that. This was the society of which her father had dreamed, in which black people were just people. At last she felt a sense of kinship that went deep—deeper than the present, stretching into the past.

When she saw Jak, and he raised the matter of freeing the rest of their companions, she had felt uncomfortable. She knew that rescue should be a priority, yet she mouthed platitudes at Jak about leaving things as they were for a few days while she gained the confidence of the baron's daughter. It would be a tricky matter to get them released, and escape would be difficult, leaving them with no chance to avoid buying the farm if they were caught.

Even as she spoke, she could see the disbelief in the albino's burning red eyes. He knew she was stalling and couldn't work out why.

Neither could she. Deep in her heart, she knew what the companions meant to her, and she knew from some of the things she heard the Pilatans say about the whitelands that there were things in this society that were merely the inverse of what they had left behind.

Mildred was divided. The ideal for the oppressed that she had heard of as a child, and the sense of historical belonging that she had never thought to experience, raged against the ties forged by a life that toyed with the big chilling everyday…ties forged by fire that couldn't be broken, no matter the color of the skin or the historical antecedent.

Right now, even Mildred had no idea what she could do to calm the raging sea within.

# Chapter Six

"It is time that you met my father, but he is like the lion in winter. Where once he was tall, erect and noble, now he is bowed by the weight of years upon him, and responsibility only adds to the burden. He takes much more time to think in these days, and so you must not worry if he does not, at first, respond to you."

Mildred chewed on her lip and nodded. She was keen to meet Barras, the baron of Pilatu, but knew that he was a man fading into the final dimming of the light. Everything that Sineta had told her over the past couple of days pointed to a man whose days were drawing to a close. It seemed that the ville's medic could do little to help, and Mildred was aware that it could only strengthen her position if she were able to assist his suffering in some manner.

"You do realize why I want to meet him, don't you?" Mildred asked.

"I have told you that there would be much opposition to releasing your friends. The untruth spoken to assist the albino will weigh against them in my father's judgment—and also in the opinions of many within the ville."

"By which you mean Markos won't like it, right?" Mildred queried.

Sineta allowed herself an indication of agreement. "I believe that you already know the answer to that question, Mildred. Markos will find it impossible to believe that people from the whitelands could treat a brother or a sister as equal. You have to understand that he is not a bad man—"

Mildred raised a hand. "I know. I can appreciate that. He's a man who has always thought a certain way, and has no experience to teach him otherwise. But I figure that he's a good guy, and if he can take the time to learn a little about the others, he'll see beyond their pale skins."

Sineta made a small moue. "If his brother allows him to think in another way from himself."

"I had kind of noticed that." Mildred smiled. "We'll just have to see."

"Then let us depart."

The two women left Sineta's quarters and walked the short distance between her adobe hut and the larger premises where the ailing baron held court.

As they covered the ground Mildred thought about the decision that had brought her to this. She had seen Jak when the gigantic wild boar he had helped capture had been carried into the ville. When she had tried to talk to him, he had simply asked her why the rest of the companions were still in jail while he and Mildred were free and she had the ear of the baron's daughter.

It was a question that Mildred couldn't, in all honesty, answer. Her conscience was gnawing at her that her companions had been incarcerated while she had been free. And yet, since awakening in the Deathlands, her world had been almost entirely white, with little cultural recognition to the people she had left behind. Not all her friends had been black, but some certainly had, and it wasn't until she had awakened in Pilatu that she realized how much of her identity had been based on that cultural heritage. However, she had damn near bought the farm with Ryan and his people, and she was as much a part of them as of the people of Pilatu. When it came down to it, they may share a common heritage, but that was out of whack when you considered that she was, in truth, over a century older than anyone else on the island of the same skin pigmentation.

It was a balancing act; she had to keep her eyes fixed ahead and her feet sure and true.

As they approached the baron's quarters, she saw Markos go in ahead of them. The sec boss gave them a saturnine glare before entering, as though annoyed that his audience with the baron would inevitably be interrupted.

Mildred felt a shiver run through her as Markos looked away. She had encountered the sec boss several times over the past few days—indeed, it seemed at times as though he were following her, for wherever she went, he would soon appear—and she could feel a frisson whenever he was near. The woman had wondered if he were keeping an eye on her, unsure of where her allegiance lay. Of course, he had a point, but she wouldn't admit that when considering how irritating he had become.

They had spoken a few times, and on each occasion he seemed to probe her about her views on the island and the people who lived here. He was blunt almost to the point of rudeness, yet listened carefully and attentively to her answers. It was obvious to her that he had doubt about her—which was, after all, reasonable—but it also seemed as though there was something more. In his earnestness, and totally serious devotion to the cause of culture and separatism espoused by his brother, Markos reminded Mildred of Rodney Stone, an intern at the hospital where she had been resident before her operation and subsequent cryogenic stasis. An intense and dedicated man, Rodney had seemed at first to be completely immersed in his work to the expense of all personal relationships. He appeared completely disinterested in anything that fell outside of the definition of work. When he'd asked Mildred for a date, she had been astounded. In his ivory tower of medicine, Rodney had appeared aloof. In fact, this had masked his inability to communicate in any other way, a problem born of his dedication.

There was much about Markos that was similar and Mildred was beginning to look at him in a different way. He was handsome, there was little doubt; and, despite his brusque manner, he burned with a passion for his world that bespoke of much hidden beneath the surface, perhaps reined in because of his brother. For she had learned that Chan was always the weaker, and their mother had died giving birth to him, leaving only their father to raise them. He himself had been chilled when the boys were still young, leaving the older, stronger Markos to provide for himself and his sickly brother. Chan was smarter, and he used this to dominate his older, stronger brother. Markos was smart enough to know that, but also felt an obligation that constrained him.

It was this constraint that Mildred was sure she felt now. There was an attraction between herself and Markos, and a man such as he would be unable to hold his peace when his reserve was exhausted. For her part, she was unwilling to examine this attraction too closely when she thought of J.B. sitting in jail. Was part of the attraction to Markos because he was black and they were both in this ville? Was it part of a dream of belonging?

Right now, she really didn't want to think about that too much. It was going to be difficult enough to obtain a release for the companions, without Markos interfering on personal or sec grounds.

Sineta led them into the baronial quarters, acknowledging the greetings of the sec guard with a regal nod as they passed. Outside, it was warm and bright, but within the building it was dark and cool, with the shades drawn over the windows and only candlelight to illuminate the room. For, as all the houses in the village, the baronial quarters consisted of one room, with separated areas for kitchen, latrine and ablutions. These small areas didn't take away from the richly textured decorations and hangings on the walls of the main area, nor from the beautifully hand-carved furniture and ornamentation that stood on the rush matting. As with Sineta's abode, there were signs of status within the community, but no sense of ostentation.

A healer stood in attendance a short distance from the baron's bedside, close enough to respond to his call, but not close enough to be a hindrance on either his guests or himself in speaking freely. Markos was seated on a chair by the side of the bed; the baron was propped up on pillows.

It was Mildred's first sight of the baron, although she had heard much of him from his daughter. Her first thought was that Barras was dying. There was nothing she would be able to do, except make his decline easier. He was stick-thin as he lay on the bed, naked from the waist up, his lower half covered with a thin sheet. She could see his ribs sticking painfully through dry skin that held a gray pallor. His cheeks were sunken, almost as much as his eyes. His hair was white, with the odd streak of gray to remind people that once it had been more than the current sparse covering. His arms had lost all flesh, all muscle. He moved while talking to the sec boss, and his movements were stiff and painful, as though any movement at all was an effort. It looked to Mildred, even at first glance, as though the baron were suffering from a cancer that had eaten away at him and was now ready to claim that last spark that kept him alive.

And yet, when he looked away from the sec boss to see his daughter and Mildred enter the room, the sunken eyes blazed with life once more and in the gaunt, drawn face Mildred could see echoes of the man he had once been. Echoes of the fine-boned structure this once-handsome man had passed down to his daughter.

"Sineta, it is early. Even though the light pains me to watch now, I can tell from the lightness of the air itself that it is still the day. You do not usually come until the darkness has fallen and the shadows of imagining fill the room. There must be good reason to change the routine of one who, like her father, lives by the habits of the hunter."

Sineta smiled, ignoring the barely disguised scowl that crossed Markos's face. She leaned over her father and kissed him gently on the cheek.

"Sineta, I would bid you leave to wait until I have finished my business with your father," the sec boss said with a barely held politeness. "I am making my report and there is little to interest you."

"I hope you will not feel this way if you have your wish and attain my hand in marriage. The consort of a female baron should not be so disrespectful…."

Markos gritted his teeth and looked away. Sineta's barb had hit home. Without looking at her, he rose to leave. As he did so, his eye caught Mildred's and she could see within a discomfort at his position.

"I would only marry for the sake of the people, to give them a baron who would try to do the right thing," he stated, looking at Mildred all the while. "There would be no disrespect to you, as that would be likening to spit in the eye of Pilatu."

Sineta softened, placing a hand on his arm. "I know you only wish to do that which you think is best. But perhaps you should be open to other ways and ideas…and perhaps you should remain, as you will want to hear what I have to say."

Markos nodded and regained his seat. "I suspect that I have some notion of your business. And it will be no hardship to stay in such a presence."

Mildred frowned slightly. He had been speaking in response to Sineta, but all the while his eyes had been fixed on her. More to the point, although she knew he would soon be objecting to what he would hear, she wasn't upset that he had been studying her as he spoke.

Barras looked up at his daughter and the ghost of a smile played across his lips. "I have known you since before you were born, as you have always been like your mother. I know that whatever you are about to say, I probably shall not like it."

"Perhaps not, but it is something that I would wish you to give some thought. Since I have known Mildred, although it is but a few days, I have come to trust what she says. She is truthful and glad to find our society, but…" Sineta paused, trying to find a way to phrase her request so that Markos couldn't explode with anger before her father had a chance to speak. "The white-landers who arrived with Mildred are not her masters, are not her enemy. They are her friends, and she wishes you to grant them their freedom, for which they undertake to help and work in the ville until such time as they can leave."

This wasn't exactly what Mildred and Sineta had discussed, but there were reasons for the baron's daughter to deceive her father in such a manner.

Sineta continued, holding up her hand to silence Markos who had risen angrily to his feet, eyes flashing fire at Mildred as though she had betrayed him in some way. "I know that the albino—Jak—led Markos to believe that he was their slave in order to attain freedom, a deception the one-eyed man encouraged and reinforced. But this was so that at least one more of them may go free. It was a small untruth, nothing more."

"Nothing more, woman?" Markos roared. "By the Lord, the albino lied to myself, to my brother and to the whole island. He could have made any amount of sabotage while he was free—"

"And has he?" Mildred asked calmly.

Markos stared at her, fury tightening the muscles on his face, eyes narrowing. "No, he has not. But that is not the issue—"

"Then what is? That a man should tell an untruth to attain freedom? That his companions should collaborate to grant him this even at their own expense? Surely that speaks of a greater nobility?" Sineta queried.

Barras chuckled. "The girl has you there, my friend. Your hot temper lets you lead with your mouth rather than your brain. You have learned over the years to control this, but intense feeling lets you down, as ever. What makes you feel so strongly this time?"

Markos shook his head. "Nothing…it is nothing."

But the old man was still sharp in mind and noticed the quick glance his sec boss gave Mildred. Barras appraised her, then spoke.

"Why did you not mention this before?"

"I needed time to recover from my own injuries," Mildred replied. "I also needed time to gain the trust of your daughter. I had to explain things to her, try to show her how I am. I couldn't expect her to take me on face value."

Barras nodded thoughtfully. "My daughter is a fair woman, and a good judge of character. But," he added shrewdly, "why now and not tomorrow, or even yesterday?"

Mildred looked at Sineta. How could she tell him the truth? That they had chosen today because they had only struck their bargain in the morning?

SINCE THAT FIRST NIGHT, when the baron's daughter had told Mildred about the island and her position, and how she wished to be free of the obligations of marriage and be the baron herself, Mildred had wondered if the woman was reaching out to her to be an ally. In return, once she had decided that she had to try to strike a balance between her companions and the almost idyllic society in which she found herself, and get them released, Mildred knew that she would need the assistance of Sineta in trying to persuade her father to authorize this release in the face of the strong opposition she expected from Markos.

It had come to a head that morning when Mildred had explained to Sineta her decision. The woman had considered Mildred's words carefully before answering.

"We must leave this island, that much you know. And the fact that you and the whitelanders have such a close bond should show all but the most intractable of the islanders that it is possible for us to live in peace on the whitelands, and that not all pale ones are the demons and ogres of legend. If they were to be released, and the islanders were to meet them and exist behind them for a short while, then it would perhaps help to reinforce this."

"But there will be those who will disagree—"

"There have always been people like that, in any situation," Mildred interrupted. "If they're not the majority, then their objections can be answered and overruled by the majority."

"It is perhaps not that easy," Sineta argued. "There are those who have gotten to know you who will consider you a traitor to your skin for suggesting such action, wondering why you have chosen to do this after seemingly settling in with us, and these people will perhaps turn against me if I back you."

Mildred shrugged. "That's a risk I'll have to take—you, too. If you help me, then I can help you. I'll support you as you need when the time comes to make your stand. I know that's what you want—shit, anyone would. You're going to take a lot of crap about your decision to assume the leadership yourself and maybe, me being an outsider, I can help you more than anyone caught up in the politics of the situation. I figure I would have done it anyway, because I feel you're doing the right thing. But just maybe having the others free will help for the reasons you say—it'll show your willingness to lead well by showing how 'pale ones' and the brothers and sisters can coexist." Mildred smiled deprecatingly. "I know I've got my own agenda, but that doesn't mean that I don't mean it, right?"

Sineta came forward and embraced her. "I believe you, and I believe in you, Mildred Wyeth. You have your bargain. There is only one thing I would wish to know—why has it taken you so long to talk of this?"

ALWAYS THE SAME question. Mildred had no idea how it could be answered, but the moment was saved by the sudden explosion of Markos, the sec boss being no longer able to contain his anger.

"Barras, you cannot seriously contemplate such a ridiculous move," he yelled, springing to his feet. "Surely you can see that this would cause nothing but discord and disharmony—"

The baron silenced him with a raised hand. The sec boss's respect for the baron was such that he ceased speaking immediately, although his staring eyes and heaving chest told of the emotion he fought to contain.

"Do not tell me what I may or may not do for my own people. Until—if—you take the hand of my daughter, you are not the baron nor the heir to the responsibility. So do no presume to tell me my duty."

"I'm…I'm sorry," the sec boss stammered. "I did not wish…I wanted merely to—"

"That is immaterial. The fact remains that you dare to speak across and against."

"But what is your decision, Father?" Sineta pressed.

The ailing baron beckoned Mildred to approach. Keeping an eye on the sec boss and noticing the way he stared at her as she moved near—a mixture of whipped-dog disbelief and anger—she approached the baron's bedside.

"Mildred Wyeth," Barras began, as though it were a statement in itself, "I have heard much about you from my daughter. She says you are a medicine woman, and that you carry much with you. Is this so?"

"It is," Mildred answered simply. "I carry what supplies I can find in my travels, and I know how to use them. But if you're going to ask—"

"I am not," he interrupted. "I know that I am on the long walk to join the lands where my ancestors dwell, and I realize that the road is not long anymore. My end is drawing near, I only ask that I have peace along the way."

Mildred nodded. "If that's what you want, I have medicine to ease your pain. And," she added with a glance at the sec boss, "I can instruct your healer, so that she can administer it. Just to make sure."

The ghost of a grin crossed the old man's lips. "That is not necessary, but a revealing gesture. You should not distrust Markos. He is a good man, if headstrong. But he will learn the truth about your comrades soon enough, if they are free to show him."

"You'll release them?"

Barras nodded, then inclined his head toward the sec chief. "You will take Mildred and Sineta to the jail and release the prisoners. They are under the charge of my daughter. Also, find the albino and make sure he understands the situation."

Markos breathed in heavily and slowly, as though suppressing the urge to comment, contenting himself with, "Your wishes will be complied with."

Barras leaned back on the pillows supporting him, closing his eyes. When he spoke again, his voice seemed somehow smaller, weaker.

"Now go, all of you. I will expect to hear from you later today, Mildred."

"You will," Mildred affirmed.

Sineta, Mildred and Markos turned to leave, the sec boss allowing the women to precede him out the door. However, when they were outside he pushed brusquely past Mildred, muttering, "Follow me now and we will get this madness over and done with."

Letting him move on a few paces, Mildred stayed Sineta with a hand on her arm.

"You've done your bit—lady, the deal is on."

INSIDE THE JAIL, the air was no longer fresh. Even the adobe walls and the lack of windows couldn't keep the inside of the building cool. The most crushing element was boredom. The five inhabitants found their conversation moving in ever-decreasing circles until it reached the point where all they could discuss was when Mildred or Jak would attempt to break them out. It was that or try to sleep. Even thinking was impossible. Monotonously, the subject would always return to the subject of escape. What had happened to Mildred and Jak, and why had they heard nothing from either?

The air was still and humid, the latrine in the corner of the room imbuing the atmosphere with a dankness. Their bedding was hard and made good sleep impossible and, although they had been fed and watered well, there had been little opportunity to bathe. They felt sweaty, itchy and in some discomfort.

"Four people approaching," Dean said to no one in particular.

"They're heading straight for here, and I'm sure I just heard Jak's voice!" Krysty exclaimed, sitting upright. Her red hair, lank with dirt, still waved around her head to indicate there was no danger in the approach.

"Jak? With others? What the fireblasted hell is this all about?" Ryan questioned rhetorically, lifting himself up into a sitting position.

They heard the footsteps and voices draw near, exchanging only the odd word, but enough to identify the sec boss Markos, Jak, and Mildred, along with a voice that none recognized.

"Millie? With Jak and the sec chief?" J.B. queried. "This is going to be interesting, if nothing else."

They heard the lock on the door turn and click after a few barked words from the sec boss. The door was flung open. At first the sudden sharp light of the midafternoon sun was blinding and it took the companions eyes a few moments to adjust. But when their vision cleared, they could see the doorway blocked by Markos's tall, muscular figure. Behind him, it was possible to see the confused sec guard standing with Mildred, Jak and a fine-boned, dark-skinned woman.

"You are free to go," the sec chief said sharply.

"Say that again?" Ryan muttered.

"You are free to go. You are no longer to be held captive, but are to be freed into the care of Sineta and the sister Mildred." He stepped back to allow them to leave.

As they stepped out into the light, Markos added, "I do not approve of this—she knows that. And I will watch you as the stooping bird watches the mouse. I am ready, should you choose to overstep any boundaries that are set for you." With which the sec boss turned on his heel and walked off, leaving the companions alone together for the first time since their landing, and in the company of Sineta.

After a joyful reunion, Mildred introduced Sineta. When they learned that she was the daughter of the baron, it became clear to the prisoners why they had been granted release. At the behest of Sineta, the companions then walked the short distance to her home, where they bathed and changed into clean clothes Sineta had brought to them by women from the ville. Their own clothes were taken to be cleaned. The women returned immediately with food and drink.

"You will be given quarters later, so that you may rest. But first you must eat and we will explain to you what has occurred."

"'We'?" Krysty asked, looking from Mildred to Jak. who shrugged helplessly, knowing that Ryan wouldn't like the situation any more than he did himself.

"Yeah, it's not that complex, but it does need explaining," Mildred offered.

And so, after they had eaten, the companions settled down to hear what Mildred and Sineta had to say. When they had outlined what had occurred and the conditions of their release, Ryan turned to Jak.

"What do you think of this?" the one-eyed man asked the albino.

Jak shrugged. "Good people here—some little crazy, but most fair. Good to me, mebbe not you. Mildred in for trouble, I think. But probably no real danger."

"And do you reckon Markos'll play this one down the line?" Ryan added.

"Good man," Jak affirmed. "Listen albino brother too much. Weird shit ideas, there. Not about people at all, but some kind of self thing."

Sineta interrupted. "Jak's right. Markos listens too much to his brother, and for all his talk I have often felt that Chan uses ideas as a shield and mask for his real self. I would not trust him, but I would trust Markos."

Ryan chewed his lip, then fixed his eye on Sineta. "Okay. Look, I don't want you to think that we're not grateful for what you've done for Mildred or for us, but we don't belong here. I figure the best thing is we get the hell out as soon as possible."

There was a general murmur of agreement from all except Mildred. She looked Ryan in the eye and spoke low and clear.

"No, Ryan. If you want to go, you go alone. I can't. I made a promise."

"But, Millie! We can't leave without you!" J.B. exclaimed.

"Yes, you can, John, and you'll have to if you want to go right now."

"You know we can't do that. You'll be ripped to pieces if we disappear and leave you. It'll confirm everything that worries Markos and the others like him," Krysty said softly.

"I can't help that. I've given my word, and I want to stay," Mildred asserted.

"But why?" Dean asked, although he thought he already knew. He needed to hear this for his own reasons.

"Because I've never been in any place where I felt I belonged, and now perhaps I do," Mildred began.

They sat and listened while she explained to them about her background and the lack of identity she had sometimes felt since awakening in the postdark world. All the thoughts that had whirled around her head over the past few days now came tumbling out, taking better shape for her as they were spoken. She told of things that they had spoken of when they were first imprisoned: of the prejudices they had seen in the oil wells and the division of people based on skin and race they had seen in other places during their travels.

All of it made sense to them, but there was one vital question that remained unspoken and unanswered. It was a question that J.B. put to her when she fell silent.

"So who's more important, Millie—us or them?"

It was a question that Mildred couldn't immediately answer.

The atmosphere was strained for the rest of the evening and Mildred was glad when a sec man arrived to show the companions to the quarters they would share in the ville. Jak was told he would be relocated with his compatriots.

As they started to leave, J.B. noticed that Mildred made no attempt to move. "You coming with us?" he asked her.

Mildred avoided his gaze for a second, then decided that she couldn't opt out in this way. She met the Armorer's eye with a level gaze.

"I'm staying here, John. That's part of the deal."

"Guess that mebbe answers my question," he said, looking away as he joined the others.

"And maybe it's just not that simple," Mildred murmured as they left.

DAWN BROKE with a clear sky and a light breeze that was chill but refreshing. Certainly refreshing enough for Ryan and Krysty to be out before many of the ville's inhabitants were awake. However, those who were up greeted the appearance of the couple as they walked through the streets with a mixture of curiosity and outright hostility.

"Remind me again why we're doing this?" Krysty whispered to Ryan as they passed a sec man who made a point of sliding the catch on his blaster, either as a totem or a reminder not to step out of line.

"Because we need to take a look around ourselves before we get assigned our work tasks," Ryan replied. "When Mildred and Sineta were talking about the ville and where it's situated on the island, they mentioned an inlet."

"Yeah and they also made a point of saying how it would be real hard to get down there unobserved," Krysty pointed out.

"True enough, but I'd just as soon check it out for myself. If Mildred reckons it's a no go, then normally I'd trust her—"

"Normally?" Krysty queried.

"Ninety-nine percent," Ryan answered. "Trouble is, this is that one percent. This ain't easy for her, but I sure as shit do not want to be trapped here at the mercy of a people that may turn against us."

"That shouldn't happen," Krysty said.

"Yeah, operative word being shouldn't," Ryan replied. "But this isn't a normal situation for Mildred, or for us. We've already talked about this, and last night did nothing to change my view on it. I don't blame Mildred—figure I'd feel the same if I was her. But I'm not."

By this time they had left the ville and were walking down a path, beaten smooth by constant use over the years. A path that led to a sandy strip of beach that marked the small bay formed by the inlet.

"Yeah, this would be fireblasted difficult to run an escape from right now, especially as we don't have any blasters," Ryan speculated as he turned and looked back up the hillside toward the ville. "Even more so as we've been followed."

"I thought as much," Krysty mused, turning to follow his gaze. Her hair coiled around her in warning, as she squinted up into the trees to see a sec man lurking among the undergrowth. His stance was nonaggressive, but he had obviously been deputed to keep watch on them. "Wait, there's someone coming," she added.

They could hear Mildred before they saw her. She appeared at a bend in the path, coming toward them. Even at a distance, they could tell from her body language that she felt uncomfortable.

"Ryan, Krysty, what are you doing?" she asked as she approached across the sand.

"Stupe question, Mildred. You know what we're doing," Ryan replied.

"I had hoped that asking you not to escape but to help me, and help Sineta, would be enough," Mildred stated.

The one-eyed man shook his head sadly. "Come on, what did you really expect? Most of the people here are going to be suspicious, some hostile, and a few might just decide to deal with us. We've got no blasters and only the word of your new ally that we'd be okay. If you were me, what would you do?" He waited, but Mildred didn't answer. Ryan continued. "You were right. If this is the only way to insure getting safely out to sea, then it'll be too difficult for us to crack without a major firefight. And I don't want it to come to that any more than you do. But I've got to check it out, have a backup plan if it all fucks up. After all, while you're helping Sineta we're going to be weaponless—"

"Only our blasters," Mildred countered. "You, John and Jak still have knives."

"Good you said 'our' blasters," Ryan noted, "but the

situation is still basically the same. We're still going to be workers, at the mercy of others.'

"Join the club, Ryan—that's what my ancestors were," Mildred said heatedly.

"Fair point." The one-eyed man shrugged. "I'm just worried that someone will get overexcited and try to get some retroactive vengeance using us as the pawns."

Mildred sighed. "Ryan, there's no real way of winning here, is there? Look, I don't figure that's going to happen. You know why I want to help Sineta. I haven't felt like this since I was a kid. And you know I don't want to let you guys down. Yeah, I'm torn here, but I need your help to help me. Prove to the idiots here that not all whitelanders are against them. As for those that would try to chill you to prove their point… Shit, there's fools like that trying to chill us every day."

"That's fair," Krysty murmured. "We should help Mildred. That way we all get to the mainland and all get what we want."

The one-eyed man pondered that. Finally he said, "Yeah, okay. I can't pretend to understand how you feel, but I know you realize why I feel like I do. But I warn you—if the shit hits, then we'll have to go in hard and for our lives."

"Wouldn't expect it any other way, Ryan," Mildred told him.

Krysty looked up at the waiting sec man, who had stepped onto the path at Mildred's entrance. She indicated his presence to both Mildred and Ryan before she spoke.

"Come on, let's get back to the ville to see what

we're supposed to be doing, before Markos and that brother of his start getting reports that'll give them ideas."

# Chapter Seven

"Father, now that we have the opportunity, we must act," Sineta pleaded, holding the old man's hand while his healer administered the injection of morphine, supervised by Mildred.

"You push me when I cannot think straight. My mind is traveling ever more like a maze, like the path of a half-crazy snake. Perhaps that is what I now am—" Barras halted as another spasm of pain racked his body, biting hard to try to prevent crying out in agony.

"Just hang in there," Mildred said softly. "It'll take a few moments to start working."

She indicated to Sineta to follow her to the far side of the room. She didn't want the baron to hear what she had to say, although, looking at the hard lump protruding from his stomach, the only sign of anything other than skin and bone on his wasted frame, she knew that in his heart he already knew what she had to say.

"Mildred, I know he is not long for this world and will soon join our ancestors, but that is why I must press him," Sineta said quickly, preempting Mildred.

"Sineta, I can't remember the last time I saw cancer like that. The tumor inside him must be huge, and it looks like it has spread over his whole body. He must be in immense pain. Any shots I can give him are not going to be strong enough. Pretty soon, he'll be too resistant to the dope to get any relief. How can he make any decisions like that?"

"But he must. He is the baron, and we cannot move without his word."

Mildred closed her eyes and sighed. "Okay, but don't be hard on him. It must be all he can do to keep lucid right now."

They returned to the baron's bedside. From the expression on his face and the misting in his eyes, the morphine had kicked in enough to give him temporary relief.

"Father—" Sineta began, but was cut short.

"I know. I have a brief time of calm in which to gather my thoughts. Find Markos quickly and bring him here."

Sineta rushed from the room, leaving Mildred and the healer alone. The baron dismissed the healer with a wave, then extended his arm, offering Mildred his hand. She took it and felt how weak his grip had become.

"Listen to me, Mildred Wyeth. I have two things that I must do before the long night draws in on me. I must authorize the evacuation of our now-barren home, and I must decide between Elias and Markos for a husband." He smiled weakly, catching a look in Mildred's eye. "You think I should let my daughter rule alone, as she wishes? Ah, if only it were that simple. I would trust her to be a good leader, but the people of this island believe that a baron should be male."

"If you trust her that much, why not make the precedent?" Mildred asked gently, interrupting him.

Barras shook his head gently. "Another time, perhaps. But this is a crucial point in our history. We have
to take to the whitelands to survive, and there would
be too much fragility in a change of convention at such
a time. Surely you can see that?"

"I can't say I agree totally, but I do see where you're
coming from," Mildred admitted.

"Markos is a good man, but distrusts the pale ones
because of his brother's teachings. Elias is more open,
but does not have the people's respect. This delicate
balance I must use for my decision. And at a time when
I cannot think. There is something else that colors my
mind and makes the choosing hard. A secret that is
passed down the baronial line and must rest with Sineta
before I go into the darkness. Something that is made
the more important by the fact of our leaving the island."

"Then maybe you should tell her now, while you
still have the lucidity," Mildred counseled.

Barras clicked his teeth and shook his head. "Again,
not that simple. It could be awkward for this to be
known when we—they—are preparing to leave. I will
stay here, for I will be gone. But the secret cannot. I
must trust you with this, Mildred Wyeth, so that you
may carry it with you and tell Sineta at the right moment."

"And what will be the right moment?"

"You will know. You have enough wisdom for that."
The old man looked away from Mildred, toward the
doorway, as he heard the approach of Sineta and
Markos. He said hurriedly, "It would be impolitic to tell
you now—another time, when you administer my

painkiller. Now I must prepare for my final great decree."

The door to the adobe hut opened and Sineta entered with Markos respectfully at her heel. The sec man shot Mildred a glance that was curious. Was it because he wondered what had been said while she was alone with the baron or was it because he still couldn't figure her out?

The baron had sat himself upright on the pillows and looked from his daughter to the sec boss. He sucked in a breath that was constrained and painful, then began.

"I had my daughter bring you here because I have a decree. You will not like it, but it is a necessity. From today, we ready the islanders to leave our home and transport all our wealth, belongings and our spirits to the whitelands."

Markos's eyes widened and his mouth fell agape. It took him a moment to regain his composure before saying, "Is this wise?"

"You dare to question me?" Barras snapped. For the briefest of moments Mildred could see the strength of the man shine through, an insight into how he had to have been before the cancer ripped through him.

"No, I would not presume to contradict the word of a baron. I would, however, wish to understand why such a decision—one that will meet with much opposition within the community and inspire resentment that will be divisive in some quarters—has been made."

Barras gave a wry grin. "Very politic. In truth, I would not wish to leave this island unless it was necessary. And in truth, you know that it is. Take your head from the sand and look around you, Markos. This island can no longer support us. Successive generations have drained it dry, and now we have to find a new home. It will not be easy to wrench ourselves away from here, but it must be done. I shall not see it, but it is important we set matters in train right now, lest it be too late."

"You mean that the word would be better received from you than from me," Sineta said bitterly.

"That is not a stain on you, but rather an acknowledgment of fact. We shall talk of this another time, when we are alone. For now, all that remains to be said is that it is up to you and Markos to inform the people of my decision and to implement the necessary measures for the people to move. Now leave me. I feel tired, and have to rest...."

Barras lay back on the pillows and closed his eyes.

"The morphine's really taken effect now," Mildred whispered. "It'll put him out for a few hours."

"Then we should leave," Markos said in a clipped, strained voice. "I have matters to attend, but I shall be at your home in two hours, if that is acceptable, to discuss arrangements."

Sineta acknowledged the sec boss. "In two hours, then." When he had left, she said to Mildred, "Although it was the decisive action I wanted, I feel this is going to be fraught with problems."

Mildred looked back at Barras, thinking of the secret he would be imparting to her trust. "Oh, yeah," she said slowly, "that's for sure."

THE MEETING at Sineta's dwelling was short and far from sweet. Markos made it known that the move would bring nothing but trouble and that he, personally, was far from happy about living on the whitelands. However, he had a job to do and he would discharge his duty to the best of his ability. Having made his position clear, Mildred noticed that he seemed to relax and shift into a different gear, acting with a clearness of head and clarity of purpose that she wouldn't have thought possible. Plans for the evacuation were drawn with speed, the sec boss pointing out areas of difficulty and overcoming them with ease. It was hard to believe that this was the same man who had started the meeting by voicing such objections.

He left in the still watches of the night, the plans complete. It was agreed that they would hold an island meeting the next morning to make matters clear and to begin the process. As he left, the sec boss ordered the night watches to prevent early rising hunters, miners, farmers and fishermen from beginning their tasks. Everyone had to be present in the main square when the meeting began.

For Sineta and Mildred, it meant a night of little sleep. The reaction of the people was an unknown that worried the baron's daughter.

As for Mildred, she wondered how her companions would feel, hearing this from someone else while she stood beside the baron's daughter. She knew that if it were her, she would feel in some way betrayed, and made wary. Yet she couldn't go to tell them now, for there could be no risk of the news leaking before the next morning.

It was an untenable position.

"I WONDER WHAT THE HELL this is about," Ryan said as the companions gathered in the main square with the rest of the Pilatans.

"Whatever it is, Millie's got a hand in it," J.B. mused, seeing her enter the square with Markos and Sineta. "Which kind of makes me wonder why she didn't tell us about it."

Doc laid a hand on the Armorer's shoulder. "I fear that is something on which you dwell too deeply, John Barrymore. Dear Dr. Wyeth is walking a very fine line at the moment, and we have to allow for this."

"Yeah, but how far do we do that before it gets to be a problem?" Dean asked.

Krysty shot him a puzzled look. "You're doubting Mildred?"

Dean grimaced. "No, not really. It's just that…well, she kind of belongs here, and I figure that stuff's important. Mebbe more important."

Doc raised an eyebrow. "You've been unsettled since we landed here, young Dean. What is it that ails you?"

"Nothing," Dean muttered, shrugging off the memories of dreams that haunted him.

"This still more interesting than waiting next hunt," Jak murmured.

There was a raised platform in the middle of the square that was used for speeches and celebrations, and the trio of Markos, Mildred and Sineta mounted it to a hum of speculation that stilled as the sec boss raised an arm.

"People, it is very rare in our history that we have to meet in such a way. And it is beyond such that we meet today, for we have something unprecedented in our history of which to speak. Our beloved Barras is too ill to come to speak, but he has given me orders and requested his daughter to speak to you. Pray be silent and listen well, for what Sineta has to say is of the utmost import."

He stood back and made way for the woman. She stepped forward and looked over the sea of faces in front of her. Never before in her life had the reality of being the baron—the leader and focal point of so many—become so apparent. It was several moments before she found her voice.

For many in the gathering it wasn't long enough. Markos's brother Chan stood in the crowd, instantly distinguishable because of his pigmentless skin, and listened in growing disbelief and anger to what Sineta had to say. She told the people of her father's decision to authorize a mass exodus to the whitelands and why. Their resources were all used up. It was a simple case of move or buy the farm. She explained that her father, herself and Markos were aware that many would be against mixing with the pale ones. These people had to face the reality of the situation.

The plan was to find a place where they could live in relative isolation, so that they wouldn't have to mix with anyone—of whatever descent—if they didn't wish to. But there would be pale ones, and there would be no point in fighting it. She hoped that the presence of Mildred's companions would help to show that not all pale ones were the enemy. As for those who just did not wish to leave the island of Pilatu—they just needed to look around. The harvests were lessening; the game was harder to hunt; the mines were running dry. The island had served them well, but now it was exhausted. The time to reenter the world their ancestors had left behind had finally arrived, and truly they were the chosen ones for undertaking this momentous task.

It was a good speech; a true speech. All the things that Sineta touched upon were true, albeit that they were angled to make her point seem more irrefutable. To many in the crowd, it seemed to make sense. Even those who were saddened by the thought of leaving the island could see that it wasn't a question of choice any longer.

Watching the faces as Sineta spoke, Mildred felt it was going better than she might have expected. There were some that looked unhappy, even angry: not least among these being the instantly recognizable visage of Chan. Markos, too, had spotted his brother, and when Mildred glanced at the sec boss she could see the mixed emotions that boiled within him.

But the faces that caught Mildred's attention most of all were those of the companions. At the back of the crowd, they stood out immediately and clearly by virtue of their skin color. She could see the amazement at the revelation, and also the disappointment. Her eyes locked with J.B.'s and, despite the distance between them, it seemed as though she could actually hear what was running through his head. His stare was accusatory. He felt that she had in some way betrayed them— could she be trusted?

It saddened and angered her that he could feel that way. Of course she could be trusted. It was just that she was caught between two loyalties, two ideals. Both were right, but neither could be completely served. Instead, she had to juggle…and sometimes the ball was dropped.

"SHIT, THIS IS GOING to make things very hot for us," Ryan muttered to his people.

"You can say that again, lover," Krysty conceded as she watched some in the crowd turn to them. Most were curious, but others were outrightly hostile. "We're really going to have to watch our backs. There's going to be some who want to use us to prove a point, and they're going to be out to chill us."

"By the Three Kennedys, one would have wished Mildred to have given us some warning." Doc sighed.

J.B. answered this without taking his gaze from the platform. "She would have, once."

Jak tapped the Armorer's arm. "Not real danger— look there," he said, pointing into the crowd.

J.B. followed Jak's finger, the rest of the companions following suit. The albino Chan was no longer looking at Sineta or his brother on the platform. Instead, he was facing the back of the crowd, his eyes scanning for signs of the companions. Two other men had barged through the crowd and were now urgently talking to him. The albino held up his hand to silence them, then smiled slowly as he located the white faces at the back of the crowd. He spoke to the two men at his side, and they, too, directed their gazes toward the companions. They listened as he spoke. When he had finished, they indicated their agreement.

"That something worry about," Jak said slowly.

"We're really going to have to be triple-red from now on," Ryan mused. "Shit, I wish we could get our blasters back. Mebbe Mildred could—"

"Mebbe she won't," J.B. interrupted coldly. "Figure that just mebbe we'll have to get the blasters ourselves."

"You think it'll come to that?" Dean asked, alarmed.

J.B. was about to answer when Krysty cut him off. "Don't say anything you might regret, J.B. And listen, I think this concerns us."

On the platform, Sineta was detailing the way work at the ville would be divided until the migration. It was important to keep the land and hunt in progress, so that there would be plenty of food. Yet there was also much to do in the way of preparation and storage. One of the most important tasks would be to ready the transportation that would take them to the whitelands. New boats were to be built, and those on the fishing fleet would be rotated so that they could be adapted to take larger cargoes of people and produce and the livestock and wags that would carry the population once they hit the mainland.

"Mildred's companions have much experience of such matters, and so they will work with us on the conversion of the boats. They will also help to oversee the storage of foodstuffs and belongings for the journey. They will work closely with us, and you will see the true qualities of the pale ones."

Ryan cast his eye over the expectant crowd that had turned with curiosity to view them. He particularly noticed the hostile faces, especially those grouped around Chan.

Sure, it would give them a chance to prove both themselves and also the point Sineta—and presumably Mildred—wanted to make.

But it would also put them right in the firing line for the fanatics.

# Chapter Eight

"Fireblast! How tough are these damn trees?" Ryan grunted as the ax stuck yet again in the fibrous wood of the trunk. Sap oozed over the ax head and down the handle, almost like glue to seal the metal into the body of the tree. The trunk gave easily at the swing of the head, but was loathe to loose the metal, making it hard and time-consuming to fell even a single tree.

And there were many to be felled. Wood was needed for the reinforcement of existing craft and the rapid building of more. Hard labor was required to gather this wood, and among the few islanders felling trees, the companions were set to the task. That was, all the companions except Mildred, who was still aiding Sineta. Although this decision made sense, it still rankled J.B. that Mildred hadn't been to see them while they set about their task.

The islanders who joined them in tree felling were among the least friendly on the island. Many of those who had spoken openly after the meeting about not wishing to travel abroad had been rounded up by Markos's sec men and put to work out of harm's way. There was little they could do in the way of sabotage and damage to the evacuation plans while they were merely chopping trees. There was one exception—

Elias, the man who was Markos's rival for the hand of Sineta.

"Though I wish the move to take place smoothly, I also know my strengths—perhaps literally," he had answered when Ryan, discovering his views and identity, had questioned his being on such a 'punishment' detail. "You just have to look at me to see why I am suited to this."

Ryan had to agree. Although he was softly spoken, Elias was a giant of a man. Around six feet four or five, he was broad-shouldered, with a thickly corded neck and biceps and pectorals that showed a great upper-body strength. He seemed to be top-heavy, as his legs weren't as well muscled. However, this was only comparatively, and served to emphasize his upper-body development. He was felling trees near the companions, and in work breaks had spoken with them, keen to discover more of the world beyond Pilatu. They had learned, in return, of his desire to integrate the community in the outside world, something he felt essential for its long-term survival, and of his quest for Sineta's hand to further this. Taken with what they knew of Markos and his brother Chan, it made the giant Pilatan a sympathetic figure who may be a good ally.

And good allies were what they would need. Even from the attitude of those around them, they knew that there would be problems. A couple of times there had been axes or knives that flew mysteriously through the air to embed themselves in trunks near where the companions worked. The sec, being dismissive, had ordered everyone back to work, thus none of the

companions had been able to pinpoint the origin of the
hostility. So they were constantly on triple-red, and
glad for an ally among the island population. What
worried the companions more than anything was that
they were unarmed. Ryan's panga, J.B.'s Tekna, Dean's
knife and even Doc's silver lion's-head swordstick,
had been taken away by the sec. They still had Jak's
leaf-bladed knives, but to keep these secret, the albino
kept them about his person, which meant that he
couldn't swiftly distribute them in time of trouble.
There would always be a crucial delay.

On the third day, Mildred came to the area where
the felling was taking place to check on the progress
for Sineta. She was accompanied by Markos.

"There really isn't the need for you to cover me like
this," Mildred snapped at him as they followed the
swath left by the already felled wood. "I can look after
myself, you know."

"I would not suggest that you are helpless, like the
rabbit caught in the snake's gaze," he answered stiffly.
"On the contrary, I would be more like to compare you
to the snake."

"Shit, thanks," Mildred replied.

Markos grimaced. "Once more you misunderstand
my intent. I would almost believe that you purposely
misconstrue my words so that they appear false and
damaging to you."

Mildred looked at the sec boss's expression and
laughed. "Lighten up, Markos. I was being funny."

"I am not good at being… 'funny,' as you put it," he
replied with an almost too solemn dignity.

"I had noticed," Mildred pointed out, followed by,

"That's better," as she saw a smile of genuine amusement cross his face. "But it's true. I can look after myself."

"I realize this, but factions against you may not. My presence may make them think again about attack, or at the very least give another pair of eyes to keep watch."

"You really think someone may try to chill me?"

He shrugged. "You are an outsider who aids change. We are going where the majority of workers have been placed out of harm's way because they oppose change. You figure it out."

Mildred glared at the sec boss. "Okay. By the way, for someone who isn't funny, that actually wasn't bad. Guess I asked for it. But you didn't want change, and I don't have to fear you. Do I?"

"I accept the inevitability of change and the tide of history as it ebbs and flows."

"That still doesn't answer my question."

"I repeat—you figure it out. But we are almost there," he added as the sound of tree felling became more apparent. They rounded a bend in the path and came upon the edges of the work party, who stopped when they saw Mildred approach. Among the workers in this section were the six companions and Elias. The dark giant stiffened on seeing the sec boss approach.

"Your posture would suggest you have a problem—and quite a large one—with our friend Markos," Doc murmured.

"You know him—and his pernicious brother. If you wish reinforcement for my views, just ask Jak," Elias muttered.

However the companions—especially J.B.—were too preoccupied by seeing Mildred again to dwell on that.

"Millie, good to see you here," J.B. said with an understatement that was obvious. "It's been a while. We wondered what was going on."

"John…" Mildred returned. "I've been busy. There's a lot to do."

"Plans going well for the evacuation?" Ryan asked.

Mildred was about to answer when Markos stayed her with a gesture. "Remember where we are. Perhaps that is a question that should not be answered here. Mebbe later."

"Yeah, perhaps you're right," Mildred agreed.

J.B. spit angrily on the ground. "When later?" he said, with barely controlled anger. "We're billeted here while you're with the baron's daughter. So what happens when we get over to the mainland, eh?"

"I can't even think that far ahead," Mildred replied. As she spoke, she realized what she was saying.

"Well, isn't that interesting?" J.B. said, a deceptive mildness to his voice.

"J.B., leave it," Ryan counseled. It wasn't an order. There was a rare softness and an understanding in the one-eyed man's tone.

Krysty moved across to J.B. and took his arm. "We can talk about this later," she said softly. "Right now we've got work to do, and I'm sure Mildred has, too." With which the redhead shot Mildred a look that asked her what the hell she meant, before leading the Armorer away.

"Yeah, mebbe we should talk about this after we get

across to the mainland," Ryan said quietly. "Seems to me that you've got some decisions to make."

Mildred chewed her lip thoughtfully before answering. "Yeah, maybe I have," she said simply.
She turned to Markos. "We should get on. Sineta wants to know how the whole of this operation is going."

She turned away to follow the sec boss through the clearing to the next sector of the felling operation. She didn't see Dean follow until she felt his hand. She whirled, ready to defend herself and wondering why she suddenly felt it necessary.

"Whoa, easy!" the youth exclaimed.

"Sorry, Dean. You just surprised me," Mildred replied.

"It's okay," he said. "Look, I just wanted to say that, well, I guess the others just haven't thought of it, but this island... Well, I just figure that mebbe you don't feel so lonely anymore."

"Lonely?" Mildred queried, puzzled.

"Yeah. Mebbe that's not what I mean," he answered, struggling for the right words. "I don't know, mebbe I mean more like... Well, you don't feel so alone."

Mildred sighed. "Yeah, I think I see what you mean. You might be right. But in some ways, I'd be alone without you guys. It's a difficult one to call."

Dean shrugged, then looked past her to where Markos was waiting impatiently. "He's waiting, and he's not happy about it. But I just wanted to say it, that's all."

Mildred grasped Dean's arm. "Okay, thanks."

"What was that about?" Markos asked her when she joined him and Dean had returned to the work party.

"Nothing to concern you," Mildred answered. "Let's get on with this."

They moved away through the trees, and the sec boss turned to Mildred with the intention of speaking. However, he froze, causing Mildred to stop dead.

"What—" she began, but he cut her short with a gesture. Indicating that she stay quiet and wait. He moved sideways from the path and into the denser growth of trees.

Mildred was suddenly very aware that she was alone in the woodlands and unarmed. Since working with Sineta, she had taken to not carrying her Czech-made ZKR, which was stored safely in the home of the baron's daughter. She scanned the lands around and listened intently. There were the sounds of the work parties, but little else she could differentiate.

No, to the left of her she could hear someone coming through the trees. She moved around and fell into a combat stance, crouching to prepare herself for an oncoming attack. She almost laughed with sheer relief when Markos appeared out of the trees, particularly when she saw the expression of surprise on his face when he took in her defensive stance.

"I thought I heard someone follow—stealthy like a true stalker, but still clumsy enough to trip some roots and move the undergrowth," he said.

"But who—" Mildred began, only to be cut off by the piercing sound of a man in mortal agony.

Mildred and Markos moved as one. Both were able to pinpoint the direction of the cry, and both ran toward it. Markos had his H&K drawn and in his hands, ready for any attack. Mildred may have had no weapon for whoever had been attacking, but her thoughts were with whomever had been attacked: to offer assistance if she could.

The cry had come from the area they had just left. Mildred felt a qualm of apprehension. Was that one of her friends? She hadn't recognized the voice that screamed, but it had been distorted by pain, forced high and keening.

Markos and Mildred burst into a clearing to find one of the Pilatan workers, back against a tree as though resting, an initial impression belied by the pool of blood in which he reclined and the spray of crimson that spread in front of him. Markos held out his arm to keep Mildred in cover at the edge of the clearing, scanning the area for the attacker; but Mildred pushed past him to reach the afflicted man.

Crouching in front of him, she could see by his blank eyes that he had already bought the farm, his life spilt onto the ground from a wound in his throat. His throat had been expertly sliced, right through cartilage and artery to the vertebrae, which showed through as Mildred tilted the head. His lifeblood had been pumped through the gaping wound in less time that it took them to locate and run to the sound of his scream.

It was then that the weapon caught Mildred's eye— a leaf-bladed throwing knife had been embedded in the tree to one side of the corpse's head.

Jak? It couldn't be. But the knife… Mildred's head whirled.

"Stay there and don't move," Markos's voice commanded. Mildred turned sharply to see who had arrived on the scene. It was Ryan and Jak, with Elias close behind. Markos narrowed his eyes. "You're here quickly," he said with suspicion. "You don't work near here."

"Don't be a fool," Elias panted. "We heard the scream and are just the quickest." He turned his attention. "The brother?"

Mildred shook her head. "No way. Sliced clean through."

"I see no ax. The murderer must still have—" Markos began.

Mildred cut him short with a curt shake of the head. "This was no ax. Far too clean. Besides…" She pulled the leaf-bladed knife from the tree and held it out. She looked cold and hard into Jak's eyes as she revealed the weapon. The albino returned her gaze with an equal iciness. Was he masking guilt or expressing disgust at the implied suggestion of her action? Mildred couldn't tell.

"I have seen no workmanship of this kind here," Markos said softly, taking the knife and examining it carefully. He kept his voice low as the clearing was now ringed by several workers from nearby, including the rest of the companions and some Pilatans who had responded to the cry of agony.

"You wouldn't," Mildred replied in the same soft tone as the sec boss. Markos followed her eyes and fixed his gaze on Jak.

"Now just wait a minute, Mildred," Ryan said in a level voice. "Think about this."

"No need think," Jak said. "Lost two, three knives when we were taken. One of those."

Markos raised an eyebrow. "And someone found it in the undergrowth on the other side of the island and

brought it over here to do this?" he intoned sardonically.

Jak looked around him, aware of the sudden swell
of voices. The Pilatans—not best disposed to the companions in any case—had turned hostile in a matter of
moments. The other companions moved close around
Jak, their body language subtly changing as they tensed
for an attack.

"Wait!" Elias stepped into the clearing, turning to
look at the gathered islanders. He turned back to
Markos and Mildred, a look of contempt clouding his
visage. "You really would condemn this man without
thinking? Even you, who are supposed to be his
friend?" he added directly to Mildred.

"The knife—" Markos said.

"No! That proves nothing," Elias shouted. "You
would not believe Jak's friends, I know—but would
you also accuse me of lying?"

"What do you mean?" Markos snapped.

"I mean I was with the pale ones from the time that
you both left until this poor unfortunate screamed," he
said, gesturing to the corpse. "Jak could not have used
the knife—nor any of his friends, for that matter—as
they were in my sight the whole time. You will have to
look elsewhere for your sacrificial lamb, my friend,"
he added with heavy sarcasm.

"WHAT THE HELL HAVE WE become that Mildred is no
longer one of us and doesn't even trust us?" J.B. asked
bitterly as they returned to work.

"Not her fault," Jak replied.

"Jak's right," Elias added. "It was made to look like

Jak. You have some pretty powerful enemies, ones who will got to the length of taking a discarded weapon and using it to incriminate you."

Ryan nodded. "That's what worries me. If you hadn't been able to vouch for Jak's whereabouts back there, I figure we would have had one hell of a fight on our hands. They wanted to lynch us."

"Yeah, and in a way I don't blame them," Krysty said thoughtfully. "That would have been a pretty good argument against going to the mainland, if we were the example of what it was like."

"How true, dear girl, but surely our priority should be to find whoever is responsible for such actions, lest the situation be allowed to worsen."

"It is easier to say than to do," Elias mused. "After all, many of the work parties are separated from each other, and it is easy to move about undetected in these woods. Come to that," he added after a thoughtful pause, "do we know that Mildred and Markos had each other in sight the whole time?"

Ryan frowned. "You think that Markos may have had something to do with this?"

Elias shrugged. "He was quick enough to point the finger of suspicion, and was he not in charge of the party that took you prisoner on the far side of the island? What better opportunity to have retrieved the knife—perhaps only for a trophy or to study—or to know where such a weapon may be."

It gave the companions pause for thought. If their enemy was the sec chief, then they would have to keep close counsel and watch one another with the utmost care.

The oppressive thought killed all conversation and each was lost in his or her own thoughts as they returned to felling trees. The work was hard and there was a plentiful supply of water. However, the humidity was such that they drank far more than intended, leaving them dry, as J.B. discovered when, with a loud curse, he turned the empty canteen upside down.

"Dark night, nothing about this pesthole is good."

"River there," Jak commented, indicating through the trees. "Mebbe fill canteen."

"Is it drinkable down there?" Ryan asked Elias.

The dark giant shrugged. "It may be a little brackish with this density of wood—the river gets blocked too frequently to flow fresh—but it will still be drinkable."

"Better than nothing," the Armorer commented in a taciturn manner as he took the canteen and headed toward the river that ran parallel to the area being felled by the work parties. As he made his way through the trees, J.B. could hear the other tree fellers at work. But his attention wasn't on his surroundings. Spinning around his head were thoughts that he didn't want to consider. If they managed to get off this island in one piece, without either being chilled by separatists or lynched by those who felt they were responsible for the death, then it was highly possible that Mildred may part company with them. Although there was a part of the Armorer that could understand Mildred's dilemma, for the most part he could only think of traveling on without her. It wasn't something that he wished to contemplate. He wasn't a man for expressing his feelings, but he had always assumed that she knew their depth. Perhaps he was wrong.

He had reached the bank of the river, which was little more than a stream, that ran sluggishly. He bent to scoop up a palmful of water to taste it and to appease the dryness in his throat. He grimaced as it hit his taste buds. It was sour and brackish, tainted by the leaves and twigs. But it wasn't poisonous and better than nothing. J.B. uncorked the canteen and dipped it into the flowing stream.

It was as he lowered himself to his full extent to reach out to catch the water at its fullest flow that he heard the snap of a twig behind him. It was a sharp crack, suggesting a heavy footfall and no small animal following its own path.

Cursing to himself, the Armorer threw himself forward into the river. The realization that he had been so wrapped up in thought that he hadn't been observing the slightest caution angered him. He couldn't believe that he'd been so stupe, so soon after they had been under threat. He had to have been simple to track, and he was relieved that whoever was in his wake had been so careless as to give him unintentional warning. He gasped in as much breath as he had time before he hit the surface of the water, flat and hard. The leaves and branches stung with the force of his flattened impact, the surface hard to him like a stone being skimmed across it.

That wasn't the only sting he felt. Before his ears were filled with water, he heard the harsh bark of a blaster. From the tone, he figured it was a Glock, and his stalker had time only to loose off a single shot. Just the one, but enough to catch him as he entered the water, a burning needle entering his hip. It felt like a graze. He had to have made the water in time to prevent a better shot. It still hurt like hell, though, the residual impact and the shock making him turn in the water. Somehow his glasses stayed on, although his battered fedora floated past his eyes as he rolled over. He felt his backside and legs hit the muddy bottom of the riverbed, soft and clinging. He kicked, churning up silt as he freed himself from the mud's grip. He reached out and grabbed his hat, not wanting it to hit the surface.

The dirt in the water stung his eyes and he could only see light reflected against the opaque surface of the river. If he couldn't see out past the scum and detritus on the surface, then it was a fair bet to assume that whoever was after him couldn't see in past the same. So unless they wanted to take another random shot, he was safe for the time being.

But not for long. His descent had been too swift for him to do anything other than take a regular breath, and he could feel his lungs burn and burst. He had to let out air and somehow break surface enough to take in more oxygen. He spasmed and coughed, bubbles of carbon dioxide exploding from his nostrils and heading for the surface, giving away his position. He ignored the pain in his hip and the dark stream of blood that colored the water around him. If he was going to break surface soon, he needed to move so that he would be harder to resight and fire upon.

Following the flow of the river, he turned and kicked, propelling himself downstream until he had no choice but to surface and gasp more air into his lungs. He hoped that the others had heard the report of the

Glock, and would have headed to the riverbank to investigate. They might not catch whoever had fired, but at least they would scare him away, leaving J.B. to escape the river in safety.

He could hear the blood pounding in his ears and see the black stars exploding in front of his eyes as he stroked, trying to keep low in the water. It was no good, he would have to surface now, before it was too late and his lungs exploded, expelling carbon dioxide and taking in the brackish water instead of fresh air.

Kicking up, careful not get his feet caught in the mud, J.B. broke surface, the air light and fresh after the heaviness of the water, his mouth hungrily sucking in air as his lungs shot through with the agonies of relief. He couldn't tell how far downstream he had traveled, and right then he didn't care. Neither was he mindful of the hidden marksman taking another shot at him. He could breathe again and that was all that mattered.

Spluttering, brackish water running from his nose, J.B. set his feet lightly on the bed of the river. It was chest-deep at that point and it buoyed him enough to prevent his heavy boots becoming bogged down in the mud. His ears popped as water ran from them, the sound now piercing and painfully clear and bright.

"J.B.! Fireblast, man, are you okay?"

Ryan was running along the riverbank, leaping over the foliage and twisted tree roots that sprung out into the water in his attempt to reach the Armorer. Krysty was close behind, her hair flailing free behind her, suggesting that the moment of real danger was past. Farther along the bank, back where he had dived into the river, J.B. could see Dean and Doc holding down a struggling man, while the giant Elias, and Jak—who looked even more deceptively small and frail next to the muscular Pilatan—stood guard, holding off a small cabal of wood cutters who were clustered around.

J.B., still clutching his fedora, struck out for the bank, hauling himself up with the help of the one-eyed man's outstretched hand. As his right leg hit the bank, no longer supported by the water's buoyancy, he felt a sharpness as pain seared through the muscle and the leg buckled beneath him.

"Fuck, that stings," he hissed. "I figured the bastard caught me as I hit the water. My own fault. Should have heard him coming before, but—"

"It doesn't matter," Krysty said, joining Ryan in helping support J.B. as he took his weight off the damaged leg. "You need to get that dressed as soon as possible. We'll have to get back to the ville."

"If we can. They might have other ideas," Ryan added, indicating the men gathered around the companions and the prone attacker.

As they approached, they could hear Elias trying to reason with the crowd.

"You do not have the ears of the deaf. You heard the shot for yourselves, and now one of the pale ones is missing, while we find this man with a blaster in his hands."

"Where is this missing man?" one of the crowd demanded.

"Here," J.B. yelled, "and that bastard shot was good enough to hurt."

Jak and Elias turned to see the Armorer hobble back toward them with the help of Ryan and Krysty. A brief smile flickered across the albino's face. It was soon erased by the words of the crowd.

"They chill one of ours, why shouldn't they pay?"

Elias shook his head. "That is not right. You heard me say that I was with them when that murder occurred. Do you still not believe me? Truly, you have worse heads than the boar you closely resemble in temper."

"John Barrymore, it is a relief to see you. I feared that perhaps we had lost you when there was no sign."

"Just keeping my head down, Doc," the Armorer deadpanned.

"I don't want to spoil the moment, but I figure we'd better get J.B.'s leg looked at as soon as possible," Ryan broke in. "We need to get back to the ville, and take him with us," he added, indicating the man still being held down by Dean and Doc.

"Why should you have any help when our people are left to buy the farm?" asked one of the crowd, a hard-faced man whose eyes were alive with hate. "One of our people is chilled by a weapon of yours, and our ville is in the hands of one who allows herself to be defiled by you. It is a pity that he did not drown."

Ryan felt J.B. stiffen at this reference to himself and Mildred, and stayed his friend with an increase of pressure in his grip on the Armorer's shoulder. "Easy, J.B. Don't let him rile you," he whispered.

Elias spit on the ground in front of him with contempt. "Is that all you can think of, when we are at a crucial moment in the history of our people? You should be left here to rot when the rest of us move on." He turned and took the Glock from where it lay on the ground, then swung around to face the group in front of him. "I will carry this blaster, so that even you cannot protest about the weapon being in the hands of the pale ones. We will leave now and head back to the ville. You—" he inclined his head briefly to the man on the ground "—will come with us, and if you try to escape I will blast you myself. Come, let us go."

As Elias leveled the blaster at them, the crowd of disgruntled Pilatans moved back to allow the companions and their captive to pass through. Dean had the Pilatan captive's arm up behind him in a hammerlock, with Doc at his side, one of Jak's knives in the older man's grasp, poised for the captive's ribs to strike if necessary. Jak led the way, and behind Dean, Doc and the captive came J.B., supported by Ryan and Krysty. The Armorer gritted his teeth and tried to put as much weight as possible on his leg to save the energy of the duo who supported him—there was some way to go before they reached the ville. The wound, which stretched from his thigh up to his hip, was still bleeding, and he could feel his leg starting to stiffen. It wasn't deep, but this was partly why the wound refused to stop bleeding, despite the effort Krysty had made to pack it to staunch the flow.

Elias covered them, walking backward, until they had rounded a bend in the path and it was no longer possible to see the Pilatans gathered by the riverbank. The giant turned so that he could walk in a more regular manner, but still kept vigilant for attack from the rear or the sides.

"Don't need to tell you, I know, but keep your ears open, Jak. I don't think we can trust them," he said.

"Already there," the albino replied. He had a leaf-bladed knife in each hand and was alert for the slightest sound.

"This is really gonna let the shit hit the wall," J.B. said through gritted teeth as they progressed. "What the fuck will Markos and Mildred make of this one?"

COMPLETELY UNAWARE at that moment of what was going on in the woods, the sec boss and Mildred were about to part company. After leaving the wood-felling sites, they had walked down to the beach where work was progressing on the refashioning of the boats. From here, they had moved into the ville itself, where there were moves afoot to pack up as much of the ville as possible for transportation while still keeping it running until such time came for them to depart. Both at the beach and in the ville, Mildred was aware that there were sections of the community that resented her presence as an overseer and were more inclined to talk to the sec boss than they were to her directly. She wondered if Sineta would have been wiser to make the round of the works herself with the sec boss rather than send Mildred, for the doctor had heard some talk among sections of the populace concerning herself and J.B., and also talk of resentment that such a mere interloper should be acting as a liaison between the baron and the Pilatans.

They couldn't know the truth. Barras was approaching the end of his life. Despite the painkillers she had given him, Mildred had known from the first that the baron's condition was critical. What had surprised her was the sudden worsening of that condition. It was as though the old man had been grimly hanging on, waiting for the deadlock in his people to be broken. The arrival of Mildred and the rest of the companions had been the catalyst and now action had finally been taken. With nothing left to live for, and the knowledge that any attempt to move him would hasten his demise, the old baron had let go and was rapidly approaching the crisis point. So his daughter was spending as much time with him as possible, deputing Mildred to fulfill her tasks. But the people couldn't be told, as they couldn't be distracted from their purpose at this time.

Mildred and the sec boss arrived back at Sineta's quarters and entered. As Mildred had expected, the baron's daughter wasn't there.

"You'd better get on with your own tasks," Mildred said wearily. "I've kept you from them enough. Lord knows, if I'm tired, you must be exhausted by the time you finish your working day right now, having to nursemaid me, as well."

Markos lingered for a moment, as if shaping the words that he spoke. "On the contrary, I would argue that it is a vital part of my duty—and a part from which I derive great satisfaction—to work alongside you."

Mildred allowed herself a smile before answering. "It's good of you, but it must be a real pain in the ass to have to follow me around."

"It is something I would do from choice," the sec boss returned.

He was looking at her intently, and as her eyes locked on to his, she felt a wave of emotion sweep over her. Qualms she had felt about consequences of any actions on the companions were swept from her mind.

Markos crossed the room and embraced her, bending so that his lips could meet hers. Mildred responded eagerly, pulling him to her fiercely.

As Markos's hands slid down Mildred's back to cup her buttocks, the couple was distracted by the sounds of a gathering crowd outside. He broke the embrace, shot Mildred a puzzled glance, then rushed to the door.

Mildred followed and was astounded to see J.B., supported by Ryan and Krysty, hobbling across the main square, his wound still bleeding, while the growing crowd stared at their captive fellow Pilatan, with Elias holding the Glock steadily trained on him.

"Mildred, J.B. really needs some attention," Ryan yelled as he caught sight of her.

"And I have something that I think, equally, is in need of your attention," Elias added, gesturing with the Glock.

# Chapter Nine

"Millie, where are you going?"

Mildred turned at the sound of J.B.'s voice. It was the afternoon following the blaster incident by the river, and after she had dressed his wound and shot him full of painkiller, it was decided that he would be unable to return to tree felling until it had healed. In fact, with the time scale under which they were now operating, it was likely that J.B. wouldn't be able to take part in the evacuation procedures.

It was Mildred's suggestion that he remain in the ville, where he could make himself useful by utilizing his skills to supervise the cleaning and packaging of the Pilatan armory. It would also give him a chance to restore to full working order the companions' own blasters, which were currently lying idle. Markos had bristled when she outlined the plan, but as the Pilatan armorer, a man named Simeon who was known to be sympathetic to integration, had raised no objection, Sineta had overruled the sec boss's objections.

Mildred had just left Sineta's quarters on her way to a meeting with Barras. She was spotted by J.B. as he left the armory to fetch more packing cases while Simeon went through the spare H&Ks.

"John, I can't stop right now. I've got to see Barras,"

she said in a bright tone, one that sounded false to her as soon as the words left her mouth. From the change in the Armorer's normally taciturn expression, she could see that it was equally obvious to him.

"Guess if it's that important," he replied, not even bothering to keep the sarcasm out of his voice.

She changed direction and walked toward him. "It's not like that, John, and you know it. But I'm under a lot of pressure here."

"We're all under pressure," J.B. answered quietly. "You're not alone. How do you think it is for the rest of us, being in such a minority?"

"You know my views on that," she snapped, then sighed as she realized how it had to have sounded. "Shit, you know that's not what I mean. Look, if this is going to come off, then I've got a thin line to walk, as Sineta has left it all to me while she looks after her father."

"Quite convenient for her," J.B. mused. "If it turns to shit, then who'll get the blame?"

Mildred shrugged. "Yeah, I know it looks that way, but trust me when I say that it isn't."

J.B. mirrored her shrug. "Whatever you say, Millie. Point is, we don't actually see enough of you to actually be kept in the picture."

"It's hard, John. There's so much to attend to." As she spoke, she looked around the square and could see Markos talking to a sec guard outside the baron's quarters. His eyes kept flicking across to her and she became acutely aware that she was being watched. "Look, I can't stop to talk now. I really have to be getting on with things. After all, he is still baron, and I can't afford to piss him off…for all our sakes."

"I guess not," J.B. said, sounding far from convinced. "I suppose I have my own work to do."

There was an awkward pause and finally Mildred said, "Look, I'll tell you what we can do. Meet me here at about nine tonight. I'll fill you in on what's been going down, and you can let the others know what plans have been made." There was also the unspoken subtext that she would be seeing J.B. on his own. Right now, she wasn't sure how she felt about that, but she didn't want to hurt the Armorer at a time when they all had to pull together.

When they all had to pull together? Who? The Pilatans? The companions? Which camp was she in, and who was she thinking of when she used the term "we"? Issues that she had pushed to the back of her mind came bubbling to the surface. Issues with which she didn't wish to deal at the moment.

"Yeah, okay," J.B. agreed, snapping her out of her reverie. "That sounds good. I'll tell the others when I see them, but I guess I'd better be going. Till later…"

The Armorer moved off and Mildred watched him go, aware that Markos was watching her. She turned and walked toward the building, trying not to meet the sec boss's eye.

"So you will be meeting with him later?" Markos questioned as she approached.

"Is it necessary for me to answer?" she returned.

He winced at her tone. "Yes, I believe it is. Partly because of what is between us, and partly because I have larger concerns to oversee. What will you be telling him?"

"Nothing that will have any bearing on your responsibilities in either sphere," Mildred replied. "Now, if you have no objections, the baron is expecting me."

"I know. I have been informed."

"Is that why you've personally taken this watch?"

He shook his head briefly. "I dismissed the guard so I could speak with you in some degree of privacy. Now I shall have to cover until the next watch."

"So you don't lose face or appear human in the eyes of the men you command?" she asked.

Markos didn't answer.

Mildred knocked on the baron's door and heard his feeble voice bid her to enter. She left Markos resolutely looking away from her so as not to betray any feelings.

The baron's quarters were in almost complete darkness. One oil lamp, suspended from a bracket near the door, lit the interior and the shutters on the windows were covered with thick curtains to prevent any leakage of light. It took Mildred's eyes awhile to adjust, during which time she made her way unsteadily and carefully across the room.

"It takes a few moments," Barras's healer said as she appeared from the shadows, her hand gently taking Mildred's arm to guide her to the baron's bedside without bumping into anything. "I am almost blind for the first minutes of duty. Thankfully there is never anything of any importance during those minutes," she added.

When Mildred was seated by the baron's bedside, and her eyes had become accustomed to the low level of light, she was able to see that Sineta hadn't exaggerated when she had described how ill her father had become. Barras's eyes were wild and bloodshot, staring out into the darkness with an almost scary intensity, seemingly fixed on some distant point. It was almost as if he had swathed the room in Stygian gloom because the river and the boatman were already fixtures on his horizon. His eyes, with their hallucinatory air, had sunk even farther into his skull, which seemed to be now devoid of flesh. He had grown, if anything, thinner than the first time she had seen him, and the painkillers were no longer of any use as anesthesia. They could keep the level of pain such that he could bear it, but they no longer dulled or deadened it. His skin held a ghostly gray tinge and had started to break out all over in sores as the cancer broke through as if fighting its way out of his body and taking him over, transforming him into something alien.

"Mildred, I'm glad you came," he said in a hoarse croak. "I fear I cannot hold on to my reason for long. Even now, it would seem that I drift in and out of this world. Sometimes it is as though my dreams become flesh, or I become a dream. I see my mother and father…my wife…they wait for me, as beautiful and noble as they were in their prime. Perhaps they will see me in that way when I finally arrive and not as I am now. Layla," he added, trying to turn his head with a painfully slow rotation, "where are you?"

"I am here, my baron," the healer whispered, coming close.

Barras nodded slowly. "You may leave us for now. Mildred is able to care for my needs while I talk, and we must have privacy. She will call for you when I am done. Perhaps," he added with the sudden reappearance of a mischievous glint, "Arun will be on duty. I know you have feelings for him from the way you mention his name."

"Thank you, my baron." The healer giggled, leaving them alone. Mildred watched her go, thinking she would be disappointed when she saw Markos outside. But it did, in a flash sadly growing rarer, show her again how the baron had to have been in his prime, and why he had been a popular leader.

Barras waited for the door to close before grasping Mildred's hand tightly. He spoke rapidly and with urgency.

"I must say this, and quickly, for I do not know how long it will be before the dreamtime once again descends upon me. And the next time may be the final time, and I become as a dream once more. Now, I am lucid, and I want you to listen carefully."

"You've got my full attention. But why can't Sineta know this?" Mildred couldn't help but ask.

Barras shook his head impatiently. "In the regular course of events, it would have been told to her and her husband before the time came for me to die. But I do not know if she will take the hand of Markos, or Elias, or will opt to continue alone. If alone, and at such a time, the knowledge of this secret would put her in more danger than a wild bore with the hunt on its tail."

"Why? Why now?"

Barras grasped her hand harder, his bony fingers indenting her flesh. "Listen, and you will understand. When this ville was first built, and the island first inhabited by those escaping bondage, they did not come empty-handed. The concept of money and riches have meant little on the island as we are insular, but our forefathers came from an outside world where such values were paramount. They knew these things meant much to those who had enslaved them, and they knew that to survive in such a world they would need riches of their own. So they took from their masters whenever possible, when they were to escape. Arriving, it soon became obvious that these things were superfluous here, and that they would have no practical use. So they were gathered and kept in a secret place known only to a few, as they would serve if we should ever need to leave the island to deal with the whitelands again.

"The store of such riches was added to when people arrived with more stolen treasures. It was always presumed that these things would be useful one day.

"And then came skydark and the hard years after. In the struggle to survive, the store of whiteland riches—for that is what they were, having no meaning to us outside of that—was largely forgotten, the location becoming a secret that was passed only from baron to baron, so that it would be known if ever a time came when the treasures of the whitelands became needed.

"So it would have continued. I would pass the secret on to Sineta and whoever became her husband, and they would pass it on to their children, and it would always be there for times of need.

"But that has changed. Now the Pilatans must move to the mainland, and the riches may be needed. I am no fool—I know that some of the treasures will mean nothing and have no value in the whitelands. Priorities for all have changed since the nukecaust and the long darkness that followed. The value of things is relative to need and desire, I know this. Those treasures have only a fraction of the value they may have held at the time they were first brought here. But they still have value at least to barons, and I have seen the horde. I have seen it, and I will tell you that it will still have value in the whitelands, and that this is the time for it to be disinterred and taken with the islanders into the whitelands."

Mildred said nothing for a moment. Barras fought for breath, exhausted by his efforts to tell his story, forcing it out while he was still lucid. She found it sad that he referred now to the islanders and the use of the treasure in the third person, as though it no longer had any direct meaning for him. It was, she supposed, an acknowledgment of impending chill.

"I still don't get why you're telling me and not your daughter about this," Mildred said finally.

Barras allowed himself a small smile. "The timing is all wrong. She has no husband, no ally to watch her back. This is the perfect time for the treasure to be taken from the people for private gain, when the whitelands are reached. There are too many possibilities for it to be snatched away. No, it must not be revealed until the Pilatans are settled upon the mainland and there is order restored after the chaos of travel. Sineta will be established as baron by then, no matter what, and it will be harder to resist her status in taking the riches.

"I want you to take the treasure…you and your companions. You are outsiders and will be able to take the treasure and protect it until the whitelands are reached. And you, Mildred, will then be in the perfect position to reveal the secret to my daughter."

"You would trust me…trust my friends, who are pale ones…you would trust us with the riches of Pilatu?"

"Perhaps I am a stupe old man whose mind is muddled by the long chilling, and you would take the riches and run, using them for yourselves. Perhaps. But I think that is not the case. I have seen you, have heard about you...and your friends. They have been misjudged by many in this ville because of their skin, but that is an attitude that will have to be changed when my people are out in the whitelands. Things are not as they were. On the whitelands, much has changed—although I grant you that much will always remain the same—whereas on this island we have been enclosed in a bubble of our making where almost all has always remained the same. Perhaps your way is better."

"Perhaps," Mildred said softly, "but if you knew my history—my real history—then you would know why this island has cut so deeply with me."

"That is good for you, Mildred Wyeth, but I must look forward to the future for my people, even if I will not be there to see it. You must promise me that you will do this for me," the old man said.

Mildred sighed. Things were getting more and more complicated at a time when she least needed it. But at least she would be able to discuss this with J.B. when she met with him later tonight.

"Very well, tell me where it is, and I promise you that it will be done."

The old man squeezed her hand. "I knew that I could rely on you. You have a nobility that runs deep. In many ways, you remind me of the woman I married." For a moment a twinkle lit his glazed eyes. "But that was all a long time ago. I must dismiss these thoughts from my mind so that I may tell you. Past the point where the trees are being felled for boat building, you will find a river—the river where one of your friends was wounded yesterday. Go upstream for half a mile and you will come to a rock cluster that has a cave entrance. Inside the cave is a fork. To the left, it becomes so narrow that only a slender man or woman may squeeze through. Once through, there is a simple lever system that lifts this shelf of rock so that many may enter, and move the treasures within freely."

"It sounds simple enough—as long as we aren't followed."

"That is your province. It is simple, true, and has only remained undisturbed for so long because none except the barons have known of its existence."

"We'll do it. In the next day or two. I'll tell you when it's accomplished. And, believe me, I'm honored that you've trusted me with this. I'll do my damnedest not to let you down." With which, she leaned over and kissed the old man on the forehead, a gesture heavy with respect.

"Go now, for I feel I am slipping into the dream-world, and I am ashamed to let any except my healer or my daughter see me when I am like such."

"I understand. Until the morrow or day after," Mildred said gently, taking leave of the ailing baron. Looking back as she made her way to the door, she saw his eyes glaze over, becoming unseeing as he entered the world that was his gateway to the beyond.

She had no time to dwell on this, however, as more earthly matters took the imperative. As she neared the door, she could hear voices on the other side. They were whispering, but the door wasn't of a thick wood and she could hear them clearly. One was Markos, and the other—similar in timbre, but slightly higher in tone, she couldn't place.

"Things are as they are and that cannot be changed," Markos was saying.

"But you are changed, and the changes are like those of the snake that sheds skin as it grows fatter."

"You dare to say such things to me, with their implications?"

"I do, and gladly. You know that her influence will pollute the purity of the idea and moral that I have—"

"You dare to speak of purity?"

There was a silence. Then the speaker broke the silence with a low hiss pregnant with suppressed menace. "That is the matter of which we never speak. Indeed you are lower than the snake to bring that into the argument. I cannot reason with you when you are in this temper and I feel so disturbed. We will continue this later."

Mildred heard the speaker move away, his footsteps fast and heavy, obviously agitated. She had paused by the door, uncertain as to whether she had been heard, but unwilling to walk into the middle of the argument. Now she judged that it was safe to open the door and exit.

As the light flooded in, she squinted at its sudden violence. The heat of the words she had heard from behind the door, mirrored in the thickness of the atmosphere.

Markos turned to her, the anger of the argument still written on his face. But he softened his tone with a visible effort. "Mildred—all went well with the baron?"

## The Gold Eagle Reader Service™ — Here's how it works:

NO POSTAGE
NECESSARY
IF MAILED
IN THE
UNITED STATES

**BUSINESS REPLY MAIL**
FIRST-CLASS MAIL    PERMIT NO. 717-003    BUFFALO, NY

POSTAGE WILL BE PAID BY ADDRESSEE

GOLD EAGLE READER SERVICE
3010 WALDEN AVE
PO BOX 1867
BUFFALO NY 14240-9952

If offer card is missing write to: Gold Eagle Reader Service, 3010 Walden Ave., P.O. Box 1867, Buffalo NY 14240-1867

## Get FREE BOOKS and a FREE GIFT when you play the...

# LAS VEGAS
### GAME

*Just scratch off the gold box with a coin. Then check below to see the gifts you get!* →

## YES! I have scratched off the gold Box. Please send me my **2 FREE BOOKS** and **gift for which I qualify.** I understand that I am under no obligation to purchase any books as explained on the back of this card.

▼ DETACH AND MAIL CARD TODAY! ▼

**366 ADL DVFD**　　　　　　　　　　　**166 ADL DVFC**
　　　　　　　　　　　　　　　　　　　　　(MB-04)

|  |  |
|---|---|
| FIRST NAME | LAST NAME |

ADDRESS

| | |
|---|---|
| APT.# | CITY |

| | |
|---|---|
| STATE/PROV. | ZIP/POSTAL CODE |

| 7 | 7 | 7 | Worth TWO FREE BOOKS plus a BONUS Mystery Gift! |
|---|---|---|---|
| 🍒 | 🍒 | 🍒 | Worth TWO FREE BOOKS! |
| 🔔 | 🔔 | ♣ | TRY AGAIN! |

Offer limited to one per household and not valid to current Gold Eagle® subscribers. All orders subject to approval.

"Uh, yeah," she replied with caution.

"You do not wish me to pry?" he questioned. His tone was sharper than his expression implied, which she put down to the discussion he had just concluded, the argument that gave her a feasible excuse to change the subject.

"No, it's not that… It's just that I couldn't help hearing as I came to the door…" She shrugged, not knowing what to say.

Markos allowed a wry, sad smile to flit across his face. "My brother. He grows more and more agitated at the notion of moving away from the island, and he wants merely to pick at his agitation like the wounded animal picks at its sores. I do not even know what he was doing here, apart from trying to pick yet another argument with me."

Mildred furrowed her brow. "How the hell did he know you'd be here? You aren't supposed to be."

Markos shrugged. "It couldn't have been difficult. He had merely to go to where I should have been and ask questions."

"I guess so. Do you want me to go find you a relief for this post, so you can continue?" It was not merely from the goodness of her heart that Mildred wanted to do this. It would also enable her to escape before the sec boss reverted to a line of questioning about her meeting with the baron.

"I would appreciate that," he returned, adding as she turned to go, "But tell me just one thing. Why do you wish to meet with J.B. tonight?"

Mildred stopped. She turned to him, deciding to hide her newly discovered reason behind a curtain of the personal, hoping it would dissuade him from prying further. "Because not everything is always cut and dried. Matters overlap, and there are loose ends to be tied. And that's all I want to say on the matter. Is that permissible?"

Markos thought for a moment, chastened. Finally he said just one word. "Yes."

"Then be happy with it," Mildred told him before leaving.

J.B. CHECKED HIS wrist chron. It was a little before nine and the ville was lit by oil lamps that glowed in the deep blue of late twilight. He had spent the day cleaning the companions' weapons until they were back in working order, although they still reposed in Pilatu's armory. He and Simeon had also inventoried and packed much of the Pilatan weaponry, leaving out only spare blasters for the sec men to carry on the journey. J.B. had counseled this as a precaution, as there was always the likelihood of running into trouble as soon as they landed on the mainland. Simeon had been only too pleased to have advice from someone who had knowledge of the whitelands, and the disposition of the Pilatan armorer had made for a more congenial atmosphere than J.B. had encountered in the woods with the other companions.

When the day's work was complete, he had eaten with the others and told them of his meeting with Mildred. Ryan was glad to let the Armorer go alone, knowing that although it would be vital for the group, there would also be matters that would be nobody's business but J.B.'s and Mildred's.

There were few people around at that hour, even though it was still early. Work for evacuation, and the preparation of personal effects, kept people inside their dwellings. Only those with business abroad, or the regular sec patrols, could be seen.

J.B. perched on the platform used for public events, waiting, uncomfortable to be alone with his thoughts at this time, and relieved when he saw Mildred approach from the direction of Sineta's quarters.

"Dark night, you look exhausted, Millie!" was the first thing he said as she came near.

"Thanks, I'll see if I can find something nice to say about you," she returned, embracing him.

He could sense some distance in the embrace, but decided to say nothing until they had spoken further. Perhaps it was just exhaustion.

"I didn't mean… It's just that you look like you've got even more weighing on you than you did this morning," he said by way of apology.

"I have. Shit, you wouldn't believe it, John. I thought things were complicated enough, but this is one hell of a curve ball."

"So you gonna tell me about it, or is it another thing that you keep in the dark?" he asked spikily.

"Oh for God's sake!" She spit the words out angrily. "I've tried really hard not to do that. Try to see it through my eyes."

The Armorer shook his head. "Can't. Don't know what there is to see," he said simply.

Mildred screwed up her face and looked around. There were few people around, sure, but for what she had to say, she needed somewhere much more private.

"Look, there's more going on than we could talk about tonight, but when I met Barras this morning, after leaving you, he told me something—asked us something—that I can't talk about here."

J.B. nodded. "Then let's get some privacy."

Without waiting for her to comment, J.B. led her out of the square and through to the outskirts of the ville. As they passed the wildlife pens, she noticed that he was still limping quite heavily: not on the side he had been shot, but on the other, where his old injuries had been aggravated by his overcompensation as he sought to keep weight off the fresh wound.

It got darker and quieter as they neared the woods. J.B. led her into a clearing and sat her in the center.

"This should be far enough. Anyone who wants to eavesdrop on us now will have to make enough noise getting here for us to know they're coming."

"I know that. I haven't forgotten everything," she said angrily.

The Armorer took off his spectacles and started to polish them. "Sorry," he said quietly. "So, why don't you start at the beginning?"

Mildred began. She filled him in on the background to the hidden horde, and why it had to remain a secret from Sineta. She detailed how they could find it, and added that Jak would be the best bet to gain ingress to open up the hidden part of the cave where the riches were stored. She finished by explaining why Barras felt that they would be best equipped to find and transport the horde until it could be given to Sineta.

When she had finished, J.B. pushed back his fedora, scratched the top of his head, then whistled softly.

"And we're supposed to be flattered that the old baron trusts us?" he said finally.

"Why not?"

J.B. gave a short, barking laugh. "Think about it, Millie. Mebbe you've not noticed, but we're not exactly popular around here. Someone tried to chill me yesterday, and another man was chilled so that we could be blamed. If Markos or anyone close to him or his brother gets a sniff of this, we'll be lynched."

"Markos wouldn't do that," Mildred said in a way that made the Armorer look at her shrewdly.

"That's as may be," he said, opting not to argue. "Mebbe you trust him, but how do you feel about that brother of his?"

Mildred took a deep breath. Should she mention the argument she had overheard between the two of them that morning? How could she without it leading to matters that would cloud the issue?

"Exactly," the Armorer said, reading her pause the way she had hoped. "He's going to be a big problem."

"But we'll do it, right?"

The Armorer shook his head. "I don't know. It's up to Ryan. I'll tell him everything you've told me, and then we'll see. Problem is, if we do it, then how do we all get out of the ville or away from our work parties, get the treasure and hide it without anyone becoming suspicious or noticing we're gone?"

Mildred sighed heavily. "Yeah, you've got me on that."

J.B. stood and looked around. "Yeah, well, I guess we'll just have to work that one out when we come to it. We'd better get back. Someone on sec will have noticed us leave, and if we spend too long out here they'll get suspicious and come looking."

They returned to the center of the ville in silence, passing a sec patrol on the way. When they were in the small square, both J.B. and Mildred noted a sec man watching them with interest.

"Markos likes to keep his eye on things," J.B. commented wryly. "And I'll tell you something else, Millie. We haven't really talked much about anything except—"

"I know," she said, cutting him off. "Priorities?"

"Mebbe. But it's not just me. Where do we all stand with you?"

Mildred shrugged. "I don't even know where I stand right now. Things are going too fast for me to step back to figure it out. But I know I'm going to have to," she added before J.B. had a chance to speak.

"Okay," he agreed. "Look, I need to get back to discuss this with the others. Tomorrow morning, right here, before we set off for the felling area."

"Yeah. Be careful, John," she said, holding him for a moment.

"Mebbe you should be thinking that of yourself," he murmured before turning to go.

Mildred watched him leave the square, heading toward the companions' quarters. What exactly had he meant by that last remark? she wondered. Glancing over to Sineta's quarters, she wondered if she should break her promise to Barras and tell his daughter. It could help if they ran into sec trouble while trying to retrieve the horde. But someone from Pilatu knowing would really complicate things.

Mildred decided to take a walk to take some time to think about things. She set off alone.

AS SHE WALKED DOWN the side streets of the ville, wrapped in her own thoughts, Mildred felt so safe that she wasn't listening for attack, or keeping the corner of her eye fixed on that spot in her peripheral vision that was always the first indication of danger. She had grown soft during the days she had spent in the company of Sineta and Markos, believing the danger would be to her companions, not to her.

She turned into the alley, thinking only of her dilemmas. Should she speak to Sineta? Was her future with the Pilatans or her companions who had rescued her as a freezie? What was she to do about J.B. and Markos? It was a problem for Mildred simply because she was a woman who had never really had to think about such things before. In the predark world she had fought every inch to become a doctor and exist to be considered a woman first and an African American second. Not because she wished to deny her heritage, but because she had felt this would be the only way on her chosen course to beat back prejudice. Maybe she had been wrong, and had forgotten things learned from her father and his teachers. It was right at the time. And then, after waking up in Deathlands, she'd had no time in which to consider such niceties—for that was what they had become. It was chill or be chilled, and survive at all costs. Given a choice, you tried to do the right thing, but what was that, now? Always, her whole life before and after skydark had been based around acting and reacting, moving forward. There had been no choices such as this to make; or, at least, no time to think about them when you had to move on with such rapidity.

So now, when it came to a point where she had to consider such matters, she found herself ill-equipped for the task. She had never had to deal with her emotions in such depth before, and she had no idea where to begin.

It was perhaps because of her introspection that she failed to notice the lantern in the alley was extinguished. It could have just been one of those things. Low on oil or a wick that wouldn't take after lighting. Maybe she would have taken no notice of it, even if she had been concentrating.

But then, at least, she would have been on triple-red. As it was, she was oblivious to the sound of breathing and the deliberately muted footfalls that padded behind her. In fact, she was halfway along the alley, at the worst possible tactical position, when she became aware. Somewhere at the back of her mind, behind the constant rollover of cogitation, a spark of instinct alerted her, flashed warning lights.

Jolted from her self-imposed reverie, Mildred suddenly became aware of the breathing and the soft, uneven pad of feet. One person—indeterminate sex—making an attempt to be quiet that would have worked in a less-quiet atmosphere.

No one trying to be that silent in a darkened alleyway had any intentions toward friendliness.

Mildred turned rapidly to face the opposition, whoever it may be. She was acutely aware that she was unarmed and not completely free of her preoccupation with her problems, which refused to be blotted out, and this would slow her reflexes. If she could spare the energy, she would curse herself. But it was already too late for that.

Her eyes weren't accustomed to the darkness as much as she would have wished. She was only aware that her attacker was wiry—height was impossible to tell as he or she had dropped into a crouch. Instinctive reading of the body language and shape told her that it was a male attacker, but beyond that he was hidden in the shadows, his head shapeless beneath a hood or scarf of some kind.

She had no time to make other judgments as he was on her. She was slow and had allowed him to make the first move. Nonetheless, he had to have had some idea of her capabilities, as he had been swift to pounce as soon as she turned. By the time she had fully rotated 180 degrees to face him, he had sprung forward and was in midair. His face was still swathed, his shape disguised by a loose cotton shawl or cape that billowed out to his rear. It was effective in more than just disguise. The material effectively blotted out the residual light from the street behind him, making it harder for her to see what he was doing.

Knowing that he would cannon into her, and there was nothing she could do about it, Mildred let her muscles relax and began to fall back. It had the desired effect. As he hit her, the impact was lessened by the momentum of her own descent, and she was ready for the hard-packed ground when she hit. It still jarred, but she didn't damage anything and the breath wasn't driven from her body for she had exhaled in readiness.

Her opponent, however, didn't have as easy a descent. Expecting her to crumple and be driven back by the force of his body against hers, he was unprepared for the lack of resistance and hadn't had the time to prepare for the unexpected force of his own landing. He grunted at the impact. Although softened by having Mildred beneath him, it was enough to drive out his breath while his own momentum made him stumble and cartwheel over her body to land awkwardly some distance away.

Before he had even come to rest, Mildred was coming to her feet, using a hand on the ground to pivot as she rose and turned simultaneously. It was risky, because if he was quick enough he could kick or strike at her hand and leave her falling on her face with one arm rendered useless. But if she came to her feet in any other way she would be facing away from him, leaving her back undefended.

There was little room to move. The walls of the alley seemed to close in on her, making the area of combat close and cramped. Surely someone in the buildings on either side would hear the scuffle? If she cried out an alarm… No, that would take too much effort and breath. She felt in her gut that this was something she would have to deal with herself.

She was on her feet and poised as her opponent hauled himself upright. As he did so, his right hand darted to his waistband and pulled out a wicked-looking knife. The blade was long and came to a vicious point. There wasn't enough light in the alley for the blade to glint, but the metal showed as a white shape, clear and sharp against the dark of his body.

It was a knife that looked horribly familiar. Mildred felt her senses whirl. It was J.B.'s Tekna that her assailant was brandishing, and he was moving toward her.

For a fraction of a second she was paralyzed by the revelation, then adrenaline kicked into her bloodstream and she was galvanized into action by the knowledge that if she didn't move right now, there would be no time later for idle reflection.

Time slowed. The adrenaline in her system made everything in her body seem to move at a faster rate, making it easier to make snap decisions without panic. She knew that one wrong move could leave her chilled. She had no intention of making it that easy for her opponent. Dropping into a combat stance, she balanced on the balls of her feet, so that her balance had a forward impetus. As her opponent thrust at her with the knife, she swayed her hips to feint to her left. It was a movement her opponent followed automatically, with little thought and complete instinct, which was just what Mildred wanted. Straightening and moving to the right, she grabbed his forearm as it came past her, the knife harmlessly slicing at empty air. Both hands grabbed at the forearm, taking it in an iron-hard grip. With some part of her mind that was still functioning, she noticed that he was covered from shoulder to fingertips, long sleeves tucked into gloves. She had no idea if her attacker was white or black, something that was important to her. If it was J.B., and not merely someone who had his knife... But he had been in the armory all day. Who could take it without his knowing?

All these thoughts whirled through her mind in a fraction of a second. The tension in the muscles of her attacker's forearm as he responded to her grip brought her attention back to the moment and focused her on the immediate danger. Hissing breath through her teeth with the effort, she thrust the arm down and brought her knee up so that it connected with his elbow. The force caused him to yelp with pain and the knife to fall from his nerveless fingers. She could also reasonably have expected the force to shatter his elbow and tear cartilage and tendon, rendering the arm useless. But whoever her attacker may be, he had reactions almost as quick as her own. Knowing that he couldn't stop the blow, he contrived to duck into the movement and twist his arm so that Mildred's knee didn't hit him square on the elbow, and he was able to absorb enough of the impact momentum to prevent serious injury.

This fractional movement was also enough to upset Mildred's balance, which had been weighted toward the delivery of her knee. She stumbled, shuffling her grounded foot to adjust balance.

It was the cue her attacker needed. He swept his own leg around so that his heavily booted foot caught her in the calf. A sharp pain shot up past her knee and the muscle went dead as the nerves responded to the blow. She felt her leg buckle and cursed inwardly as she knew she had to fall. She let go of the man's arm and tried to lessen the impact of her fall, but to little avail. She stumbled back, trying to make a yard of space for herself, or at least to fall against the wall of the building behind her, so that she wouldn't be prone. But it was no good. She fell awkwardly onto the hard ground, feeling the breath explode from her lungs. Her shoulder jarred awkwardly and painfully against the adobe wall behind her. She pitched herself sideways to prevent her head from cracking against the wall, leaving her at best stunned, at worst, unconsciously and completely vulnerable.

She took the force of the ground on her elbow and shoulder and tried to use any bounce in the earth to act as a lift as she rose to a sitting position. She was still vulnerable, but at least she was facing her attacker and might be able to parry an immediate blow.

However, there was no such blow. Instead of moving in to strike empty-handed, her opponent had opted to try to retrieve the Tekna. Definitely for use in the attack, but perhaps also because it would be incriminating if found?

Why the hell had none of the Pilatan sec heard the fight, or been alerted? Where the hell were they? Usually, it was impossible to avoid them.

No time to think about that now. The assailant's move had bought her a precious fraction of a second in which to recover her balance and poise, to act rather than react. Pushing herself upright, Mildred ignored the throb in her calf, still aching from the kick, and moved toward the masked man. In the enclosed space of the alley, it took but a moment, and he only had time to look around from his action of picking up the Tekna before she was on him. Not trusting her aching leg to support her steadily, she used it to kick at the man. With his back half turned to her, it wouldn't be a truly effective blow in the manner of a head shot, but catching him full in the ass pitched him forward so that he sprawled on the dirt, the knife dropped.

Mildred hissed in pain at the impact of the kick. She hadn't pulled the punch at the last, but was aware that her damaged leg carried less force than usual, and still hurt like hell. It was as well that she hadn't trusted it to support her weight.

The masked man was scrambling in the dirt, rolling to face her as he tried to right himself. He lay with his legs apart, and she considered taking a kick at his exposed testicles. It would disable him, but she would run the risk of him grabbing her foot and pitching her off balance. Her eyes flicked across the ground, searching for the knife. There it was, to one side of him, still within reach, but seemingly forgotten as he struggled to right himself.

"Hey, what's going on down there!"

The shouted exclamation from behind made Mildred start. She hadn't heard anyone raise an alarm, so it had to be one of the regular sec patrols that she had cursed for their absence a few moments before. She felt the automatic urge to turn to reply, but reason took over and she kept her eyes fixed firmly on her still-prone attacker. The imperative had shifted. His priority now would be to get away fast, while she wanted to keep him right where he was, so that he could be unmasked.

"I asked a question. Freeze and don't move a muscle," shouted the sec man as he began to move down the alley. She could hear his running feet. A few seconds and he would be at her shoulder. Time enough for her attacker to make his getaway if she let him.

The masked man struggled to his feet as Mildred advanced.

"No, you bastard," she raged as she launched herself at him. He had left the Tekna on the ground, so he was still unarmed: level playing field. Mildred's leap was tempered by her injured leg, which still refused to move properly, but she was still fast enough to catch him full-on as he clambered to his feet.

Once more, the masked man grunted loudly as he was thrown to the ground, Mildred on top of him.

But that was when it started to go wrong. As she hit the ground, she had the bizarre feeling that she had bounced back up. The sec man had arrived at the rear of the action, unable to see what was happening with any clarity, and had elected to take out the first party he could lay hands on...which just happened to be Mildred.

"Okay, let's break this up," he said with a sharp exhalation of breath as he plucked at the back of Mildred's shirt and pulled her up, throwing her back against the wall. He was a huge man-mountain, several inches taller than the woman and almost as wide as the alley. And he could throw her with some force, as he demonstrated with ease.

Mildred moaned as she hit the wall...hard. Her spine jarred, her ribs ached and she was unable to breathe. All she knew was that he had pulled her off the man who had tried to chill her, and he couldn't be allowed to get away. Unable to even try to explain, she knew she had to act. She forced herself forward so that she staggered toward the sec man as he bent to pick up her still-prone assailant.

If she had been thinking clearly, she would have realized what a stupid move it was. If she just left the sec man alone, he would mop up the mess. But she could only focus on the thought of her attacker getting away. She stumbled as she threw herself onto the back of the unsuspecting sec man, hitting him with very little force, her balance taking her to one side. Unfortunately, he hadn't expected her to move after he had thrown her against the wall, and she caught him by surprise and off balance. With one massive hand still on her attacker, the sec man pitched to the side, catching his temple on the adobe wall.

It was enough for him to break his hold as he fell. And enough, with the sec man out of the frame and Mildred stunned and falling against the far wall, for her attacker to scramble down the alley, covering ground as he regained his senses, exiting into the street beyond.

"You stupid bastard," Mildred gasped between breaths that ached in her bruised ribs.

The sec man drew his H&K and clicked the safety. "We'll see about that. I think you owe me an explanation."

"I think you both owe an explanation—and to me."

The alley was flooded with light as Markos appeared with a flaming torch that cast shadows over the giant sec man and Mildred, who squinted with the sudden illumination.

"I—" the sec man began, but Mildred cut him short.

"Markos, someone tried to chill me. I fought him off—knife's down there. He got away because of this guy…" she managed to gasp between labored breaths.

The sec boss's eyes were drawn to the Tekna. "Which way did he go?" he rapped, a steely edge to his voice. Mildred didn't try to speak, but indicated the far end of the alley.

Markos gave a curt nod and set off down the alley, his legs covering the ground with ease. He disappeared around the corner at the far end and the alley was plunged into darkness.

"I didn't know who was protagonist and who—" the giant sec man began, only to be cut off by Mildred for the second time.

"Save it. Not in the mood right now," she rasped.

She was in even less of a congenial mood when Markos arrived in the alley, his blaster drawn and J.B. preceding him.

"John?" Mildred gasped. The Armorer was limping, as when she had left him earlier. Limping like her attacker. But he was still dressed as he had been, and showed no signs of injury from combat. He didn't look like a man who had just been in a no-holds-barred fight.

But what the hell was he doing here? He had to have been close, as Markos had only been gone a matter of moments.

"Millie! Dark night, what's going on?" he said, making to move toward her, but stayed by the jab of Markos's blaster in his ribs.

"Wait, my friend. I think you owe us an explanation."

J.B. whirled angrily. "What—"

"Look, John," Mildred cut in, indicating the Tekna that still lay on the ground.

J.B. followed the line of her arm and started when he saw the knife. "What's that doing here?"

"A good question," Markos murmured mildly. "It is yours, is it not?"

J.B.'s eyes narrowed, and his voice became a thin whisper. "It's been in the armory. Anyone with access could have taken it."

Ignoring this, Markos directed his next question to Mildred. "Was it this man who attacked you?"

Mildred looked at the Armorer. She hadn't mentioned her attacker's limp, as this would lead to an obvious—to Markos—conclusion. But it was in her mind.

"I don't know…" she began. "I can't be sure. The man who attacked me was swathed from head to foot, masked." She shook her head.

J.B. was furious and saddened in equal measure, a mix of emotions he couldn't come to terms with. His voice was barely audible, even in the quiet night. "You're not sure? You think I could…" His voice trailed off as he shrugged his shoulders.

Mildred couldn't look the Armorer in the eye, turning away as she answered. "Why are you here? You were going back to the others when I left you."

"I had to think about…what we talked about," he said cautiously. He couldn't reveal the secret entailed to Mildred, yet his necessary reticence made Markos all the more suspicious.

"How very convenient," the sec boss murmured.

J.B. glared at him. "So what was Millie doing here?"

"Yeah, okay…I had to think about what we'd talked about, too," she said. It was an admission that cast a different light on J.B.'s seemingly feeble excuse.

"So you cannot prove it was this man who attacked you?" Markos asked bluntly. "You will not say that it is?"

"I can't."

"But can you say it was not he?"

Mildred paused. Could she? It was a pause that brought anguish to the Armorer's face. Finally she said, shaking her head sadly, "No, I can't."

Markos looked at J.B. with barely concealed contempt. "You may go…for now. But I shall detail men to watch you and your friends. Where there is doubt, I must make sure."

J.B. left the alley without looking back at Mildred. She said nothing as Markos also dismissed the giant sec man. She said nothing when Markos told her to go and rest. She didn't respond when he held out a hand to her as she passed him. She didn't even notice his puzzled and hurt expression as he stood at the head of the alley, watching her go.

She had too many other things on her mind.

MILDRED TOLD Sineta only the barest details of what had occurred, and only to explain the condition in which she arrived back at the baron's daughter's quarters. She was quiet, and Sineta didn't push her.

The women retired for the evening and Mildred figured that she would sleep from sheer exhaustion. But that was denied her. She couldn't settle, her mind endlessly chasing arguments around in circles until she could find some kind of resolution that ceaselessly evaded her.

For so long she had denied a part of herself. She had been Mildred Wyeth, one of a team, despite the fact that she had a fundamental difference. She was black. In the days before the nukecaust, that had made a difference. Maybe it still did, but in a subtly changed way. Black was like mutie, despised by some and tolerated by others, but mostly ignored in the struggle to survive. Being in this community had put her back in touch with that lost part of herself, and that was good. But was it that great when it came to making her doubt J.B.? Leaving aside the relationship they had built between them, and her feelings for Markos, there were more pressing issues. J.B., Ryan, Krysty, Jak, Dean…even disagreeable, argumentative Doc—they had been through so much together, made bonds of loyalty forged in fire. The fire of battle and the promise of buying the farm. Things that went deeper than age, race and sex—the knowledge that they would pull together without it even being spoken of or thought about.

And she was doubting that, denying it?

The time to strike out for the mainland was near. Within the ville there were the same divisions as when she first arrived. Those who wished separatism wouldn't move on or accept cold reality. Was she overcompensating for all those years and edging toward them? Why else did she think J.B. had been behind the attack, if not because he was a different color?

There was a rift between her and the companions. But perhaps this was a good thing. It made her examine herself, her priorities and loyalties. Without the rift, she couldn't have realized how much both her own color and also the loyalty of her companions meant to her.

In the end, the ideals of the island were pitched against pragmatism and experience of reality in the world outside.

Some wanted nothing less than war. But who makes the sides in a war?

# Chapter Ten

For the next couple of days Mildred kept some distance between herself and the rest of the companions. Although she wanted to know what Ryan had to say about Barras's revelation, and if they would act upon it, she was also aware that J.B. had been stung by her suspicions and that at least some of his anger would communicate itself to the others. She wanted time for this to subside, and for herself to gain some kind of equilibrium after the wild seesaw of her own emotions had stabilized.

Besides which, there was work to be done. The preparations for the exodus were nearing completion. The tree felling had been completed and the companions were now at work on the beaches, helping to build boats and seaworthy rafts from the wood they had helped to fell. It was an easier situation for them, as the beach was nearer the ville and, in a more open environment, it was easier to keep alert and to look out for your back. Not that this was as necessary as before. The radical separatists who had been detailed to tree felling weren't allowed to work on the boats and rafts. Markos, in consultation with Sineta and Mildred, had felt that it may be too tempting for those radicals who were in favor of sabotage to loosen a few joints, slacken a few ropes, and so delay or scupper attempts to leave the island.

Mildred, meanwhile, had neared the completion of her own tasks. The Pilatans had the majority of the personal belongings and the tools of their trade packed and ready, leaving only the necessities for the time up until departure. The treasures of the ville, the armory, and the paintings and writings that charted the history of the ville were also carefully packed, along with food supplies and farming tools.

There was, however, the one treasure that still remained unclaimed, and time was growing short. Mildred had stalled Barras when he had asked to see her, but the old man was growing impatient and nervous on the matter.

"I do not have long, Mildred Wyeth—a matter of days, mebbe not even that," he had whispered to her on her last visit. "How can I join my ancestors on the long journey knowing that I have let them down in the this manner, that I have betrayed my people?"

Mildred looked at him. She couldn't argue with his self-diagnosis. He was little more than ashen parchment skin stretched over a skeleton that seemed to shrink into itself with each passing day. His eyes were cloudy, so that she could no longer tell if he was focused on this world or one that he could see beyond this life. His voice was little more than a harsh, croaking whisper.

She would have to act soon, or she was sure that he was right. He would buy the farm without being satisfied. When she'd left the baron on that day, she decided that she would have to act immediately.

It was a decision ratified by the events of the next morning.

"MY FATHER IS NEARING his end," Sineta said softly as she and Mildred prepared for the day ahead. It was neither question nor statement. She continued. "The time for us to depart grows near, but still I feel I should spend more time with him."

"So you want me to cover something for you?" Mildred questioned.

"The livestock is to be fitted for the crates that will carry them to the mainland. Horses will be loaded singly, but Markos believes that the pigs and goats should be crated in small numbers."

"Makes sense," Mildred agreed. "And you want me to go and oversee the fitting while you spend more time with Barras?"

Sineta fixed Mildred with a puzzled look. "Yes...are you sure that is all right?"

"Yeah, sure," Mildred said in an offhand manner that she knew sounded false as it left her lips. The truth of the matter wasn't that Mildred resented covering for Sineta, which was possibly what the baron's daughter believed; rather, Mildred was concerned that Barras, nearing the big chill and beginning to lose his grip on lucidity, would say something to Sineta about the hidden treasures that Mildred was supposed to have recovered. To hear about it in the ramblings of her dying father and not from Mildred would naturally arouse suspicion. And if she told Markos… The sec boss was already growing distant from Mildred, their earlier attraction replaced by a self-imposed restraint. This would only add to his…what? Suspicion? Confusion? She no longer knew what he felt. Which made him a loose cannon in the equation.

"If there is a problem, you would not hesitate to share it with me, would you? We are, I would hope, bonded by more than just our skin," Sineta said softly.

Mildred shook her head. "No, there's no problem," she said slowly, hoping that her lie wouldn't show through. "It's just that the end is near for Barras, and I've kind of grown to like him," she continued. "It's going to be tough for you when he goes."

"It is good of you to consider me in this manner," Sineta said softly, "but it is something for which I have been prepared for some while."

Mildred sighed inwardly with relief. In truth, it hadn't been a complete lie. She did feel concern for the baron's daughter and was truly worried about how Sineta would react when her father bought the farm. She had merely used this to divert Sineta's attention from the true cause of her apprehension.

With mixed feelings, Mildred made her way across the short distance to where the livestock was housed and farmed. She was relieved to be away from Sineta's questioning presence, but tense about the possibility of fulfilling her promise to the baron.

She arrived at the livestock pens to find chaos. Markos and the giant Elias—whom she recognized from his tree-felling detail with the companions—were chasing a goat that had escaped its pen and was running riot among the pigs. The livestock farmers, meanwhile, were concerned with preventing the spooked pigs from breaking the walls of their pens and trampling the crates that lay empty and looked all too fragile at the side of the goat enclosure.

"Damn this creature, why does it not respond our directions?" Markos yelled as he and Elias tried to form a pincer movement that would direct the creature back toward its own pen. To the sec boss's intense annoyance, the goat failed to yield to his direction. With a bleat of fear mixed with triumph, it slipped under his outstretched arms and ran free once more.

"It is a free spirit, and not one of your lackeys that you can direct like a machine," returned Elias with a throaty laugh as he watched the creature circle the pigpen, scattering squealing pigs in his wake.

"Then if it is like you, think like the goat and give me a suggestion that has more practicality," Markos snarled in frustration.

"Things not going so well?" Mildred announced her arrival with a comment that failed to keep the amusement from her voice.

"I'm glad that you find it a source of pleasure that we struggle to prepare for our travels," Markos snapped with a petulance and pomposity that showed how hard he was struggling to keep his dignity.

"Lighten up." Elias laughed. "Man versus beast and beast is winning…there's a lesson in there somewhere, I'm sure."

The goat came hurtling out of the pen, yelping after a bite on its hind quarters from an enraged pig had left it floundering. Sensing their chance to drive it out, the pigs had united into a driving force that had, like a sentient battering ram, forced it toward the gate of the pen.

The terrified creature, skirting around Markos and Elias, too startled and surprised to react in time, headed for the open woods beyond the pens. It was also heading straight toward Mildred.

In the fraction of a second she had, Mildred dropped to her haunches and looked the goat in the eye. Its wild, glassy eyes showed nothing except terror. It wasn't seeing anything in front, merely running blind. Unfortunately, it also gave her little idea of which direction it would take to get past her.

She would have to guess. The goat was upon her, and on some instinctive level she saw it begin to sway toward the left as it shifted balance to swerve around the obstruction in its path. As it passed, she threw herself to the right and grabbed it around the neck. She had only the one chance and she had to make it count. She grasped the tensed muscles of the creature's neck, feeling the hardness of its tendons and flesh beneath the greasy coat. It resisted her attempt to dig in for a firm hold, and she found her fingers slipping on the heavy oil of the goat's hair.

"Oh, no, you bastard, you're not getting away and making me look like an idiot,' she muttered as she clung on for dear life, wrapping herself around the beast, slowing its momentum and dragging it down. She felt it wriggle and whip like a snake beneath her, bleating in a mixture of fear and anger as it found itself constrained.

"Don't worry, don't worry, it's okay," she repeated

over and over in soothing tones as she held on to the goat. Around her, the livestock farmers were penning those pigs that had escaped and calming those that had remained. Things were returning to a calm mirrored by the creature she still held: its thumping heart against her own chest beginning to slow.

"I think you may cease to grip so closely. I'm sure Markos won't want you to smell too much of goat. Or maybe he would," Elias said with heavy humor and a sly glance at the sec boss as he took the goat by the neck, gently guiding it back toward its own pen after Mildred released her grip.

"I know one thing for sure. I could do with a bath already," she said as she rose, attempting to dust herself down but finding she was covered in an almost adhesive layer of goat grease and farm yard mud.

"Why are you here?" Markos asked brusquely and without ceremony, trying to cover his embarrassment at Elias's blatant amusement.

"Sineta sent me to check how things were going. She's with her father again."

Markos nodded solemnly. "I fear it cannot be long now."

"Frightened he's going to buy the farm without naming you?" Elias asked as he returned to them. Although his tone was seemingly light, there was an element of malice shot through.

"You would dare speak of the baron in such a manner—" Markos began, visibly bristling.

"It doesn't matter how he speaks of him," Mildred cut in. "It doesn't change what's happening or why I'm here. So, how are things going?" She was in no mood to listen to the two men sparring for points, and her last question was delivered in a manner that would brook no argument.

Markos told her briefly that the penning of the livestock was going well, had been going very well until the point at which she had arrived, and that they were on target to be ready for the appointed date. He then pointed out that he should be elsewhere, and excused himself.

"Seems like he can't wait to get away," Elias remarked as they watched the sec boss leave. His implication was clear and Mildred found herself taking a strong dislike to the giant beside her.

"Might be more than one reason," she said pointedly. "So, you want to stop being interested in things that aren't your concern and show me what I want to know?"

Elias nodded and began to lead her around the pens and the area covered by the livestock farm. Sensing the guarded hostility in her stance, he changed his tone and was serious as he gave her a full report of the livestock farming activities. When he had finished, and they had come full circle, he excused himself, saying that he had to carry on with his allotted task. It was only then that a certain amount of sarcasm filtered through into his voice, causing Mildred to watch his back with a degree of skepticism as he turned and walked away.

Something told her that his anger and dislike of Markos had been turned on her, as well. There was something about the giant that made her wary, but it wasn't anything that she could pin down exactly, which made it all the more unsettling.

Mildred stood watching him for a moment, then
turned and walked back toward the ville. To return to
the baron's quarters and Sineta, she had to walk
through the housing on the edge of the ville. At this
time of day—it was now midmorning—this part of the
ville was deserted, the populous being either occupied
at the center, the beach, the farms, or out hunting. It was
quiet, and Mildred walked freely, pondering what role
Elias played in the drama of Pilatu. She was aware that
he was Markos's rival for Sineta's hand, and why Barras had made him such; she also knew that the baron's
daughter didn't trust him. To what lengths would he go
to gain power now that the Pilatans were to move to
the whitelands, particularly in view of his rival
Markos's own opinions?

It was a measure of Mildred's distraction at the manner in which she had become embroiled within the culture and politics of Pilatu that she had slipped into a
reverie despite the attack a few nights before. Her attention wasn't focused on the outside world, and it was
only when chippings from the adobe wall to her left hit
her ear, and she saw the cloud of dust thrown up by impact, that she realized that she was being fired upon.

Any cogitation on island politics was pushed to the
back of her mind as instinct took over. Mildred threw
herself forward into a roll, eyes darting back and forth
for a place to take shelter. Where the hell was the firing coming from? Another shot pockmarked the earth
in front of her, throwing up another cloud of dust.

Mildred thanked the Lord that whoever was firing
at her had lousy aim, and tumbled toward the doorway
of a house. She was acutely aware that whoever had

fired had access to the armory for the simple reason that the shots had made no sound. Whoever was shooting had a blaster with a fitted silencer. Even in the almost total silence of the deserted street, there was no sound to alert her or to give her an indication of position. The only thing she was able to determine was that her assailant must be some distance away for even a silenced blaster to be silent.

She jerked away and narrowly avoided receiving a splinter through her eye when the next shot took a chunk out of the door frame where she was taking shelter. Time to move out.

As she scuttled across the street, keeping low and moving quickly, trying to present as small and awkward a target as possible, she figured that he had to be firing from somewhere over to the right. From the low angle of the shots, he had to be fairly high. In one of the houses or on top? Taking a second to glance up as she moved, she could see no one on the rooftops. But could she stop to scan enough to take in distance? After all, he had to be some distance away.

No time. Another shot hit the dirt in front of her, kicking up a cloud.

Where the hell could she go? There were no open doors, and if the ones she tried were locked, she would present an easy target in the time it would take her to find this out. Dammit, where could she go? Maybe she could double back and try to make the last alley she had passed. If she took the one on the right, it would make for an almost impossible angle and her assailant would have to reveal himself in some way to get a better shot at her.

She turned back, spinning on her heel. It was a clumsy maneuver when she was still trying to keep low and small, but the sudden change of direction should— she hoped—compensate for how slow it would make her. A hope that was confirmed when the next shot hit the wall of a house farther in front of the direction she had turned from. It could buy her the few moments she would need to make the alley.

However, the assassin had to have had reflexes that were better than his aim, as the next shot hit the wall beside her.

"Shit!" she cursed, not expecting to have her direction tracked with such speed. She could see the alley up ahead to her left after she had reversed direction. It was only a few yards away.

Mildred felt a stinging blow across her forehead, as though someone had tried to carve their initials with a red-hot poker across her head. She was aware of nothing else except the ground coming up the short distance to meet her.

She didn't feel herself hit. She was already unconscious.

IT WAS ONE HELL of a headache. She didn't think she had been out for long, but it had been long enough— certainly long enough for two sets of footsteps to approach her from the same direction.

Part of her wanted to cry out to them for help, but a small voice inside told her to play possum until she was sure they were friend not foe. It was the right call.

"Is she chilled?" someone murmured. It was a voice she couldn't quite identify because it whispered, but it was familiar. The other, when it replied, was immediately identifiable.

"She's not moving, and not talking, and that's something for which we must be joyous," Elias said in a quiet voice barely louder than his companion's.

"This is not the time for humor," snapped the unidentified voice. Mildred desperately wanted to open an eye to see who it was, but knew this would bring certain death.

"Who said I was being particularly funny?" Elias returned. "She talks too much, and is a pain in the proverbial ass, whether you mean posterior or animal. She's come between Barras, Sineta and my attempts to wheedle my way into that loathsome woman's favor. The only good thing I can see about her, as far as I'm concerned, is that she's taken your brother's mind off being my competition."

"Do not bandy words or push whatever luck you may have left," the second voice raged, attempting to keep a low voice despite the level of rage causing his words to be little more than a venomous hiss.

So the second voice belonged to the albino Chan? Mildred found it hard not to show any amazement as she lay there. The arbiter of integration and the prophet of separatism made for strange bedfellows. What could have brought them together, and why was their venom directed toward her?

More to the point, what the hell was she going to do lying here playing possum with two enemies upon her, at least one of whom was armed?

They were within feet of her now and would soon determine that she was still alive. Not for long, she was sure. But as long as they kept arguing, it gave her some time to think.

"I wouldn't get overexcited if I was you," Elias said with that sardonic calm that Mildred had found so infuriating earlier and that seemed to have the same effect on his uneasy ally. "I believe it was my shot that actually claimed the bitch, rather than yours. That gives me the moral advantage, I believe."

"You?" Chan spit. "You have no idea of what the word even means. Do not talk to me of such matters. This is pragmatism, pure and simple."

"Of course, whatever you say…and your motives are pure at heart, are they?" Elias mocked.

"My motives are not your concern, although they are fuelled by the likes of yourself."

Elias sighed. "Whatever you say. I would suggest, however, that rather than discuss philosophy with this creature sprawled in front of us, we would be better employed disposing of her."

Chan snorted. "We haven't even checked whether or not she is breathing."

"Then all the more reason to do so. If she's still alive, we carry her off and finish the job where we're going to dispose of her. I don't have any particular desire to be caught with the half-chilled or chilled by any of your brother's lackeys. Even you would find that hard to explain to him. Besides, I have plans for her."

There was something in the tone of his voice that made Mildred want to shiver, something she was barely able to suppress. At least they didn't plan to chill her then and there when they inevitably discovered that she was still alive. It would buy her a little more time, and that was all she had.

She felt a foot prod at her, tentatively, and with some disgust that managed to communicate itself even into that gesture. She stayed limp and allowed the sharp toe of the booted foot to jab her several more times in the ribs without giving way to the desire to gasp at the pain.

"Still breathing—I can see that—but not responding. She's either unconscious or playing. If the latter, then I'll just emphasize to you that you keep that blaster trained on her and blow her fucking head off at zero range regardless if she so much as makes a move," Elias commented.

She stayed still and silent, allowing the giant to turn her over. He was as strong as he looked, for she felt the lightness of his touch as he flipped her over with ease. She felt blood from the crease along her forehead run back into her plaits and was thankful it didn't run down to her eyes. That would make the next part of her act easier.

"No surprise that she is unconscious," Chan muttered, "not with a graze such as that."

"Pity it wasn't a straighter shot and took the bitch out with a blast through the brain," Elias returned with venom. "Now, my sweet little child, let's just see how far from conscious you really are."

As he spoke she felt the hard pad of his thumb on her eyelid. She rolled her eyeball back into her head, which took considerable effort to keep it there as he held her eye open for some time. She wasn't sure how long she could keep it rolled back.

"Yes, I would say that she is well and truly unconscious," Elias pronounced with some satisfaction. "Now we should get her out of here. It's far too public for my taste. There will be some blood on the ground. When I lift her, scuff the earth to cover it."

"I am not as stupe as you seem to believe," Chan returned petulantly. "I had already considered this point."

Mildred felt herself be lifted up by the giant Elias as though she were nothing more than feather, and was flung unceremoniously over his shoulder. He strode off, each step bumping her stomach on his hard shoulderblade. She could hear the scuffling of Chan's feet as he covered the bloody signs of her shooting, and then the patter of the lighter man as he ran to catch up with Elias.

Elias was dangerous because of his size and strength. Chan was a lightweight in every way. She had already sized him up as neurotic. But they were two, and she was alone. More than that, she was quite possibly concussed from the bullet crease and may find it hard to act quickly when called upon. And, finally, they were both armed, and she wasn't. The only advantage she had was surprise, as they believed her to be unconscious. Somehow, she figured that it wouldn't be enough.

They walked for some distance, the two men bickered all the while. The longer they walked, the more she would learn. But to what end?

"I don't like this. We should have finished the job there and then," Chan said.

"And let her be found? There would be an investigation and sooner or later it would be discovered that we have nothing in the way of an alibi. Where would we be then? Would you be able to talk your way out of that with your brother?"

"But the longer we are in possession of the accursed woman, the greater the chances of being caught," Chan argued.

"Not this way," Elias said with confidence. "I have watched carefully the patterns of the security patrols, and I know for a fact that there is no work going on out here. The wood for the boats has long since been felled. All we have to do is keep things relatively quiet. Not difficult with these silenced blasters," he added. "I thought it rather a master stroke to use the one-eyed man's blaster. If anyone checks the armory, they'll find it has been recently fired."

"Would anyone?"

Mildred felt the giant shrug beneath her. "I doubt it, but it would supply a neat and rather confusing finishing touch."

"You have approached this entirely with an unbecoming sense of humor," Chan snapped.

"Oh, come now," Elias replied calmly, "is not the whole thing quite absurd in many aspects? Who would consider the prospect of either of us deigning to work together? You are well-known for your bigoted and inflexible views, whereas I am known for my forward-looking attitude."

"I— You are the most—"

"And your complete lack of a sense of humor. I really should have added that," Elias cut across the albino's protest, almost musing to himself. "However, I will grant that you showed a commendable streak of ingenuity when you came to see me."

"Pragmatism. I could not do it by myself, and I could see that you have your own reasons to be self-motivated."

"Ah, yes, greed. A fine thing. After all, if you don't look out for number one, no one else will."

Mildred felt herself being lifted off his shoulder. Knowing he would drop her with little regard for pain, she allowed herself to relax and to not anticipate her landing. It was hard and painful. She hit the ground on her back, her head bouncing on the ground. She figured they had to be near the river, for the ground was softer here and there was the sound of running water nearby. Had they carried her down to where the treasure was hidden? How the hell had they found out about it? From their conversation, she had assumed that they were aware of both its existence and its whereabouts. She was about to find out how, as they continued their conversation, as if oblivious to the fact of her even being there.

"It is not a noble sentiment, but I can only concur with your somewhat crude way of phrasing it. I had read the legends of the old treasures of the whitelands in the archives of our people, but I had thought the secret lost forever until I heard Barras tell this bitch about it. To know that he had kept the secret for long enough was bad, but to know that he was imparting it to an outsider and for pale ones was intolerable. It belongs to the Pilatans."

"And of course you'll be giving your half to them," Elias said with heavy sarcasm.

"You know perfectly well that I will not," Chan returned with an unexpected fire. "They do not understand what it is to be black. You do not. You think that it is acceptable to mix with outsiders. You think that it is so terrible to want to keep ourselves pure? And yet those fools and morons treat me as different because I am an albino. They treat me with contempt...worse, with pity. Because I have no skin pigment, they do not think of me as being black. You sought power for your views by marrying the baron's daughter, and so did I—although a high yellow beauty like her would not condescend to the likes of me, still I had my brother. He, at least, they all see as a black."

"Uh, excuse me, but strictly speaking, if you have no pigment, then you aren't actually black, are you?" Elias said mildly.

"Of course I am!" exclaimed the albino. "Being black is not about the skin pigment!"

"Then why do you object so strongly to white-landers?"

Mildred listened to the silence. Elias's mocking tone elicited no verbal response from the albino but heavy breathing as he fought to contain his temper. If she was lucky, they might actually kill each other at this rate, and save her the worry of having to escape. Yeah, as though she should be that lucky. Desperately she sought some way of gaining an advantage over them once she had used the surprise card.

Their argument continued.

"You will use your half of the money to squander," the albino said, sneering, "whereas I intend to set up a community where those such as myself can live in peace, apart from whitelanders and cartoon blacks such as yourself."

"Interesting definition of squander, I would say," Elias commented wryly. "But I really feel that we're wasting time now."

"Something I have been saying to you for some time," the albino snapped.

"So I've suddenly grown weary of your tattle," Elias commented. "I feel it's time to complete step one. Once she's chilled, we'll get the treasure out and leave her corpse there. By the time anyone figures out that she's a little more than just missing, we'll be well away from this accursed island."

There was a pause.

"So who'll do it?" Chan said nervously.

Elias sighed. "Oh, really, do I have to do everything for you?"

The taunt worked. "No, damn you. I'll see to it," the albino snapped.

On her back, eyes still closed, Mildred heard him move near. She thanked her luck that it was the lighter and less competent of the duo that was approaching. He would be easier to take by surprise and to overpower. She could get his blaster and perhaps use him to shield herself to make a difficult shot for Elias. It was a slim chance, but the only one she had.

As the albino leaned over her and she felt the muzzle of the blaster rest against her forehead, she opened her eyes suddenly, ignoring the searing pain of the daylight—even shielded as it was by the albino's body—and looked Chan straight in the eyes.

He gasped and started back, the blaster pointing away from her. Before Elias had a chance to ask him what was wrong, or for him to answer, Chan found himself kicked sideways as Mildred swung her leg up with as much force as she could muster. There was little momentum she could give it, and she was still weak from her head wound, but the kick was strong enough to catch him in the ribs and to catapult him sideways. She rolled after him, feeling the breeze of the first shot from Elias as it threw up splatters of damp earth where her thigh had been moments before.

"Don't fire, for the Lord's sake, don't fire," Chan yelled, his voice pitched high with fear.

"Then get out of the damned way," Elias snorted as he tried to take a clear aim.

With one hand, Mildred grabbed the blaster that had fallen from Chan's hand when he'd been pitched sideways as she grabbed the albino around the throat with the other. It was a difficult maneuver, and the albino was slippery, but at least she had the blaster.

"You dimwit, you didn't even have the safety off," she yelled at him as she flicked the catch.

Elias fired again, the shot whistling past both of them at head level.

"What are you doing?" Chan yelled. "For the Lord's sake."

"Not so loud," Elias ordered. "There are still security patrols—"

He was cut short by a blast from Mildred that tore up a clod of earth to his left. Her usually deadly aim had been spoiled by the albino's movements, which she still sought to contain.

This was a stalemate, and one that couldn't continue for long. Sooner or later Elias would tire of this and just fire through Chan, or the albino would wriggle free and she would be an open target.

What she needed was a miracle. What she got was something close.

"Mildred! Duck!"

Mildred didn't think about what was happening, or where Jak had sprung from. She just threw herself to the ground.

The explosion from behind her was a signal that Jak's .357 Magnum Colt Python had been called into play. It was lucky for Chan that he had also reacted to Jak's call, as the slug would have hit him if he had stayed on his knees instead of flinging himself away from Mildred when she released her grip. The slug tore a great chunk out of the ground in front of them.

Elias had already turned and begun to run for cover. Jak sighted and loosed another shot, which took a chunk out of a tree to the left of the giant's shoulder as he ducked behind it. The wood cut into his shoulder, making him scream but doing nothing to delay his progress. Chan was close behind him, scuttling for cover as Mildred had just a short while before.

Mildred sighted with the blaster she had taken from Chan and fired. But at the last she pulled the shot and it flew wide of the intended mark. Now wasn't the time to take them out.

Jak had stopped firing. He had appeared on the far side of the shallow river and was wading across, unable to stop to take aim if he wished to reach the other side rapidly. His main concern was Mildred's safety, and that had been assured. However, he couldn't understand why she had pulled the only shot she had loosed, and asked her as much as soon as he reached her.

Mildred shook her head. "If I chilled Markos's brother, whether or not it was with Elias, then there would be a whole shitload of explaining to do, and I'm not sure that Markos would want to hear it straight off. And when we get those bastards, I want it to be clear what they've been up to."

"You be safe till then?" Jak asked.

"I figure they'll go to ground, maybe thinking we'll go straight to Markos or Sineta. Which also means they'll have to act fast. I reckon they'll be back tonight to try to get the stuff out of the rocks and make a break for it. But what the hell are you doing here?"

Jak shrugged and smiled. "Was on errand to livestock, getting stupe measurements for crates and boats 'cause of fuckup…lucky fuckup. Saw Chan and Elias on roof. Not trust one, and seeing other with him made curious. Then blasters out. Didn't know firing on you till followed them when you picked up. Followed out here and kept tail. Didn't know how bad you injured, or if you making out unconscious—body not quite loose enough," he added with a hunter's grin. "Anyway, saw you move and figured time right."

"Sure as shit was," Mildred agreed. "I was never more pleased to see you."

She hugged the albino with sheer relief.

When she let him go, he said, "So if they come tonight, we tell sec?"

Mildred grimaced. "Can't tell them outright. I figure I should make sure Markos is out here at that time and he can stumble on it. But there'll have to be backup."

"How you get him out here?" Jak asked. It wasn't an unreasonable question, but it made Mildred feel awkward. The flare of attraction between herself and the sec boss had been secret, and she wanted it to stay that way.

"I'll figure that out," she said lamely.

If Jak was surprised by that, he didn't betray the fact. Instead he continued. "We tell Ryan, and all of us get here—surround it and ready to help if necessary."

"No," Mildred said emphatically, "I don't want that. This is a Pilatan legacy, and if it comes out because of two blacks who are stopped by outsiders—and pale outsiders at that—then it'll divide the people when they really need to pull together. Half of them won't want to believe that either Chan or Elias are behind this, and if whites are there…"

Jak nodded. "Just me, then. That work?"

Mildred nodded. "You're an albino. You're acceptable in that sense. Yeah, I figure you and me can give Markos the backup he needs."

"Okay, but should fill others in anyway," Jak pointed out.

"Yeah, that's fair. Let's do it."

As they made their way back to the ville, Mildred realized that her doubts about both J.B.—and by implication, the rest of the companions—and Markos had been proved wrong. Both were good men in their separate ways. Chan had obviously been her initial attacker. He was of a similar build to the Armorer and had adopted J.B.'s limp to aid his disguise. Both he and Elias had used their moralistic stances to hide their real selves until revealed this day—and then only to Millie and Jak. It may prove harder than she thought to convince the sec boss and to convince Ryan that she should handle this with so little manpower.

Something that Markos and Ryan shared was their complete integrity. She knew the one-eyed man would understand why she and Jak would have to do this alone.

# Chapter Eleven

"You want to what!" Ryan exclaimed when Mildred had outlined her plan.

"I want it to just be me and Jak," she reiterated. "It can't be any other way."

"But, Mildred, it's going to be—"

"Are you saying that we can't handle it?" She bristled.

Ryan sighed. "Of course I'm not saying that. You know better. But we always play the odds. That's why we're still here and the people we've had to come up against have mostly long ago bought the farm. Seven is better odds than two, that's all."

Mildred paused. "Yeah, I know that's what you're saying. And you know, most of the time I'd agree with you. But this has to be different, and I've explained why."

There was a long silence. The companions were grouped in their quarters, Mildred having dragged them away from their work—allegedly under the auspices of Sineta—in order to have this conference. They were all fully armed, having reclaimed their weapons from the armory that morning. That was why Jak had been carrying his Colt Python. The only exception was Ryan, who was incensed when Mildred and Jak revealed to

him where his SIG-Sauer had found a new home. The
rearming was part of final preparations, as the armory
was now crated ready for transportation. The loading
was the task from which they had been pulled by Mildred.

The late-afternoon shadows were long over the
street where they were housed and without any lamps
the inside of the adobe hut was dark. Jak and Dean
were acting lookouts at the front and back, still keeping an ear on the proceedings.

Finally, Ryan said, "Okay, I'm with you on this, but
I still don't like it that you're not playing the odds."

"Mebbe there's a way that you could stack them a
little," Krysty mused thoughtfully.

"There is?" Mildred responded. "How?"

Krysty shrugged. "You're planning to stop Elias and
Chan and then present it as a fait accompli to Sineta
and Markos, right?" She waited for Mildred to agree,
then continued, "So why don't you let them see it going
down? Take them with you."

"But, Krysty, how the hell can I explain to Markos
about his brother?" Mildred asked. "Sineta, I could
handle. She'll understand why Barras didn't tell her,
and trusted me to do it for her at this time. But Markos
is too proud, too stubborn."

"So don't tell him it's his brother who's involved.
Just tell him about Elias, and say you didn't get a look
at the other man involved as he was masked."

"You really think he'll go for that?" Mildred asked
skeptically.

"Think about how much he dislikes Elias," Krysty
pointed out.

"I can understand that—look how he had us deceived," J.B. commented. "Markos was aware of how he was, but prove it when you're that blunt and he's Mister Nice Guy all the time."

Mildred turned to the Armorer and smiled. Of course J.B. would understand Markos. "Yeah, maybe if I play on that, I won't have to let on about Chan until he can see for himself."

"Markos good fighter," Jak chipped in quietly from his position near the window. "Night make hard for two on two. Could be better bet."

"Okay," Mildred affirmed. "Let's do it."

MARKOS LOOKED PUZZLED when he entered Sineta's quarters to find Mildred and Jak waiting for him, along with the baron's daughter.

"You sent word that there was an urgent matter to be settled between ourselves," he began. "I fail to see—"

"It is," the fine-boned woman interjected, "but as of yet, I have no idea as to its substance. That is what Mildred and Jak have to tell us."

Markos sucked in his breath. "Why do I get bad feelings that the two of them are involved?" he murmured. "Particularly when I see another injury on you," he added, indicating the crease on Mildred's forehead. Although it had been dressed by Krysty, even under a bandage it suggested nothing but trouble.

"Because it's not a pretty story," she said simply before going on to outline the attempt on her life, and how Jak had saved her at the side of the river.

"There is one thing that is a mystery to me," Markos mused, interrupting her. "Why they did not chill you when they had the chance, and why they took you to the river."

"Because they wanted to hide my corpse," Mildred explained. "And as for why they took me down to the river…" She turned to the baron's daughter. "Sineta, there's something I have to tell you. Something that happened between your father and me. And I need to tell you why he did what he did."

And she began to tell her about the legend of the whitelands treasure and why the baron had entrusted her with the information. Sineta stayed silent and listened carefully, but Mildred could see that Markos was almost bursting with anger and indignation that the baron should trust Mildred and her friends and not his own people. A view he expressed when Mildred had finished.

Sineta waited for him to finish before speaking.

"Can you not see that my father was right? At such a time as this, when there is upheaval and the disparate elements that make a community have to be pulled together in both spirit and physical being, the gathering of the old treasure would be a distraction that would pull us apart. People like your brother would wish us to remain and not take this back to the ones from whom it was originally plundered. And yet, right now, they have acquiesced to the need to journey on and are working together with the rest of us. To have this treasure taken from hiding and presented once we are on the whitelands is the only way to proceed. Of course I am hurt that my father chose one other than myself to impart this knowledge, but my feelings do not matter when set against the needs of the community that I must serve. If I can live with that, cannot you?"

Markos sighed. "You are right, of course. The post I hold, and of which I am proud, dictates that the community must come first, and that is how it should be."

Let's hope that you still see it that way in a couple of hours, Mildred thought.

Jak walked toward the door.

"Dark falls. Mebbe should go."

THE WOODLANDS along the river were in darkness by the time that Mildred, Jak, Sineta and Markos reached the riverbank. The night sky above was clear, the moon illuminating the woods enough for them to be able to find their way. Jak took the front, surefooted and able to see in the gloom. He returned at intervals to report that the way ahead was clear. Although there were paths scored through the woods by the activities of the tree fellers, Mildred guided them through thicker patches, wanting to keep the party as hidden as possible. As the rest of the companions had regained their weapons just that day, so Mildred had claimed her Czech-made ZKR target pistol, which she held loosely, feeling the familiar grain of the butt against her palm. Jak had his .357 Magnum Colt Python, and Markos his H&K, which he held across his body, loose but firm in his grip. Sineta was the only one who concerned Mildred when it came to weapons. The baron's daughter carried a Glock, which was gripped tightly in her fist. The tension in her grip revealed that she was unfamiliar and ill-at-ease with blasters.

If it came to a firefight, as it undoubtedly would, could the woman look after herself? Mildred figured that she'd have to keep an eye out for the soon-to-be baron of Pilatu, otherwise she could find herself buying the farm before her father.

Jak appeared through the trees like a wraith, seemingly able to wrap himself around the shadows cast by the trunks.

"Clear ahead. No sign yet."

"Are you sure they'll be there tonight?" Sineta whispered.

Mildred affirmed. "They've got no choice, sweetie. They know I'm still alive, and they know how much I know. Even if I didn't go to you and Markos, then they'd figure that I'd get Ryan and the others to snatch the treasure tonight, before they had the opportunity to act. If they're going to get their hands on it, then they have to move tonight."

"If only we knew who the other party was," Markos mused. "Elias I can understand, and his motivation of greed. I make no secret of the fact that I have neither liked nor trusted him. But I cannot think who else would sink so low, particularly if, as you say, this is a man who is a separatist. They are motivated only by a burning sense of dignity. It just does not make sense."

"Sometimes things people do just don't, Markos," Mildred answered, feeling uneasy about how he would take the revelation when the time came. "So let's just stop talking about it and get down to the bank, try to take up a position where we can see them. Okay?"

Sineta and Markos agreed, and at an indication from Mildred, Jak led them through the trees and down to the river.

It looked so calm under the wan silver light of the crescent moon above. The water flowed sluggish and slow and the crop of rocks coming out of the riverbed rose in relief against the trees beyond. The ground on the bank in front of them—the place where she had earlier fought for her life before Jak's timely intervention—looked serene and undisturbed, as though it had never seen human intrusion.

"Not here yet, and not many places hide," Jak whispered, breaking her reverie. "I take rocks, find crevice to hide. You three stay together. Cover away from any paths. Elias not good woodsman, so take easiest path."

"Can you be sure of that?" Markos queried. "What if they stumble on us from the rear?"

"Trust him," Mildred said softly. "If Jak figures that's how Elias will come, then that's how he'll come."

"Besides," the albino added with a sly grin, "signs there of where left earlier. Triple stupe even figure come back that way."

Markos raised his hands in a gesture of surrender. "Okay, I take your point. But how are you going to get out to the rocks without risking them seeing you as they approach?"

"Two things—one, I find route there that not make water ripple, two—" he added with a sly grin "—I checked. Elias and other not anywhere around yet."

Mildred uttered a short laugh. "Okay, Jak. You take up your position and we'll take up ours. Then I guess we'll just have to wait for however long it takes."

The albino set off without another word, melting into the shadows of the woods. The remaining three moved toward their position of cover in order to take up observation. Markos kept glancing toward the river, but couldn't see or hear a sign of Jak.

"Remarkable," he murmured. "I would not have thought…I suppose—"

"Don't doubt it." Mildred sighed. "Look, if Jak says he's there, then he's there. Okay?"

Markos shrugged, but said nothing further as they gained a secure position and settled down to wait.

LEAVING THE OTHERS, Jak had skipped over the root systems that treacherously lined the floor of the woods and wrapped himself around the trunks of the trees until he was at the very edge, with only the bare stretch of ground between the woods and the river to traverse. To his left there was a patch of shrub that would provide cover. Jak dropped to his belly and slid across, moving fast and crablike to gain the cover of the shrub. In daylight, he could be spotted, but under the much dimmer moonlight he was able to use the cover of shadows to remain unseen.

From the shrub to the water was a matter of a few feet. The real difficulty would be to gain the water without causing too much of a disturbance. At the same time, he had to make sure that his blaster stayed out of the water. Jak wrapped the Colt Python in a piece of plastic he had secreted in his pocket before they'd left, figuring that he would need to do this. He then stowed the blaster in an inside pocket of his camou jacket. He'd also thought long and hard about how he would tackle the problem of the river. To the left, just downstream, was a small clump of wood—discarded branches and leaves overgrown with creeping vine. It would provide more shelter, especially in the gloom. He made the cover in quick time. From here he just had to slip down the bank and into the slow, sluggish current. Legs together, narrowing the angle of his body as much as possible to cause the least disturbance, he slid into the water, crouching into mud of the riverbed until only his shoulders and head were above water. Then, taking a deep breath and sighting the rocks to give him direction, Jak slipped under the water and struck out for the crop.

It took him only a few strokes to come to the base of the rocks. He found a crevice that came up out of the water and broke the surface in a narrow inlet that was deep in shadow. He exhaled and gasped in two quick breaths before looking up to see where he had arrived. He was on the reverse side of the crop to the cave entrance. It was narrow, but it was simple for him to climb up and around, keeping close and on the far side of the bank where he was certain Elias and Chan would come: here he could move freely and with speed.

As he reached the angle where he would, for a fraction of a second, be exposed before gaining the cover of the cave entrance, he paused and looked deep into the wood. Ceasing to breathe, and filtering out the familiar sounds of his own central nervous system and blood flow, he could hear nothing that would indicate their approach. He could see the slightest movement of the branches around the position where Mildred, Markos and Sineta were stationed. He could hear the occasional rasp of breath from one of them when the night sounds dipped. But he could hear nothing else apart. Chan and Elias weren't hunters, and even with their best efforts he would be able to hear them from some way off.

He would have a wait ahead of him, but it meant that he could move with ease right now. His mouth curling into a grin of satisfaction, Jak slipped around the edge of the rocks and melted into the mouth of the cave. Once in the darkness, and with a good view of the area along the riverbank, he took the Colt Python from his inner pocket, unwrapped it before restoring the plastic to another pocket, lest it should prove useful, and checked the blaster. It was as dry as a bleacher bone. From habit, he checked that the blaster was fully armed. Satisfied, he holstered it before hunkering down to wait, eyes trained on the bank, the only sound his shallow breath. There was no movement at all.

Over on the bank, Markos had been watching the whole while. Despite the fact that Jak had relaxed himself when moving around the rock, Markos hadn't seen him. All he'd noticed had been the slightest flicker of movement that may have been nothing more than the scuttling of a cloud across the moon.

ELIAS AND CHAN HAD BEEN in hiding for most of the afternoon, bickering with each other. The giant couldn't resist goading the albino, and for his part Chan would always rise to the bait, unable to understand how the giant could be so casual when everything seemed to be going wrong.

"Tell me something—would your brother believe two outsiders? Would Sineta be upset about her father saying nothing to her about the legends? Of course not, and of course, if you were paying attention. So listen to me. We go back tonight. Mebbe they'll be waiting for us and mebbe not. If that bitch has got her whitelander friends to get the treasure out, then we just chill them."

"How the hell do we do that when we've only got one blaster between us?" Chan had demanded.

Elias fixed him with a glare. The sardonic humor that always seemed to be in his eyes had suddenly faded. "We would have more than one blaster if you hadn't been so damned useless. And we'll do it because we have to. We have no choice now, no going back. I do not intend to travel to the whitelands knowing that Mildred and her little friends have that knowledge as power over me. Is that clear?"

Chan had nodded, his throat too tight and dry to speak. As with many others on Pilatu, he had always thought of Elias as untrustworthy but harmless, too laid-back to be of any danger.

The look in the giant's eyes told him that he had been wrong. And the thought of being alone in the woods with this revelation was a more frightening prospect than taking on the companions.

So now, as the night hit its stillest and darkest watch, he found himself stumbling after the giant as Elias made his way through the woods, from the copse where they had taken shelter to the riverbank by the outcrop and caves, where the whiteland treasure lay hidden.

They followed the same path as they had taken that afternoon, only traveling in reverse. It wasn't long before they gained the riverbank, with the crop a few feet out into the water, rising to a peak with a cave beneath.

"There it is, just sitting there waiting for us," Elias said with a chuckle. "See, my cowardly little friend. It's not that hard, is it?"

"I CAN HEAR SOMETHING," Markos mouthed at Mildred and Sineta as the sound of the two men thrashing through the woods reached their hiding place.

Mildred nodded and pointed in the general direction of the sound. Markos assented.

"Wait till they are in the open," he said softly.

"Wait until Jak moves," Mildred amended.

Markos looked puzzled. "But surely—"

Mildred shook her head. "Just do it."

She looked around at Sineta. Even in the dim light of the half moon it was plain to see that the woman was anxious and hyped up in anticipation. Despite Sineta's willingness to be here, Mildred found it obvious that the woman had never been in a fighting situation before, and she was terrified, even though prepared to fight.

Let's hope her nerve holds, Mildred thought, taking in the tight grip that Sineta had on her blaster.

She looked back in the direction of the sound. They were nearing the clearing that delineated the riverbank and would soon come into view. Now was the moment of truth. Looking at Markos's face, intent but impassive, prepared for combat, she wondered how he would take it when his beloved brother came into view.

The brush at the edge of the woods was swept aside and Elias strode out onto the riverbank, looking around him. His eyes—even at this distance—blazed, and Mildred sucked in her breath. It looked like the giant had cracked under the strain and was quite mad, which would make him completely unpredictable.

His companion stayed hidden while the giant looked up and down the bank and across to the outcrop, where Jak remained silent and still in the shadows. Elias saw nothing and assumed that the cave was empty. He turned to the brush, where his companion stayed hidden, and laughed loud and harsh, gesturing with his blaster.

"Come out, you cretin. She has done nothing as yet and we have all the time in the world."

Mildred looked at Markos, whose eyes were intently trained on the scene.

"Now we'll see who his accomplice is," the sec boss whispered, cradling his H&K.

From the brush, peering out as though disbelieving of his compatriot, Chan cautiously emerged.

Mildred braced herself, watching Markos's face. The sec boss appeared to pay the revelation no heed whatsoever—although if she could have seen in clearer light, Mildred would have noted a hardening and tightening around his jaw.

"This is too easy," Chan said in a voice that, although not loud, carried across the space between himself and his brother in hiding. "She must have said something, if not to her pale friend then to that cretinous Sineta and my fool brother."

"What? You dare to mock your wonderful brother?" Elias chided.

Chan spit on the ground. "He pretends to love me, but he is like the others. He cannot see me as anything other than freak because of this. He is the hero, stupid as he is, because he has a black skin, and he is the one who would have a chance of marrying the baron's daughter, even though they would produce brainless cretins."

"Markos, no!" Mildred hissed as she felt the sec boss brace beside her, his calf and thigh muscles propelling him upward, the catch on his H&K snapping off.

"Let him," Sineta said, also scrambling to her feet, her tension unleashed by his action.

"Shit, this is not good," Mildred muttered to herself as both Markos and Sineta broke cover, running for the riverbank.

SILENT IN THE CAVE, Jak watched as Elias and Chan bickered on the bank and then Markos and Sineta—without Mildred—broke cover and walked openly toward the two bandits.

Although no one could ever have told as much from his still-impassive expression, Jak was amazed at what was happening. Mildred hadn't broken cover, which suggested that the other two hadn't listened to her. That was their choice, but it was a choice that was likely to get them chilled. Jak couldn't see for sure, but it looked to him as though only Elias was armed. That cut down on the odds, but it still meant that both the sec boss and the baron's daughter were offering the giant a clear shot on either or both of them.

Cursing inwardly, Jak uncoiled from his position and began to move toward the lip of the cave.

It looked as if he'd have to make his move before he would have wished.

MILDRED WATCHED them walk into the open in sheer disbelief. She, too, had moved out of cover, but was keeping low. Something that Markos and Sineta were failing to do. She would have expected this from the baron's daughter, but not from the sec boss.

"Stop right there. Don't move a muscle or twitch an eyelid, unless you want to join our ancestors."

Markos's voice was firm and carried over the distance despite not being loud. It made his brother turn and gasp, falling to his knees as the shock and his accumulated fear finally got the better of him. Elias, on the other hand, was made of sterner stuff.

On hearing the voice, the giant whirled and fired. The shots echoed across the last few words uttered by the sec boss. He laughed maniacally as he fired, falling sideways to avoid being a sitting target for any return fire.

One of the shots hit Markos in the shoulder, throwing him backward, his H&K falling from nerveless fingers. He stared wide-eyed at his shoulder, the shock of seeing his brother followed by his rash action and his injury throwing him into a paralyzed confusion.

"Oh, fuck it," Mildred muttered under her breath as she moved forward, breaking into a run. The tableau in front of her eyes presented her with two distinct problems. First, Chan was scrambling toward where Markos's H&K had landed, with the intention of laying hands on it. That would make him a threat, which he hadn't been up to that point. Second, Elias was standing with a blaster in his hand, sizing up a shot at Sineta. For her part, the baron's daughter was facing the same dilemma as Mildred. She stood between the two threats, not knowing which one to go for. Her

Glock was uselessly pointed somewhere between the two. Mildred could make a snap decision and act. In fact, if she had been standing in Sineta's position she would have had no hesitation in taking out Elias first, then pivoting and taking out Chan with a second shot. But she wasn't in that position. From where she was, running, there was no way she could do both. And Sineta, for all her raw courage, had no idea of which to go for first, and no experience to guarantee a good shot.

Mildred could only take one of the options, and she knew which one it had to be when she glanced across toward the outcrop and saw Jak emerge.

The albino hunter jumped nimbly from the mouth of the cave and into the river, hitting the bottom with a stride that already propelled him across nearly half the distance to the shore. As he jumped and landed, he unholstered his Colt Python and extended his arm, the heavy blaster dwarfing his small, scarred white hand. His arm was at full extension, rock-solid as he took another stride. He saw Elias bring the blaster up toward Sineta to get a clean shot.

Jak didn't hesitate. In a fraction of a second he sighted along the barrel of the Colt as he strode forward and squeezed the trigger, almost with a caress. The recoil from the powerful blaster didn't even jolt the tensed muscles of his forearm and bicep, the arm remaining rock-solid.

Elias didn't know what hit him. One second he was shaping to blast Sineta, whose hand he had once sought in the pursuit of power; the next he knew nothing as he was despatched to join his ancestors.

Sineta saw Elias level the blaster and tried to turn to fire, but she knew she was too slow and was preparing to meet her forefathers when she saw the giant's head suddenly explode in front of her. One second his malevolent glaring eyes and vulpine grin framed her imminent demise, the next they had disappeared as his skull split open and a spray of blood, brain and bone splinters spewed out around his head, mostly to her left. The corpse, now with just half a head, tumbled sideways.

Sineta screamed.

Mildred had ignored the shot from Jak and the woman's scream, concentrating her attention instead on Chan. If she had stopped and taken aim, she could probably have chilled him before he reached the H&K, but her momentum was such that it would have taken a fraction of a second too long to actually come to a complete halt. Her best bet was to keep running and to throw herself at the albino, stopping him gaining the weapon.

Chan was reaching for the H&K when he felt Mildred cannon into him. He hadn't looked up to see her coming, so had taken no evasive action when she threw herself across the last couple of yards. He was kneeling, but she pitched herself low and he was flung back—and away from the blaster—by her sudden appearance and impact. Unfortunately for Mildred, the momentum of her flight carried them back toward the woods. As they landed she hit the side of her head on an upraised tree root.

Desperately, Mildred fought to cling to her faculties, even though stars exploded inside her head and the world turned upside down. She felt her limbs grow heavy and unresponsive, refusing to react and allowing Chan to squirm out from under her. Her ZKR slipped from her grasp and before she had a chance to drunkenly fumble for it, the albino had seized it and taken hold of her arm, twisting it up behind her and holding the blaster to her head, dragging her to her feet.

Mildred's vision cleared with the sudden lurch of fear that greeted her realization of her position. In the brief moment that she had been knocked almost senseless by the tree root, she had enabled Chan to gain the upper hand, the very thing she had hoped to avoid.

In front of her she could see the chilled Elias; Sineta, on her knees and gasping for breath; Jak emerging from the water, still holding the Colt Python, and Markos, one arm hanging uselessly to his side, the other grasping the recovered H&K.

The sec boss scrambled to his feet and looked behind him.

"Jak, no!" he exclaimed. "He's my brother—leave him to me."

"Okay, but if Mildred chilled, you next," Jak said, letting the Colt drop to his side.

Markos turned back toward Mildred and Chan, taking a slow step forward. Mildred felt Chan's grip tighten, the barrel of the ZKR press into her temple.

"Don't think you can appeal to any familial sentiment," Chan blurted. "I cannot be swayed by that which I do not feel."

"You mean that our lives were a sham? That they meant nothing? Do you really believe that I cared for you, protected you, for nothing?"

"Yes, for something—to make you feel good, to make you feel big. The big, strong brother to look after the weakling freak. How good that makes you, my brother…and how small that makes me."

"It is what you do now that makes you small," Markos replied sadly, leveling the H&K.

"Think before you do that," Chan yelled. Mildred could almost smell the fear on the albino as his breath rasped in her ear. "Think, my beloved brother. You would have to be a fine shot to chill me before I could fire on the bitch…the bitch you want more than anything. You think I do not know that? And you think that does not disgust me more, to know that you would go with someone degraded by the whitelander? So think—fire on me and you will lose her, for if I do not chill her then your shooting will not be good enough to take me without going through her."

"Are you willing to wager your life on that?" Markos asked quietly. The H&K was still raised and the sec boss was as still as a standing stone. His eyes were barely visible in the wan moonlight, but Mildred could see that there was a fire in them. He would not back down; did his brother know him well enough to realize that?

Chan began to pressure the trigger on the ZKR.

"I—"

The shot was single and loud in the quietness of the night. Mildred closed her eyes and waited for her brain to explode as Chan pulled the trigger of the ZKR.

It didn't happen. She felt his grip relax and heard the ZKR clatter on the roots at their feet. She let her jaw drop. She was so startled that there was nothing she could do. Hardly daring to turn, she slowly pivoted to see the albino at her feet, a hole in the middle of his forehead, a spreading dark pool at the back of his skull indicating the size of the exit wound. His eyes were wide, his mouth open in shock, much like her own. But unlike her, his were eyes that would see no more in this world.

Turning back, she could see Markos calmly standing, his blaster still leveled.

"He should have tried to appeal to me as a brother. That worked all our lives, and I never realized how he really felt. Fear and danger are strange things, are they not, in the manner of which they betray the truth."

Jak rushed past the sec boss to Mildred.

"You okay?" he asked, bending to retrieve the ZKR, which she took from him without thinking.

"Yeah, at least I think so. Shit, Jak, I think I might actually be in shock," she said in amazement.

Jak led her back to the edge of the riverbank, where Sineta now stood, shaking her head.

"What do we do with this carnage?" the woman said quietly.

"Figure we leave these for carrion, come back in daylight and get the treasure for your father," Jak said.

Sineta nodded with an air of finality. "Yes. It should be done like that."

Mildred walked back to where Markos was standing, looking down on the corpse of his brother. "You hear that?" she asked gently.

"Yes…yes, I have no business here. Not now," he said softly.

Mildred took his arm and they walked back to Jak and Sineta. The baron's daughter was trying not to look at Elias's mutilated corpse. Jak indicated that they should leave and gently guided her past the corpse. Markos didn't look back.

The moon was beginning to wane, sunrise only an hour or less away.

IN THE COLD LIGHT of morning, it was easier for both Sineta and Markos to return to the riverbank. Jak, Ryan and J.B. preceded them with three of the sec force to bury the corpses of Elias and Chan, which showed signs of investigation from the predators of the woods. By the time the main party had arrived, the bandits were beneath the soil. Markos didn't speak of them as he asked Mildred for all the information regarding access to the treasure that she had been told by Barras.

Going across to the cave, Markos entered with two of his men and Ryan, J.B. and Jak. The wiry albino hunter was the one chosen to take the pothole route into the inner cave where the treasure had been secured. When he triggered the entrance mechanism and the party gained entrance, it was easy to see why the baron had wished the treasure to be recovered before the Pilatans left their island home. Carefully wrapped to provide as much protection as possible, there were precious metals and jewels both loose and in settings. There was also paper jack, which was now useless in a post-skydark world. In any case, the damp of the cave had permeated the coverings and the paper had rotted and mulched.

It took little more than an hour to remove the treasure from the cave and to take it across the short distance to the shore, where Sineta and Mildred watched as it was unwrapped. Some of it would be useful on the mainland, but it seemed very little for Elias and Chan to risk—and lose—their lives over. And very little for Markos to lose much of his life over. For the sec boss had been subdued since the previous night. It was as though all he had believed had been proved to be false. His ideals had been fired by the words and ideas of his beloved brother, just as his actions had been directed toward the protection of Chan and all that he believed. Protection of a brother who he thought had loved him, but had used that belief as a mask behind which there was only loathing and manipulation.

The sec boss was subdued as they took the treasure back to the ville, where Sineta showed it to her father, and the treachery of Elias and Chan was revealed. Barras was dismissive of the now-chilled bandits, glad only to see the treasure recovered in time for the exodus.

It was only a few hours before the baron flew to join his ancestors.

IN THE DAYS that followed the death of the baron, the preparations for the journey to the whitelands were subdued. Sineta assumed the baron's role in total, and Markos backed her in a public address in which he condemned his brother for his hypocrisy. He also stated that he found it hard to agree wholeheartedly with leaving the island of Pilatu, but would back Sineta one hundred percent. His personal views could not come before the only viable future the Pilatans could have. As he spoke, Mildred could see that he was a troubled soul, but he had resisted all attempts she had made to see him and talk to him about what had happened, and about their relationship—such as it had been.

Sineta and Mildred did, however, speak about marriage. The baron's daughter had met Markos to discuss her father's notion of marrying either the sec boss or the charismatic Elias.

Before Sineta had a chance to speak, the sec boss had sardonically pointed out that the latter had been a very bad call, and as for the notion of his marrying her, well, that had been at the instigation of his brother, who had wished to use him as a political tool. The idea of marrying for the pursuit of power was one that he found distasteful and, with all respect to the new baron, he would be only too glad if the subject was never again raised.

So work continued. The deaths of Elias and Chan had shown the divisions between the peoples of Pilatu as something of an artificial divide and even the most hardened of separatists had worked harder to prepare for the exodus. Their views remained unchanged, but they would fight for their beliefs when the Pilatans had gained a new homeland that was more fertile and able to support them.

The boats were finished and loaded. The adobe homes were stripped of all but the barest last-minute essentials. The animals were loaded during the final day, and the night was given to muted celebrations. Muted because of the arduous journey ahead. Muted because the islanders were sad to be leaving their home after so many generations. And yet there was a mood of optimism engendered by the gaining of the treasure—which would provide valuable jack and barter in the, to them, new world—and by the accession of a new baron who would prove to be strong. Barras had been a good man, but of necessity his long illness and decline had left the ville in limbo for some while.

On the morrow, the journey would begin: but before this there were still matters to be addressed.

DEAN HAD BEEN keeping his head down and getting on with the work allotted to him, yet he had obviously been preoccupied. Ryan had tried to talk to him, but the youngster had been reticent to speak to his father. Doc had also tried. He had always been able to converse with the youth; even he could get little more from him than a vague admission that something had been troubling him.

Krysty had been able to tell for some while that there was a matter weighing heavily on Dean's mind. Yet she could also tell that he wasn't yet ready to talk about it. Until now, that is…

Dean was sitting at the back of the adobe dwelling they had called home for the past few weeks, staring out into the night. He had crept away from the celebrations in the center of the ville and was staring up at the sky, so preoccupied that he didn't hear Krysty approach. He started when she spoke.

"You want to watch that. It could be dangerous," she commented, seating herself beside him.

"Sorry…I guess I was thinking," he replied.

Krysty sucked in her breath. "Oh, that's dangerous, too much thinking. Especially when it cuts you off from everyone. Mebbe it's best then to share the thoughts, make them seem less heavy?"

"I don't know," Dean said nervously, scraping the ground with his boot. "It sounds kind of stupe to me, so mebbe you'll think I've gone as crazy as Doc if I tell you."

Krysty laughed. "I'm not sure if that's even possible, but tell me anyway. It won't go any further and it may just help."

"Okay. Here goes…" With which he began to tell her about the dreams he'd had since the mat-trans jump. "They seem— Hot pipe, it seems like sometimes the dreams are real and this is the dream. And that feels really weird. And that's not all…"

Krysty watched closely. Dean was on the verge of saying something important but was having trouble framing the right words. Finally they came, and they were profoundly shocking.

"Sometimes it feels to me like Rona's still alive and that I have to find her. That it's some kind of message. And being here is a part of that, 'cause I've seen what it's like to have family and to belong."

"And you don't feel that we're your family and that you belong with us?"

"No, yes, I mean—" Dean stuttered. Pausing to take a deep breath, he began again. "You, Dad, Doc, Jak— all of you are family. But it's different with Rona. I was with her from when I was small. I didn't even know my dad until after I was taken from the Brody school. That time before I was only just getting to know him…all of you. But I don't belong, any more than any of us belong. Not like Mildred does with these people."

"But, sweetheart, Mildred's chosen to go with us

and to stay with us, once we reach the mainland. She's decided that she belongs more with us, despite any racial or cultural heritage."

Dean, who had been watching closely, had a notion that Mildred's decision was based on something a little more personal than Krysty would have him believe, but said nothing of this. Instead he said, "Yeah, but she's had a chance to make that choice. Until I find out what happened to Rona, then I'll never know."

Krysty chewed her lip. "I thought Sharona had rad sickness—cancer—and was buying the farm. That was why she entrusted you—"

"I know, I know," Dean interrupted. "But I've just got this feeling that she's still alive. A feeling that I can't explain. But I know I've got to do something about it."

Krysty frowned. "Okay. When you've got to do something like this, then you've just got to…but wait until we get over the water and promise me you'll talk about it with your father."

Dean nodded. "Yeah. I know I've got to talk to him about it. And I promise I'll do it then."

MILDRED WAS ALSO FACING a testing time in talk. During the evening's activity, Markos had approached her to ask if they could talk. She had arranged to meet him later at Sineta's quarters and was waiting with some apprehension when he arrived.

"It is good of you to meet with me," he said stiffly as she admitted him to the house.

"Is it really that hard to talk, especially as you're the one who asked?" she replied with warmth.

He smiled wryly. "No and yes in equal measure. I

feel as much of a fool as my brother called me for being sucked into his schemes, and yet I have no one now that I can turn to for advice."

"And you want advice from me?"

He shrugged. "Perhaps. I still feel uneasy about traveling to the whitelands and mixing with the pale ones…and yet I know this is foolish, as my own brother and Elias have shown that treachery and deceit are not endemic to color. I have also seen your friends, worked beside them now, and know them to be good people. But I cannot shake that feeling that is within me."

Mildred took his hand and led him to the table in the corner of the room, seating him on one of the chairs while she took another.

"You know, you shouldn't be too hard on yourself about this," she began. "You've had a lifetime of your brother telling you something, and you know, he wasn't without a point."

"You can say this?" Markos asked, surprised.

"Look, there are things about me that you can never know and would never understand…things that you would find hard to believe. But, for whatever reason, I know what it was like before skydark came across the world. And there were plenty of reasons for black people to feel the way that you and the other separatists feel about the whitelands. There was a time when we couldn't use the same restaurants, the same latrines, the same wags. Couldn't have equal housing or equal jack, and were treated like pieces of shit. Things began to change, but it was forced, and there were those who felt that it would always be that way. They wanted a separate land for blacks, a separate nation. They were right.

It was forced. But the point is that with each generation it got a little less forced on each side, and eventually people would have seen no difference. Just because it doesn't happen in the span of your lifetime doesn't mean it'll never happen. You fight for your sons and daughters as much as yourself.

"And things have changed since the nukecaust. Yeah, I've seen people get picked on because they're a different color, a different race, but also because they're from a different ville or are muties and so different. That's what it's all about—difference. It doesn't matter what they make that difference, it's still about fear of being something else. Just like you've got the fear of the pale ones being different. Makes you the same as them.

"But now, it's about your ville rather than your color. People live together and pull together to survive. No one gives a damn that you're black if you're helping them bring in the harvest or pulling them out of a hole. As long as none of you buy the farm, that's all that matters."

Markos pondered this. Finally he said, "I wish I could truly understand that. I can see the sense of your words, but there is a part of me that questions their veracity. These are different things."

"Oh, yeah, they're that, all right," Mildred replied. "But you'll see and soon enough." She fell silent for a moment, thinking of J.B. and the rest of the companions, people she would pull with and chill for. "Yeah, you'll see soon enough," she reiterated.

# Chapter Twelve

Exodus began shortly after daybreak with the Pilatans gathering the last of their belongings and moving away from their old homes and toward the inlet bay, where the boats lay waiting with their cargoes of animals and belongings, the former quietened by fear and a lack of understanding about what was about to occur. There was a subdued, melancholy air about the islanders as they loaded the boats and prepared to cast off.

Sineta and Markos would be the last to board their vessels, the sec boss because he was determined to oversee the final moments of the exodus and make things run as smoothly as possible and the new baron because she felt a great sadness at departure and a sudden desire to stay, even if it was on her own.

Krysty, on the same boat as Mildred, observed Sineta as she cast a last look around.

"Perhaps you should go and be with her," she whispered to Mildred.

Mildred shook her head. "No, she needs to be alone right now. I can understand that. After all, she'll go down in Pilatan history as the woman who led them away from their homeland. It must be kind of hard to know that posterity will label you that way, even if you had no choice."

"It could be a good thing, in the long run as well as the short," Krysty countered.

Mildred smiled. "Yeah, but would you think of that right now?"

Meanwhile, on the shore, the last of the islanders had boarded their boats, which were moored off a wooden pier built out into the depths of the inlet. Everyone and every animal had walked the long, planked pier to board the boats, which were then anchored a short distance away to allow the next boat to tie up and finish loading. It was this changeover that took time, and so it was past noon by the time that all the boats were finally ready. The islanders had never had to deal with more than two boats at a time during the days spent fishing, and so were ill-equipped for a mass exodus. The waiting had increased the air of melancholy that hung like a pall over the small fleet. As Sineta and Markos—the last two Pilatans on the island—took the walk down the wooden pier to board their boat, it was as though they were walking into a fog that threatened to envelop them.

The last boat cast off from the pier and, under the direction of a Pilatan fisherman and the sec boss, took the lead as the other boats lifted their anchors and began to heave to and follow in the wake of the craft that was to take them away to a new life.

Krysty, Mildred and Jak were on one boat. Ryan and Dean on another. J.B. and Doc traveled on the lead boat. They hadn't been split as a deliberate decision. Places on the boats were allocated according to a draw that had been made in the ville square the night before. Its purpose was to alleviate any possibility of argument among the islanders; the only exceptions had been the fishermen, who were to pilot the boats and so were exempt from any random process.

Although a fair means in one way, it also divided families and friends who would have wished to face the perils of the sea together. The apprehension this lottery engendered did little to detract from the general air of depression that lay over the traveling party.

The sea was calm as they headed out into the open water before turning to round the island and make their way toward the mainland. There was a strong breeze that caught in the patched sails of the crafts, billowing the material and driving the heavily laden boats through the water. Ryan peered over the side of his craft as he joined the ship's pilot, Orthos, at the tiller.

"Moving low in the water," the one-eyed man commented in a neutral tone.

The sailor fixed him with a stare that probed for any meaning, then spoke in an equally neutral tone.

"It is true that we sail close to the waves, but there is yet enough buoyancy to keep us afloat."

Ryan returned the sailor's stare. "I wasn't commenting on your people's abilities as seamen, but I'm on this ship, too, and it's not that long ago that my people were caught in the white water."

Orthos was silent for a moment, pondering his answer. "Very well, I will agree with you that we are too low in the water for my liking. Nothing must be said, as panic would be a greater enemy, but I feel that we have too much in too few ships. If only they had given us more time…"

Ryan nodded. "Do you reckon we'll be able to ride out the roughs?"

Orthos gave a small shrug, his face still impassive. "Trust, hope and faith are all I can offer, but a helping hand from you and your son if things get rough would not go amiss. You have both experienced the waters and you could be of use."

Ryan nodded; words were unnecessary. He turned to find Dean and to prepare him for what may lay ahead.

However, not all the sailors were as forthcoming as Orthos. For on another boat, Doc had also drawn the matter to the attention of the Armorer.

"John Barrymore, I feel it necessary that you should perhaps glance over the side of this craft," the old man said in passing. J.B. did so, whistling softly to himself when he saw how low in the water they sat. Glancing around, he could see that the sailor on the tiller was a man unknown to him.

"Figure I should mention this, Doc?"

The old man shrugged. "They would be poor sailors if they were not already aware of the matter. I fear they were given little choice in the matter, egged on by the exegeses of time."

"Yeah," J.B. replied slowly. "I think I know what you mean and you're right. But no one else seems to be aware," he added, looking at his fellow passengers, who were either too wrapped in their own sadness at leaving their home or too busy being seasick to give the matter much thought. "I figure that at least some of us should be prepared for any trouble when we hit the rough sea. Let's go and have a few words with the guy on the tiller."

"I would concur with that," Doc muttered, following the Armorer as he threaded his way through the crowded interior of the boat.

As J.B. approached, he knew that it was going to be difficult. He now recognized the man as one of the hostile separatists who had been on the tree-felling parties with the companions.

"What do you want, pale one?" the sailor asked, a malevolence in his voice that he barely disguised.

J.B. held up his hands in a gesture of surrender. "Hey, I only wanted to say that I've noticed that we're a little low on the waterline. If there's any problems, we want to help," he continued, indicating both Doc and himself.

The sailor sneered. "We are able to handle our own problems without help from outsiders."

J.B. was on the point of answering, but bit hard on his tongue. Perhaps things would be different if there was actually a crisis, but arguing now would achieve nothing on either side.

"Okay, have it your way," he said simply, turning away.

THE FIRST FEW HOURS of the voyage were little more than tedious as the convoy of Pilatan ships sailed out and around the island on a flat sea. Following the lead boat, which was piloted by Sineta and Markos under the direction of the island's most experienced sailor, the convoy proscribed an arc that took them out beyond any reefs that may lay in wait to snag a boat that sat lower than usual in the water. The heat of the afternoon sun and the glassy surface of the water made for a smooth passage, and the people on the boats were lulled into an almost comatose state by the calm.

That changed with a shocking suddenness as the convoy rounded the island and hit the stretch of water that lay between Pilatu and the mainland.

The calm, glassy surface suddenly gave way to white water that rose up as the crosscurrents of the channel churned the water and pulled beneath the surface.

As the lead boat hit the first conflicting current, it was as though the prow had slammed into concrete. The timbers moaned and protested as the force of the water hit them; and the rigging moaned, wind dropping from sails that were suddenly flung out of alignment. All around the island, the rigging had been angled to catch the wind, but now it was proving impossible. The motors fitted to each boat would have to be brought into play. They had remained unused up to this point as each skipper had wanted to save the fuel and resultant horsepower until necessity dictated. That time had now arrived.

"Fire the engine," Markos yelled. But there was no responding cry as the call had been lost amid the panic that the sudden impact had triggered. Shaken violently from their repose, the people on board the boat had responded by panicking, the very thing he had hoped to avoid.

Cursing, the sec boss plunged into the throng below, only to find himself thrown off his feet as the next crosscurrent hit the boat, showering the inhabitants with cold salt spray as the boat was flung sideways with the impact. Regaining his balance, it was hard for the sec boss to fight his way through. He also noticed that the craft was beginning to ship water as it dipped over and under the riders, taking on water at the prow. More than ever, it was important to get the motor running so that they could cut through the crosscurrents as quickly as possible.

Sineta came down and moved among her people, her presence alone reassuring them. Although the baron was trembling inside, she remained outwardly strong and calm, organizing the people so that they began to bale out the excess water the boat was shipping. The activity wasn't only necessary to keep the top-heavy craft afloat, it also helped to focus the people aboard and to quell any panic in the need for action.

By the time Markos had the engine fired and the boat began to cut through the water, headed for the peninsula, the Pilatans were baling as fast as they could.

On the ships that followed, there were similar problems.

"Brace yourselves, here it comes," Mildred yelled, keeping her eyes fixed on the boat in the lead and on the first indication of turbulence that broke the surface. Forewarned by the difficulties of the first craft, those behind had braced themselves for the impact, but there was still little chance of being truly prepared for the sudden shock of first impact.

"Watch out above!" Krysty yelled over the noise— the crash of the waves on the boat, the groaning of the timbers, the yelling of frightened Pilatans and startled animals, and—most ominously—the squeal of rigging that had been torn loose.

Above them, the mast had splintered under the conflicting stresses of sea and wind, and the heavy wood and sails toppled to plummet onto the deck below.

Two Pilatan women and a man stood in the direct path. All were transfixed as the rigging fell, unable to move as a crippling terror paralyzed them. The man—much older—had to have been the father or uncle of the two women, who huddled into him. He spread his arms uselessly around them, in a feeble imitation of protection. It would serve to be of no use when the heavy rigging hit them.

Mildred was out of range, but she saw Jak, sure-footed even in the pitch and yaw of the wave-tossed boat, head toward them. The albino moved swiftly, gathering speed and momentum as he slalomed around upright bodies and hurdled those who were prone. He seemed able to do this without looking at the deck, his gaze fixed on the rigging above as it fell toward the trio, seemingly in slow motion.

When he was about seven feet from the three Pilatans, the albino tensed his muscles, the cords standing out on his thighs and calves, blood pumping in his ears, and threw himself through the air, spreading his arms wide to encompass the width of all three bodies.

He didn't see them as he hit the obstacle of unmoving flesh. His head was tucked down into his right shoulder to offer his neck some protection from the impact that he knew was inevitable. He felt himself hammer into them, the momentum he had built up almost stopped dead by their frozen terror. But not quite. The force of Jak's weight—as slender as he was—going at top speed was enough to drive all three of the terrified

Pilatans backward, stumbling steps halting and falling
into a heap.

The rigging hit the deck with a splintering crash,
smashing deck planking where they had stood but a
fraction of a second before. The impact seemed to gal-
vanize everyone on board.

"Get that engine running!" the lead seaman
screamed over the sound of the whiplash waves. The
engine throbbed and roared, battling against the currents as the ship's tiller was turned to direct it toward
the shore and the peninsula.

"Hot pipe! Did you see that!" Dean exclaimed to his
father as they watched the rigging fall on the ship in
front.

"Let's hope it doesn't do that here," Ryan commented, casting his eye over the rigging above.

"Hey, you wanted to help? Then give me a hand
with this," yelled Orthos, who had left the tiller to
come down to the main body of the boat. "We need to
gather the sails in while the engine's fired—that'll stop
it going."

Dean and Ryan joined the sailor and other fellow
travelers in pulling down the ropes and sails from the
rigging, letting them rest on the deck once the billowing air had been pushed from beneath them.

"Engine won't fire," yelled a seaman, running to
them.

Orthos swore. "So long since I've used the engine,
I don't know if I could fix it."

"Let me try," Dean said quickly, pushing to the rear
of the boat where another seaman was struggling with
the ignition. Without a word he stood aside as Dean

hunkered over the machinery, studying it. He tried the self-starter again; it refused to fire. Pulling the wires from the switch, he tried again, this time by hotwiring. The engine fired.

"Good job it was just a screwed-up switch. Don't know what I would have tried next." He laughed.

"Long as it works, don't worry about it." Orthos grinned. "Come on. We're shipping water and need to bale. No rest for any of us until we're through this."

Unfortunately for J.B. and Doc, the cooperation of the other boats wasn't to be echoed on their own vessel. It was shipping water faster than many of the others, as it was weighed down heavily with much of the livestock. Although the engine had fired and the rigging was secured, the boat was still slow because of its weight and was struggling across the white water.

The Armorer and Doc had both moved to help bale water, but were stopped by the sailor who had been on the tiller.

"Don't move," he said, holding a Glock.

"We only want to help," Doc said calmly.

"Think I trust pale ones to be helping? This is our ship, our journey. Leave it to us."

"For God's sake, man, what do you think we are likely to do?" Doc countered. "Why should we do any harm? If this ship goes, we go with it. We are all in this together."

The separatist sneered. "You're in nothing with us, you stupe old man. I—"

But his attempt at justification was cut short by another wave that swept across the deck. It caught him off balance and threw him toward the rail. Losing his grip on the Glock, which fell to the deck, he toppled over the rail and just managed to catch hold as he fell toward the waves. He screamed with pain as the jolt almost pulled his arm from its socket.

At the same moment the damage from the battering waves caused the ropes on one of the livestock cages to snap; three terrified and enraged bulls stumbled from their captivity and onto the deck.

"I'll get him. You try to keep them away," J.B. yelled to Doc.

The old man nodded, understanding immediately that it was a necessity to keep the frightened beasts from the rail near the struggling man. Moving toward them, Doc tried to cut off their progress, shooing them back toward the opposite rail. He beckoned to others to help, and soon there were several Pilatans helping him to round up the cattle and direct them back toward their cage. As the frightened creatures entered what had to have seemed like a secure haven, Doc took a length of rope proffered by a sailor and secured the cage.

Meanwhile, J.B. rushed to the rail and reached over for the separatist's other arm, which flailed by his side. He knew that to grab the already strained arm would possibly cause dislocation. He had to take the strain from that limb if he was to save the man.

"Give it to me," the Armorer yelled, reaching for the free hand.

With a look of disbelief and incomprehension etched on his face, the separatist took J.B.'s proffered hand and the Armorer locked on to his wrist, using his other hand to reach over as far as he dare to grab beneath the man's elbow. Heaving with all his strength, he pulled at the heavy body, tugging it up. The deck was slippery, and he was only too well aware that the boat was still pitching. But he ignored it as he heaved the man upward.

The separatist got his other hand on the rail and J.B. released his grip, reaching over to the man's belt and pulling him onto the deck.

J.B. collapsed beside the gasping man, his own strength temporarily drained by the rescue.

"I—I thought…" panted the separatist.

"Leave it," the Armorer breathed through bursting lungs. "Let's just get out of this channel."

Even as he spoke, the last of the boats breached the reaches of the white water and was gaining calmer seas as, battered but still in one piece, the Pilatan convoy struck out for the peninsula leading to the mainland.

ALTHOUGH THE WATERS were now calm, there was still the matter of passing the jagged shards of rock that jutted from the still waters as they approached the peninsula.

Looking up from their boats, the companions could all see the green hillside and the barely concealed entrance to the redoubt where they had arrived a few weeks earlier. And, beyond the swollen bulb of land formed by the green sward, there was the narrow strip of slate rock that formed the eroded peninsula that linked the hillside to the mainland, with the break in the central section where the slate had given way and crumbled down to the sea below. All along the cliffside that stretched on each side of the peninsula were sheer slate faces, with no way of gaining the lip of the mainland. For all of them, it recalled the reason they had headed for the island.

But, approaching it from this angle, there was perhaps a way in which they could gain the top of the cliff and so attain the mainland.

Where the narrow strip of slate and rock had tumbled into the sea, there was a scree now covered with moss and sea slime. It wasn't a particularly steep incline, although it would be slippery, and they would have to take great care. If they anchored the boats at low tide and then unloaded into the shallows, it would be possible to climb this incline and reach the remains of the peninsula bridge that took them onto the mainland. The obstacle that had prevented the companions from previously using this route was now eliminated. Prior to this, they would have had to scale down one side, then up another, risking the tide. Now, with boats that were anchored in the shallows, they could make their way from ship to shore with a haven at each end when the tide began to rise.

It still wasn't going to be easy. But at least it would be less of a risk than to be caught by the incoming tide.

Markos and Sineta anchored their boat, directing the seamen on the best position. That was something that the sec boss and the baron had determined on maps of the area in consultation with Mildred before leaving. Following the lead of their baron, the other boats took up anchor positions, forming a crescent that bridged the gap between the two sides of the rock bridge.

Jak looked up at the sky. "Sun low—not get everyone out by nightfall," he commented.

Mildred followed his gaze. The late afternoon was turning into early evening, and she reckoned they had two, maybe three, hours at most of a reasonable light left to them. There was little chance of discharging all the boats by that time. Some would have to spend a night on the water, as attempting the climb by moonlight would be an invitation to disaster. The notion of having the islanders divided by night wasn't appealing. No one was sure how far it was to the nearest ville, and so any possible attack; neither did they know what kind of predatory wildlife stalked the hillsides.

"I'd feel a whole lot better if some of us were first up," she said. "Markos is a good sec chief, but he's never been on the mainland in his life. They've never—any of them—fired a shot in anger at real human opponents."

"Nothing can do. Just chance." Jak shrugged.

As they spoke, the first party of Pilatans left the leading boat and began the ascent. Markos and Sineta took the lead and, as she watched them, Mildred reflected that the death of Barras and also the chilling of Chan had drawn the two closer together—not in the sense of a marriage of convenience that the two dead men had wanted, but that a mutual sense of loss had driven them to work harder in a time of adversity.

The ascent was difficult. The slime and moss that covered the scree was soft and slippery underfoot, making it hard to get a grip on the rocks. And the small stones that lay beneath the slime were apt to fall away suddenly in showers of gravel that covered those following and made a foothold all the harder. Both Markos and Sineta took the slope virtually on all fours, testing each hold as they went, despite the shallow angle. It was the only way that they could insure a safe grip.

It took them nearly half an hour to reach the top of the rocks, during which time they were virtually defenseless should there be an attack from above. The sec men on the boats, and Ryan and J.B. with their longer range blasters, provided the possibility of covering fire. However, at that distance, it would be hard to provide an effective defense, even though the bare rock-slate peninsula offered little cover of its own and would make an attacking force of any kind an open target in its own right.

When Markos and Sineta attained the flat of the rock, they lay panting.

"If it is this hard for us, then how will the animals and the old cope?" the baron gasped eventually.

"As with all endeavor—because they have to," Markos replied when he had caught his breath. As he spoke, they were joined by the next wave of Pilatans from the first boat. These carried ropes coiled around them. Markos allowed them only a short while to recover before instructing them to proceed with the plans they had been given.

The Pilatans threw the ropes down to the rocks below, past another wave of ascending men and women. The older, more infirm Pilatans were being assisted by those who were stronger, and at times the ascent was reduced to a crawl—but still it continued, never actually grinding to a halt.

At the bottom of the scree, there were those who had helped to unload crates and packages from the boat.

They waited patiently, then took the proffered ropes and attached them securely to the crates. Each one had been designed and packed specifically so that it would be of a suitable weight for what next occurred. While the man down with the crate pushed from behind, grasping the tied rope firmly as he pushed, the man above pulled and acted as an anchor, taking the strain of the crate's weight and also acting as a counterweight for the man behind the crate, lest he should slip. Depending on the comparative strengths of the two men, it actually speeded up the process of ascent.

When the first boat was empty, it was turned by the last seaman aboard, the tiller tied so that it headed out toward the sheer cliff face, away from the semicircle of companion craft. The seaman left his boat, letting it scupper itself on the rocks and leaving a gap where the next boat in line could come in to land its crew and cargo. The loss of the boats was regrettable, as they had taken such resources to put together. But they were now of little use, and to leave them as empty and soon to be rotting hulks would only make it harder for the other craft to maneuver into shore.

Up on the smooth surface of the peninsula's rock bridge, there were now enough Pilatans for Markos to form a sec patrol that ventured to the point where the rock ran seamlessly into the green of the mainland, establishing a bridgehead that would enable the landings to continue with a greater sense of security.

Mildred, Krysty and Jak were on the next vessel to land. Descending from the boat into the shallow water, and feeling the cold drag at their feet, they were surprised at how hard the climb truly was. The angle might have been shallow, but the shale, moss and slime made it treacherous. Jak ascended the quickest, as surefooted as ever over the surface, barely seeming to touch it as his hands and feet found secure holds where it seemed none could exist. When he reached the top, he took one of the lengths of rope that was now lying idle—there being no crates to be hauled up as yet—and threw it down.

"Krysty!" he yelled to the red-haired beauty below. She and Mildred were helping the ascent of the three Pilatans who had nearly been chilled by the falling rigging. They were still in shock, and also had minor injuries from the landing they had made when Jak had cannoned into them, deflecting them from a certain chilling. Their ascent had been slow, and both Mildred and Krysty had doubled back to assist them.

Krysty looked up and saw the rope fall toward her. She grabbed at the end as it reached her, knowing what Jak wanted her to do. She took the rope and pulled down a long length of slack, Jak feeding it to her. While she was doing this, Mildred—having also guessed Jak's plan—explained to the distressed Pilatans what she wanted them to do.

The redhead wove the rope around the three Pilatans, tying each one securely into place. She also included herself and Mildred in the equation, so that there were five people tied into the rope, two of whom would provide motive power. Signaling to Jak, she and Mildred continued their ascent, with the albino anchoring and pulling at the top of the scree. It was much easier for them to help the Pilatans in this manner and they soon gained the ridge.

"Nice work, Jak," Mildred said in thanks.

The albino shrugged. "Pity save one chill then see fall so near."

Meanwhile, below, another ship was scuppered and another moved in to take its place. The unloading continued, but the sun had started to sink and the light was becoming dim, making it dangerous to continue. When the current ship had discharged its load, Markos strode to the lip of the incline and discharged his blaster three times into the air.

It was the prearranged signal in case of such an occurrence. There were two ships left at sea, and these would have to wait until the morrow before they could unload. Meanwhile, up on the rock of the peninsula bridge, the Pilatans built a fire and makeshift shelters from crates to protect themselves from the biting wind that came with the dark, settling to an uncomfortable but necessary night on the rocks.

On board the two remaining ships were Ryan and Dean, and Doc and J.B. For the former pair, it would be an easy night. They were among those who would work with them, and who didn't see them as enemies. For the latter two, this was still not the case. Despite the fact that J.B. had saved the life of the separatist who would have chilled both Doc and himself, the general atmosphere was still against them. Added to this, the livestock on board were still disturbed by the events of the voyage and prowled their cages, making it hard for anyone to rest. Tempers were frayed and getting worse in such an atmosphere.

"Truly, I would never have been so pleased to partake of an invigorating scramble in such unseemly circumstances," Doc remarked to the Armorer, with no lack of wit as they took turns to keep watch while the other tried to sleep.

On the mainland peninsula, the night winds howled and swept along the bare rock, making it hard for those in the makeshift shelters to rest.

"It is not perhaps how I would have envisaged our first night in a new land," Sineta said to Mildred, Krysty and Markos as they huddled around the fire.

"In truth, it could hardly have been any different, if one chose to reflect," Markos considered at length. "Whatever happened, we could not establish a comfortable and even semipermanent camp immediately."

"That's true, but it doesn't stop it being so damn cold," Mildred countered.

Farther up, at the point where the stone and slate gave way to topsoil and grass, Jak joined the sec men who were keeping watch on the land beyond, taking his turn with the rest of them. It was gesture that was appreciated by sec men who had no experience of the mainland.

And so the night passed. Dawn broke and the first of the remaining ships moved into position as soon as the light was sufficient. It unloaded with ease, and it wasn't long before Ryan and Dean were reunited with their companions. The ship was sent off to join the others, now little more than matchwood against the rocks.

The tide had receded during the hours of darkness and it would be a race against time to bring the final ship into position and unload it—including the livestock—before the waters began to deepen once more. Only if it was unavoidable did anyone wish to wait the hours until the tide went out once more.

On board, J.B. and Doc helped to prepare the animals for unloading. They were released from their cages one at a time and led down a gangplank into the shallow waters. Once at the bottom of the incline, they were roped with the lengths thrown down from the top of the slope and were then guided up. Here they were put in the charge of Pilatans who were ready for them, penned in crates until they were all on the level.

It was a slow and painstaking process, with many of the frightened animals refusing to make their way up the slope, the Pilatans at the bottom of the incline forced to beat them to make them move from fear and pain. The resultant cries from the beasts did nothing to quell the fear among those still on board the boat.

J.B. and Doc were among the last to start the ascent. They both stood at the bottom of the scree, the water of the incoming tide lapping at their ankles as the seaman deputed to scupper the last boat set its course and clambered down and into the calm waters as the craft headed for the graveyard that the rocks had become. They helped the man onto the drier land of the slope and, as he began to climb, they watched the boat crash into the side of the cliff.

"That's it, then." Doc sighed. "No way back for any who may regret it, now."

"No way back for us, either," the Armorer added. "And unless we move it, we'll risk being drowned in this damn tide."

They began their ascent, some distance behind the others. Doc found the moss and slime hard-going, his hands and feet scrabbling for holds, his lion's-head swordstick tucked into his belt. Once or twice he lost his grip completely and felt himself begin to slip and fall backward, but always J.B. was there to grab him and help him up again.

By the time that both men had reached the summit, they were exhausted. Ryan and Dean were there to help them up over the edge.

"Thanks for sending a rope down for us," J.B. panted.

Ryan grinned. "They've used them all on the animals. Guess they didn't think you'd need them."

"Great. I'll do the same for them sometime," J.B. gasped.

Climbing to their feet, both men could see that the train of Pilatans and their animals were ready to begin their trek. At the head of the convoy were Markos and Sineta, with Mildred, Krysty and Jak waiting for them. They were facing the beginnings of the grasslands and Sineta looked back to where the four men were standing. She said something to Markos, who turned and beckoned to the four companions.

"I guess they want us to take the head with them because we know the mainland," Ryan said wryly.

"But, Dad, it's different here from elsewhere and we—"

"I know," Ryan said quietly. "But you know what, Dean? They've got to discover that for themselves."

# Chapter Thirteen

The caravan of Pilatu made its way across the terrain for two days. Progress was slow, slower than had originally been envisioned by Sineta as the wags had been ditched and many of the older Pilatans found it hard to keep pace on foot. There were horses in among the livestock, and the younger, fitter members of the tribe gave up their mounts to assist their elders. Sineta herself was one of the first to do this, followed by Markos. The companions, who had also been given mounts so that they could keep pace with the caravan leaders and also scout ahead, also gave up their seats, although Doc was incensed when Sineta insisted that he retain his mount, on account of his age.

The area presented the weary caravan with no great threat. Rolling green hills led away from the rock peninsula where they had landed, forming a bland green barrier between themselves and the great lands beyond, the inclines making it impossible to see what lay over the crests of the hills.

"Perhaps it will be better on the other side," Markos said to Ryan as they rode on the first day. "If it stretches like this for any great distance, then how can it be farmed? Where is the shelter?"

"It'll be different, all right," the one-eyed man

replied. "You don't know how different…but I'll be glad when we're beyond this."

Ryan shivered as yet another cold gust swept along the hills. Certainly, this was hardly the most inspiring introduction to the mainland that the Pilatans could have wished. The hills were covered with a thin layer of topsoil that was enough to allow the sparse growth of grass and moss that softened underfoot but allowed for nothing else to take root. The rock beneath the soil was flat, so there were no outcrops to stop the winds from howling across the flat plain that rose in an incline to the crest.

With the slow progress that they made on foot, it seemed as if they would never reach the crest to see what lay beyond. The Pilatans moved slowly, and even to reach the crest of the long, undulating hills meant trekking a greater distance than the length and breadth of the island they had left behind. The scale of the mainland was something they couldn't even imagine, let alone adjust to with ease. And with each passing hour that they walked, they grew more and more apprehensive about their undertaking. Was this land too big for them to assimilate? Would they be able to find somewhere that had the resource and reassurance of their home?

It was something that the companions could do nothing to assuage. The vast plains of grass, rising upward, bespoke of a massive land movement at the time of skydark, which had stripped this long stretch of land and formed a new coastline that hid from view the land that lay beyond. Under their own steam, they would have made the distance in a day, and be able to view the area beyond for possible shelter before nightfall. But with the heavy caravan slowing them, it meant a night camping on the plains.

As darkness fell, the temperature dropped to below zero, with the wind chill taking it down a few degrees more. Even with the temporary shelter they were able to rig from the crates and belongings they carried with them, it was still hard for the Pilatans to make anything in the way of warming conditions. It was hard for them to keep fires going in the teeth of the winds, as they had never had such conditions to contend with on the well-sheltered island. The companions passing among them had to teach them how to shelter and nurture their fires.

There were also complaints about water running low. Many of the older Pilatans were fearful that they wouldn't be able to find another supply before their own ran out. Jak rigged plastic sheeting they had brought with them to catch the dew, and also hunted out a small spring that he was able to detect by a slightly more verdant growth of grass and moss. It wasn't much, but it did help to alleviate fears, which may have been just as important as the actual production of water. For the caravan to proceed on the morrow, the Pilatans had all to be in the frame of mind to continue.

"I know we are slow," Markos said to the companions as they gathered around their own small fire, "but we should—if we can continue even at this pace—attain the crest of the hill by nightfall tomorrow."

"I hope so," Mildred replied. "Another night like this won't be good for the older and weaker people. We need to get off this plain."

"I'm sure we will, and that we'll find better conditions," Sineta said with a confidence that Mildred couldn't share.

"Don't place your hopes too highly," Mildred said carefully. "We don't know what's going to be on the far side of the hill. It may be good land or it may be little more than a dust bowl." She saw Sineta's face drop as she spoke, and continued rapidly, so that the woman wouldn't be too dispirited. "I'm not saying that it'll be a disaster, but you have to take in the fact that conditions change so quickly here. You always have to expect the unexpected, otherwise you won't be able to adapt and survive."

Markos smiled grimly. "It seems that we have been in isolation too long, perhaps become complacent because of this."

"It's not anyone's fault," Mildred said softly. "It's just going to be a lot to learn quickly. And you'll have to."

AS DAWN BROKE, the Pilatans stirred to wakefulness and prepared to continue with little ceremony. There wasn't a single one of them who couldn't wait to crest the hill, no matter what may lay on the other side. The morning was dull and overcast, the wind chill seeming to cut straight through cloth and flesh, cold to the bone with every step. And the distance ahead, on an upward incline, was enough to suggest a good day's march. They broke to rest on three occasions, partly for the people and partly for the livestock, who were unused to walking such distances, and some of whom had the extra burden of the crates. On each break, many could barely wait to continue, preferring the relentless toil to sitting, waiting, in the biting cold.

But finally they reached the crest of the hill. A short plateau stretched ahead, just enough to make a view of the land beyond difficult. The distant peaks of hills and mountains were all that could be seen, shrouded in the mist of clouds that lay low in the overcast skies.

"Must drop down into one hell of a valley," J.B. remarked to Ryan as they trudged across the plateau.

The one-eyed man agreed. "Problem is, what do we do if the drop is too steep to get down easily?"

The Armorer glanced back at the caravan stretching out behind them and then forward to where Mildred walked with Markos and Sineta.

"Dark night, how's Millie going to deal with that one?" he murmured.

The same thoughts had also crossed Mildred's mind. Seeing the mist-enshrouded vista ahead, she had wondered what course of action could be taken if it proved impossible for the Pilatan caravan to descend on the other side of the hill. And, looking along the ridge that stretched on either side for as far as she could see, she had to admit that she had no ideas. She prayed that it wouldn't be necessary to try to come up with any.

"Oh my sweet Lord—look at it, it's beautiful," Sineta breathed with a tone of awe in her words.

Mildred snapped out of her reverie and took a few steps forward to where Sineta and Markos were viewing the land on the reverse of the plain. Stretched ahead of them were undulating forests and woodlands, with stretches of bare scrub between. In the far distance could be seen at least two villes, both dozens of miles apart.

The view stretched for maybe eighty to ninety miles by her reckoning, and showed a fertile stretch of land with a population, probably sheltered by the arid plain they had just traveled across. There was opportunity for the Pilatans here, and proof that it could sustain a population…even, in fact, giving them populations to trade with.

But would they have an easy access to this promised land? Looking down, which, she noticed, both Markos and Sineta had so far failed to do, she could see that there was a sharp incline toward the bottom of the valley, as the land had been pushed sharply up by earth movements. However, it wasn't so steep an incline that it would be impossible to traverse. Rather, it would require a deal of care. There were pathways that could be used, made by ridges in the rock. And along the way there was much vegetation that could be used for handholds. The livestock would be a little more difficult to manage, but even so…

"Figure we can do this?" J.B. said in her ear, making her jump.

"John, don't do that, for God's sake!"

"Sorry." The Armorer grinned. "I didn't realize how deep in thought you were. But what do you reckon?"

She shrugged. "It's not so bad."

"For us and the fitter Pilatans, mebbe not," he cut in. "But what about the older ones and the animals?"

"Yeah, I know. But what can we do? It's got to be done."

As the Pilatans gathered on the edge of the plateau, they were all stunned by the scope and richness of the land that lay beneath. Too distracted, in many cases, to recognize the perils of the descent into the valley. Mildred had torn Markos and Sineta away from their admiring glances at the world below to discuss the descent. When she pointed out the only route, both had decided that the manner of their descent should be left in the more experienced hands of the companions. They were also of the opinion that the descent should begin quickly: partly because a delay would give the members of the caravan a chance to fret about their route, and partly because there were only a few hours until the light faded.

While Markos, Sineta and Mildred organized the caravan into some kind of order in which to make the descent, Jak went ahead to scout out the best possible route. The albino covered the territory swiftly, moving with ease down the narrow paths and among the undergrowth. It was simplicity itself for him to cover the distance, but he was mindful of the mixed abilities of those who would follow in his wake. Picking the widest paths, and those with the best vegetation for handholds, he marked the twists and turns of the route with branches torn from the trees. By the time he had returned to the top of the ridge, the Pilatans were organized in order of descent and Mildred had gathered the companions to her.

"Ryan, Jak, J.B.—you guys go down ahead of us and make relay points, so that there's help fairly close at hand for any that may need it," Mildred said. "Krysty and Dean—one of you go to the middle, the other to the bottom. Take these," she added, handing them medical supplies she had prepared during Jak's marking of the route. "That way we've got first aid to hand if it's needed along the way. I'll stay up here with Markos. Sineta's going to be one of the first down, and I want Doc to go with her. The last thing we want is for an accident to happen to the baron, so I'd appreciate you really keeping a close eye on her, Doc."

"It shall be done. You have no need to ask," Doc said with a small bow.

"One more thing," Ryan interjected. "I figure we're far enough away from any of those villes not to have trouble from them, but we've got no way of knowing what kind of wildlife is out there."

"Keeping distance, but can smell it. Could be problem," Jak affirmed.

"Okay," Mildred stated. "I'll make sure they know to keep their blasters ready and be triple-red."

Ryan nodded, then looked at the darkening sky. "Good. Let's do it, then. I don't like the look of the clouds. The last thing we need is rain on top of the worsening light."

Moving swiftly to get the process under way, the companions separated and moved into position while Mildred prepared the caravan. Doc and Sineta were the first to make the descent.

"I find that the best thing to do is not to look too closely at the drop that beckons, but rather to concentrate assiduously on the path in front of you," Doc advised the baron as they began the descent.

Taking a quick glance across the open lands to one side of her and the angle of descent, Sineta nodded. "I will take those as wise words, and well worth adherence," she said nervously.

But the route Jak had selected was a good one, and on those few occasions when she felt herself beginning to slip, or her confidence did likewise, making her believe that she would tumble, the vegetation by her sides and the sure hand of Doc Tanner sustained her. They passed Jak, Ryan, Krysty and J.B. along the way without requiring help. When they had reached the bottom, the baron looked up at the crest of the hillside, where those following in her wake could be seen streaming down the paths.

"I think, if we all have a guide as good as yourself, then we may make it unscathed," she murmured.

"Why, thank you, madam," Doc demurred.

The Pilatan progress down the side of the incline was erratic. There were times when the slower members of the tribe held up those that followed in their wake, but there were no casualties and little need for the companions who were stationed along the way. However, when the livestock were led down, things were slightly different. The herders who had led them across the plain, and who had been in charge of the animals on the flat island of Pilatu, found it difficult to keep the beasts in line. The sheep and pigs were terrified, but were so closely roped as to be unable to break. Horses, coming down singly, were nervous but able to keep their footing. The cattle, however, were another matter. Roped together, but of varying strengths, and with each one pulling against the others in fear, it was inevitable that at one point a rogue would try to make a break, risking pulling the entire herd off the path and tumbling them down the steep incline.

It happened despite the best efforts of the herder at

the front of the line, who darted around the fretting beasts, barely keeping a foothold himself, to try to calm the rogue steer. He grabbed at the yolk of the beast and heaved with all his strength to try to keep it on the track. The beast reared as far as its bounds would allow, the hoof catching the herder in the groin and causing him to double up in pain, losing his grip and falling off the path.

Jak was the nearest, and it was as well, for the albino hunter was the best equipped to deal with the immediate problem. Clambering swiftly through the undergrowth, he stopped briefly to check that the fallen Pilatan herder was alive. The man had saved himself by grabbing at a laurel bush and was in agony but safe from falling further. He could be dealt with later. The most immediate problem was for Jak to calm the steer before it charged the whole herd off the path. If they hit uneven ground and more than one should stumble, there was every chance that they would hurtle themselves to their doom.

The beast was still rearing, but had not as of yet made a strong break, the combined force of the stubborn cattle around it preventing the break it would wish. But its companions were becoming agitated and would soon try to get away from the disruption, which would only cause further confusion.

Ignoring the rearing hooves of the steer, Jak ducked under so that he came up between the front of the agitated beast and the flicking tail and stamping hooves of the creature to its front. It didn't give the albino youth a lot of space in which to safely move, but he stoically ignored the beast to his rear and looked the rogue steer fully in the face. He could feel its hot breath, erratic and fetid, on his face. Its teeth were bared, and its eyes wild and glassy with fear.

Smiling grimly to himself, Jak ducked to one side of the creature, his fingers probing the tough, corded muscle of its neck. He found the area he wanted and pressed hard, his fingers moving in a small circle until they found the exact spot. He pinched and the beast momentarily blacked out and stumbled before recovering, this time in a much more sedate mood.

Jak moved among the other cattle, calming them, before leading them down the incline, stopping to send Krysty after the injured Pilatan herdsman.

Once the cattle and the injured man had been recovered and taken to the base of the slope, it meant that the Pilatan caravan had reached their target in one piece. And just in time. The heavens opened in the deepening twilight.

"Better find a place to camp, and quick," Mildred said to Markos and Sineta. "Let the livestock calm down and get some rest before we begin the real trek." And pray to God nothing else happened between now and then, she added to herself.

THE PILATAN CAMP had been struck a few miles farther into the interior, using the shelter of a wooded area not unlike one of those found on their island. This had been Mildred's suggestion to Markos, which he had seized upon, understanding her point that it would be simple to set up sec patrols in an environment similar to the one they had recently left behind.

A fire was set and camp was made while the sec

boss deputed a sec patrol and sentry posts to be established at the four compass points, covering the community while they took a much-needed rest.

The forest gave them shelter and increased the ambient heat at ground level, making it less imperative to build a large fire. The smaller blaze was shielded to stop the glow illuminating the area and giving away their position.

"It shouldn't matter too much," Markos told Sineta, "as the nearest ville's some good few miles away. But we're not sure what kind of predators may be lurking in the darkness. So a patrol and four compass point posts to check in with should keep us covered. I believe we may be able to rest easy tonight."

"I wish I could believe that so easily," Krysty muttered to Ryan, keeping her voice low so that only the one-eyed man could hear.

Ryan studied her. The redheaded woman's hair had flattened to her scalp and curled into her neck, giving her a worried look that echoed that which her mutie sense was telling her.

"You know what it is?" he asked.

"Could just be that Markos is a bit too overconfident. They don't really know what it's like out there and he's making assumptions about the area just because it looks like the island."

"Yeah, that's got me a little concerned," Ryan mused. "Figure we should mebbe give them a little hand."

"I don't know if Markos will like that," Krysty commented.

Ryan smiled. "Who says he has to know, unless it's really necessary?"

The one-eyed man gathered his people from where they sat or lay around the camp. When they were together, he explained the situation as it stood. He continued. "The best thing for us to do is try to shadow the sentry posts and follow the patrol. Which won't be easy, 'cause they're not stupes, just not used to the mainland yet. Hopefully, they won't have to learn the hard way, but…"

"I follow patrol." Jak spoke with an assurance that prevented his next comment from sounding like arrogance. "Mebbe they know others behind them, not me."

Ryan agreed. "If you follow them, I'll take one post and J.B. you take another. Then Krysty can cover one and Doc and Dean the last."

"What about Mildred?" Krysty asked with a frown.

Ryan looked over to where Mildred was in conversation with Markos and Sineta. "You know, I think this is one time when we really shouldn't say anything to her. She'll feel obliged to tell Markos, and then it could all be shot to shit. If nothing happens, then no one need be any the wiser."

"And if it does? Will the good doctor not feel betrayed?" Doc quizzed.

Ryan grimaced. "That's a chance I'll have to take."

"Not just you," J.B. said quietly, "all of us."

The one-eyed man shrugged. "If things go triple-red, then I figure they'll be too glad of the help to say anything."

J.B. wasn't entirely satisfied with the answer. He knew that Mildred would feel betrayed initially, and although she may understand the reasoning behind

Ryan's action eventually, it would only serve to put more distance between them when they had some to repair. But, as he looked across at Millie in conversation with the Pilatan baron and sec chief, he knew that there was no other practical course that Ryan could take.

"Okay, let's do it," he said finally.

The companions slipped away from the camp one by one, to avoid calling attention to themselves. Ryan went first, to take the north sentry point. It was in a heavily wooded area and he had to tread carefully to avoid making any sound. Once he had them in sight, he shinnied up a tree and waited in the branches, with a good view of the area surrounding. Krysty took south and followed a similar course.

For Doc and Dean, it was slightly harder. The eastern sentry post was on the edge of an open plain and the sparser covering of foliage meant that they had to hang back farther than they would have liked to keep concealed and not give away their position.

"I just hope it doesn't kick off here, if there's going to be trouble," Dean whispered. "We're a fair way away from them."

"My dear boy," Doc countered, "if we are going to see any action from the local wildlife, it'll probably come through us before it reaches them." He smiled wickedly. "Let that be a consoling thought."

Meanwhile, the Armorer had made his way to the western point, where the sentry post was set up by a stream, giving a wide view of the opposite bank. The soft gurgling of the stream gave him good cover as he made his way toward the post, keeping in the cover of rushes that had sprung up by the bank. He settled there, figuring it was a good position for concealment, although the cold water and mud around his ankles promised a freezing night ahead.

It was Jak who had the most difficult of the assignments and yet was the one best equipped to carry it out. He was the last to slip away from the camp, having no initial notion of where the roving sec patrol may be. The only thing he could do was pick any point from which to begin and listen to his instincts.

Having made his way out into the wood, so that the noises of the camp were filtered from his consciousness, Jak stopped and hunkered down, stilling his breathing so that he was as immobile and as quiet as possible. In this state, he was able to focus his senses and maybe determine a direction for the sec patrol.

Wherever they were, they were out of range. He could hear nothing and his only choice was to take a direction and proceed as swiftly as possible. If he was traveling in a counter direction, then he would find them quickly. If not, it would take him longer than he would have wished to catch up with them. He shrugged to himself, stoically realizing that there was no easier way.

"THIS NIGHT IS TOO LONG for my liking," one member of the four-man patrol whispered as they slowly made their way from one post to another. They had traversed the woodlands between the sentry points and had gone as far as the beginnings of another flat plain.

"Do not have fear because of the darkness," a second replied sardonically, "for the larger animals al-

ready share that fear and will not be seen until the daylight."

"Easy to say," the other replied sharply.

A third spoke with a weary tone. "Cease this petty
squabbling. Neither animal nor man would be out
tonight unless they had cause."

"I had not thought of that," the first mused. "Could
there be other patrols such as ourselves for which we
should look?"

The second laughed softly. "Truly, paranoia is a
wondrous beast. You saw yourself that the nearest ville
is at least a day's march away."

The first man turned to his accuser in the moonlight
and smiled. "Not everyone has to march. Listen…"

In the distance they could hear the sound of a wag,
high and whining across the plain.

"Adopt secure positions now!" the patrol leader
barked, the banter of a moment before forgotten. Following his lead, the patrol fanned out and adopted defensive positions along the verge of the woodland,
waiting for the wag to approach, for the note of the engine deepened into a drone and increased in volume as
it headed toward them. Scanning the plain, it was now
possible to pick out the shape—with lights extinguished—of what appeared to be a jeep, with at least
three men on board.

"Do not fire unless we are seen. If they wish to pass
and not enter the wood, we do not alert them to our
presence. Understood?"

The other patrol members didn't answer, taking it
as an order rather than a question.

Away to the west, Jak had just passed a sentry post,

having seen J.B. on watch and alerting him to his presence with the softest of birdcalls. The Armorer had returned the signal and let Jak pass, now knowing that the barest sound of his passing wasn't an unknown danger. Jak scouted around the post without anyone even realizing he was there, and continued on his search for the patrol.

It was soon after that he caught the sound of a wag engine on the night air. Realizing that it could only come from an outside source, and having no idea where the sec patrol may be, Jak increased his pace so that he could intercept the wag to ascertain its purpose. Within a few minutes, the engine had grown louder and Jak had arrived at the point where the sec patrol had positioned themselves.

Swiftly and silently, Jak climbed a tree so that he had an overview of the situation. He could see the wag clearly on the plain and could pick out four men in the pale moonlight, all armed. Below him he could see the four patrol members, armed with Glocks and H&Ks, which were the standard Pilatan sec hardware. The patrol was focused and ready to fight. The approaching patrol wouldn't be. They were either an outlying sec patrol themselves, or nocturnal hunters. In either case, their primary concern would be the wildlife and they wouldn't expect a four-man sec patrol to blast them.

Seeing that the Pilatans were adopting a primarily defensive stance, Jak decided to sit back and wait. He wouldn't intervene unless strictly necessary, for his sudden presence could throw the Pilatans into confusion. A conflict was looking likely, however, as the wag was headed with an almost unerring accuracy for the spot where the sec patrol was hidden.

"They're not going to turn away," the patrol leader whispered. "Be ready."

"Do you think they've seen us?" asked the patrol member who had earlier voiced apprehensions.

"Do you think it matters?" the patrol leader snapped.

There was no time for any kind of reply as the wag swerved into a turn that would take it along the edge of the wood, obviously the extent of its patrol route. This would have alleviated the need for any kind of action on the part of the Pilatan sec patrol, if not for the fact that the angle of the turn was about to send the back wheel skidding over at least one of the concealed Pilatan sec. They had no choice but to make their presence known.

As one, they sprang out of cover, firing at the wag. In the quiet of the night—broken only by the throb of the wag engine—the sound of blasterfire cut through the air and penetrated into the woods, reaching the Pilatan camp. Markos immediately mobilized some of his sec and set off in the direction of the noise, leaving others to protect the camp. Sineta and Mildred were left behind, the latter suddenly noticing for the first time the absence of the other companions.

Meanwhile, at each of the sec posts, the incumbents went to triple-red, sending one member of each party toward the sound of the firefight. The companions, watching these posts, elected to stay with the majority, hoping that Jak was on hand.

The albino hunter pulled his .357 Magnum Colt Python, but stayed up the tree, electing to see how the firefight would develop. From where he was, the sec patrol seemed to be doing just fine.

The jeep screeched to a halt, the engine stalling as some of the H&K fire splintered the glass in the windshield. Jak could hear the men in the wag curse and yell in confusion, falling from the stationary wag and attempting to return fire, but not being able to see the Pilatans against the darkness of the backdrop, the dark clothing of the sec men blending them into the trees as they dropped back to take cover, firing as they went.

It looked for a second like stalemate, as the sheltering outsiders began to return fire steadily, spraying the area with blasterfire, blindly attempting to hit something…anything.

The Pilatans, on the other hand, had a clear night sky backdrop across the plain on which to pick out the men crouching in cover of the wag. Their returning fire was more sporadic, but closer to the bone. The men behind the wag had themselves concealed well enough to avoid being chilled, but there was no way they could emerge from that small area of cover.

Things would have to change—and quickly. Jak decided it was time for him to enter the scenario. He dropped from the tree, planning to circle around from a distance to pick off some of the outsiders from the rear. It would take all of his skill as a hunter to make an unseen approach, but he was sure he could do it. He began to move across the wooded area to the rear of the Pilatans, but pulled back when he heard the members of the sec posts approaching. There were also the sounds of men coming through the woods to rear of him—sec men from the camp.

Jak swore softly to himself. There was no way now that he could go through with his part of the plan without making himself known. He went back up the tree. The Pilatans would have to sort it out for themselves.

On the contrary, it wasn't necessary for the approaching forces to muster and mount an attack. Under a sudden barrage of concerted cover fire from the outsiders behind the wag, one of the four men scrambled into the driver's seat of the jeep and attempted to start the engine. It whined and squealed three times before catching, all the while slugs from the Pilatan sec force ricocheting off the metal body of the wag. As it caught, and the outsider gunned it into life, the other three men scrambled in, firing recklessly into the woods as they did. The sheer consistency of their fire prevented any of the concealed Pilatan sec men from taking a concerted aim. The outsiders were able to gain the wag and keep firing as the driver turned it, then put his foot down, hammering the accelerator as the wag bumped over the plain, back in the direction it had come.

The Pilatan sec men kept firing at the retreating wag, even as Markos and others from the sec posts and main camp reached the scene. Breathlessly, the patrol leader told the sec boss what had occurred.

Markos nodded solemnly. "I did not think that any ville would send scouts this far out. I fear that we will have to adapt sooner than we expected to the ways of the mainland."

"But we defeated them, sir. That is all that matters," the sec patrol leader said with a barely concealed note of triumph in his voice.

It was a feeling echoed by the others. What Markos had to say to them, Jak didn't wait to hear. He had something else worrying him and he swiftly traversed the distances between the compass point posts, gathering the companions with a few words of explanation as he went. While he journeyed to the next post, the companion keeping guard returned to the main camp.

Traveling counterclockwise, Jak met J.B. last of all. The two men returned to the main Pilatan camp to find an upbeat mood pervading those who had been told of the skirmish by returning sec men and considered that they had made a good show of strength. The companions, on the other hand, were more subdued...particularly Mildred.

"Dark night! I knew we should have mentioned this to Mildred," J.B. muttered to Jak.

The albino shrugged. "Too late worry now. She should know more important things worry about."

As they approached the gathered companions, Mildred was about to speak when Jak cut her short.

"Earlier not matter now. We've got big trouble."

"In what way?" Mildred asked.

"Wag from a ville, four sec...regular patrol by look of it. Now know we're here and in firefight. Be back in daylight, with more sec, find out what fuck's going on."

"So is that a problem? It's what you'd expect," Mildred replied.

"Yeah, what we'd expect," J.B. said pointedly. "Trouble is, Jak's heard them talking to Markos. He's cautious, but he seems to be the only one. And take a look around you. They think they've won and that it stops here. They sure as shit won't listen if you tell them it never ends, so it's up to us to keep alert till the morning."

Mildred nodded. "Guess you were right to shadow them, then. I just wish you'd told me."

"Couldn't." Ryan shook his head. "You were with Sineta and Markos when we had to go for it. There was no way we could safely tell you. Believe me, that's all it was."

Mildred pondered that for a moment. "Okay, it's easy to forget that these people have got a lot to learn and they've got to learn it the hard way. I just hope there's enough of us to cover their asses and ours when the shit hits the wall."

THE PILATAN SEC POSTS had been remanned and the patrol had returned to the central camp full of their victory. Despite the best efforts of the sec chief, the people of the camp had celebrated their "victory" over the outsiders and were still sleeping when the sound of wags could be heard roaring across the plain.

Markos was instantly awake and found that the only ones prepared to meet the intruders were the companions, all of whom were awake and fully armed. Rearming his H&K, he hurried across to them, kicking awake Pilatans as he passed.

"You knew this would happen," he said to Mildred. When she nodded, he added, "You never made the point."

"How could I?" she countered. "I heard you try to make the same point, and no one was listening. So why do you think they were going to listen to me?"

He conceded the point with a shrug. "No matter now. It sounds like a heavy force, many wags...but I doubt they'll be able to get them through to here."

Ryan shook his head. "Probably just for transport. The ville seems to be a long way off. But then they'll pour through the woods, and they could be coming from all angles. And remember, they know this area probably better than we do. I think I'd have preferred it if they could have driven right up to us. At least we'd know where they were."

Markos spoke grimly. "I'll divide us up into parties, send them out to counter any actions. Will you help me rouse the people?"

Ryan nodded, and the companions separated, moving among the sleeping and half-awake Pilatans, rousing them as they went. Their actions were greeted with a mixture of fear and hostility—fear at being attacked and some residual resentment that it was whitelanders who were telling them to get up to prepare for battle.

Markos sent scouts out to the sentry posts to see what was happening and to recall those sec men so that they could be briefed. The job of the scouts was to send back reports with the returning sec men, then keep a roving brief, so that they could plot the progress of the outsiders.

Swiftly, the mood in the Pilatan camp changed. As they fully awakened and could hear the arriving wags, the Pilatans realized that they were in for their first taste of a firefight on the mainland. They rapidly checked and primed their blasters, and assembled in front of Markos, who received the reports of the incoming sec force. He turned to the assembled Pilatans and the companions, and spoke concisely, rapidly.

"They come from the one area, across the plain where the skirmish took place last night. There are ten wags, with approximately five or six people on each. This means that we outnumber them, but they appear to have machine blasters. They may have grens, mebbe even rocket launchers. We cannot know their firepower, therefore must assume the worst.

"I will divide you into small groups and assign posts. We will concentrate our efforts in the direction from which they will come, but also have outlying parties to flank them. You must be alert and shoot to chill. Use the natural cover. They undoubtedly will."

With which, Markos moved among the Pilatans, dividing them into groups and mixing some of them with the companions. "They have experience of firefights in the whitelands—listen to them," he told the relevant groups. But despite this, J.B. and Krysty were put into small war parties where there was hostility from diehard separatists who weren't comfortable with the idea of listening to pale ones.

Before the groups set off into the woods, J.B. managed to snatch a few words with Ryan, telling him of the residual resentment. "Another thing—I don't like the idea of so many people with blasters wandering about in such a small wooded area, blasting at anything that moves."

Ryan agreed. "I know. We should be drawing the enemy out where we can get a clear sighting of them. It'll be too easy to blast our own out there."

"Yeah, I'll go with that," the Armorer agreed grimly. "Good luck out there."

The war parties were about to move out when a scout returned with further information. The wags had rolled to a halt and discharged their cargo of heavily armed men, with a guard of four left to cover them. The men had fanned out and were now in the woods.

"We outnumber them heavily, so the odds are on our side," Markos added when he relayed this to the baron, "but we need to proceed with caution."

Sineta agreed, clutching her blaster. She turned to Mildred as Markos gave the order to move. "I fear I shall not be of much use in the conflict to come."

"You concentrate on keeping alive, sweetie," Mildred told her. "We're a far-flung group, so the chances of you being risked are low. Markos has made sure of that—"

"But I must lead my people," Sineta protested.

"You can't lead them when you're chilled," Mildred countered, cutting her short. "He's done the right thing in the circumstances. Now just stay close to me and don't argue about it, all right?"

The Pilatan war parties moved out into the woods and straight into trouble.

The wooded areas they had to traverse were thick, and it was impossible for them to move stealthily. The same was also true for the incoming attack parties, but the sounds by which they could have been tracked were obliterated by the noise of the Pilatans. Blaster-fire filled the air in staccato and irregular blasts, and the air became thick with cries of surprise and pain.

Leading his party, J.B. signaled them to halt, as he was sure that he could hear the enemy approach.

"Why are we stopping?" questioned a separatist who had bridled at the Armorer taking the lead.

"So I can hear what's going down," J.B. whispered, adding, "and keep your voice down, for fuck's sake. Don't need to give away our position."

The separatist took a step forward.

"What are you doing?" J.B. whispered.

"You may be frightened, pale one, but I am not," the separatist replied. "And I take no orders from you."

An astonished J.B. watched the man move openly through the wood, then signaled to his party. "Follow. We'll have to cover him."

Cutting a swath through the foliage, the separatist came across a group of outsiders as they tried to make their way stealthily through the woods. It was hard to know who was the more surprised at the sudden confrontation.

The separatist looked at the stunned war party. They consisted of a white man, two blacks and a Hispanic. Addressing the black men, he said, "But you are my brothers. Why should I make war with you? We can talk about this, can we not? I would rather—"

He was cut short by the startled exclamation of one of the blacks, who was the first to snap out of his stunned reverie.

"Nuckin' hell! Take the freak down before he stops talking and starts firing!"

And as he spoke, the black opened fire with his Uzi, the slugs cutting the separatist almost in two with a neat line of fire across his abdomen. The sound of the blasterfire galvanized the others in the war party and they all began to open fire. Blasterfire was directed at the already chilling separatist, who was hit in the chest, head and stomach, his body reduced to a spray of blood, ribboned flesh and splintered bone, suspended in an upright position only by the momentum of the slugs that poured into him.

"Take them out, now!" J.B. yelled, swinging his Uzi around and firing through the chilled separatist as he swung an arc of hot metal across the gathered war party. The stunned Pilatans behind him snapped back to reality and took aim, also beginning to fire.

The offensive war party retreated rapidly into the woods, leaving behind two chilled—the white man and one of the blacks—and J.B. certain that at least one of the others had been hit and was losing blood.

"Let us pursue them," snarled one of the Pilatans, now roused to anger and, like the others, realizing for the first time what combat could entail. But J.B. stayed him with an arm.

"No, let them go. It's too easy for them to rig an ambush out here. Fall back."

"Retreat? Like cowards?"

"No—like people using our brains," J.B. replied. "We pull back and lure them into the open."

With which, the Armorer started to track back toward the clearing where the Pilatan camp had been established.

As they reached the campsite, they found that more parties were following this course. Certainly, all the companions had encountered similar problems to his own, and the talk among the Pilatans was of other separatists who had met the same fate as the man in J.B.'s force. Their confusion was partly echoed by Markos, as he came over to where the companions had gathered.

"This is a completely alien situation to me," he began without preamble. "We have lost several of our people, although we have made dents in their personnel to compensate. But my people cannot adjust to the idea that other blacks will fire on them. Surely we have solidarity that runs over any other consideration?"

"Keep that attitude up and there won't be any Pilatans left to make a new home," Mildred said harshly. "I've tried to tell you—it doesn't matter what color you are out here, only that it's your ville against the rest. Whatever it takes to survive. And you're going to have to get used to shooting blacks as well as whites and Hispanics and whoever else. Got it?"

The Pilatan sec boss nodded shortly. "But I am out of my depth now."

He turned to the one-eyed man. "Ryan, I would like you to take over the action. Then we may have a chance. I am not good enough—"

Ryan cut him short. "Markos, cut the self-pity. You're a good sec chief who's never had this kind of experience before, so learn from it. You're still the boss, but take advice when it's offered…like now." Markos chewed his lip and assented, so Ryan continued, outlining his strategy.

"I see your point," Markos said briefly. "Let's put it into action."

Ryan charged Jak and Mildred with relaying the plan to the individual groups along with Markos. The albino and Mildred were the two companions in whom all the Pilatans had trust, and this wasn't a time for any last residual traces of resentment to surface. As soon as they had finished, the Pilatans sprang to action.

Small groups ventured to the lip of the woods and established sentry posts up in the trees. While they did that, others formed a small circle of covered wags in the center of the clearing, with the livestock gathered inside, some of the Pilatans remaining to make it seem as though a full-scale retreat into the center had been ordered and implemented. The remainder of the Pilatans, along with the companions, then made their way to the sentry posts, where they established a series of positions in the upper reaches of the foliage.

From the reports of the different parties, Ryan had realized that the opposing forces had retreated when faced with the onslaught. They'd had time to regroup and would be making a second offensive. They would be suspicious that they were meeting no resistance as they moved through the woods, but when they caught sight of the covered defensive position, with the Pilatans within arranging things to look like the whole community had pulled back into cover, they would attempt to rush the wags, leaving themselves wide open to attack from above. The key would be keeping silent and still until the right moment.

Jak had volunteered to scout the woods to try to bring back advanced warning of any encroaching parties. The albino had disappeared silently into the undergrowth sometime previously and Ryan now could feel the tension and suspense spreading through the Pilatans as they were—literally—suspended from the foliage.

Jak appeared suddenly and without warning, seeming to melt like a shadow only to reform to shinny up the tree where Ryan was waiting.

"Coming. Down to mebbe forty-five, forty-six. In one party. Not all men, either. They have one woman."

Ryan smiled slowly. It was working out better than he could have hoped. The opposition was seeking safety in numbers and was traveling in one phalanx that would keep them together and all nicely in one place for the ambush. It was puzzling that no one had spotted the woman before, and odd that she should be the only one as sec forces that used women usually had a more equal mix. But no matter. She was still the enemy and that was all that counted.

Jak moved from tree to tree, spreading the message. Ryan settled in to wait. There was no longer that air of apprehension. Action was coming, and soon.

Within minutes it was possible to hear the outsiders moving through the undergrowth, their mass making more noise than previously. Slowly they came into view. In a pyramid formation, watching the area around them closely and never thinking to look up. Ryan caught sight of the woman. There was something familiar about her that he couldn't place. He put it from his mind as the two men in front reached the lip of the clearing and saw the people gathered in the center.

"They pulled right back, man, easy pickings," the front man whispered, the words reaching Ryan's ears, he was waiting so close to them.

"Let's charge them, get it done, before they have a chance to open up and fight," came another voice.

And then the action began. The outsiders charged into the clearing, opening fire on the covered wags. The Pilatans inside began to return fire. It was a calculated risk, as they had padded the walls of their enclosure as much as possible, but were still at risk from injury or buying the farm from heavier caliber blasterfire. But they had only to hold out until the offensive party had come completely into the open.

Which was now.

At a signal from the one-eyed man, the Pilatans in the trees dropped to the ground and began to fire at the outsiders. In the sudden confusion of noise and the hail of fire that hit them, many of the offensive party didn't realize what had happened. Those who did whirled around and tried to return fire, but realized that they were in no position to defend themselves.

The phalanx broke apart, as the offensive party made a break for the woods, trying to circle the Pilatans while still returning covering fire.

Very few made it to the woods. The clearing was littered with the chilled corpses of the offensive party, caught up in the crossfire of the two Pilatan groups, with some also suffering at the hands of their own as the confused party tried to return fire in opposing directions.

The Pilatans broke, also, following the opposing force through the woods. Some escaped, starting the wags and speeding across the plain to wherever they had come from, but most were still and chilled either in the clearing or in the woods.

When they were sure that the woods had been secured, the companions and Markos assembled the Pilatans in the clearing, moving the corpses.

"We have done well and we have learned much today," Sineta said to the assembled throng. "We must move on now, before we invite further hostilities, which would be unnecessary on both sides. We will attempt to find ourselves a place where we can build our own ville, and then perhaps we shall not be treated with such disdain."

"Well, I wouldn't bet on that," Dean murmured to his father as they split into groups to bury the chilled and prepare for departure. There were only a few Pilatan casualties, but Sineta wished them to afford their enemies the same respect.

"Neither would I," Ryan replied as he began to dig. "But mebbe they've learned a lot about the mainland in one nasty, quick lesson. What do you reckon? Dean?" he added, when his son didn't reply.

Ryan looked at his son, who was staring in openmouthed disbelief at the edge of the clearing. Following his son's gaze, Ryan could see the woman from the war party standing at the edge of the clearing. There was something familiar about her, but more importantly, why was she still there when the others had long since departed?

"Dean, what is it?" Ryan asked again.

Dean shook his head in disbelief and said only one word by way of explanation and reply.

"Rona…"

# Chapter Fourteen

"Sharona?"

Ryan couldn't believe that his son was correct. The woman at the edge of the clearing seemed much older than Dean's mother would be, if she had lived. But she had bought the farm. Rad sickness was why she had sent the boy away from her. This woman appeared gaunt, different than he remembered. Although there was something about the eyes... Perhaps that was why Ryan had looked twice at her, with an uneasy sense, when he had seen her in the war party.

But why had this woman remained behind?

Even as those thoughts crossed Ryan's mind, the woman was stepping forward into the clearing, so that both he and his son could see her clearly.

"Dean..." the woman said softly in a voice that sent a chill up Ryan's spine, a voice that dragged up echoes from the past.

"I knew you were coming," Dean stated flatly. He didn't know what to think. All those dreams and that sense of longing.

She walked forward slowly toward the younger Cawdor. Dean broke from beside his father to run to embrace her.

Ryan watched, still stunned at the sudden reappearance of a woman he had long since believed chilled. Away to one side, both Jak and Krysty stopped in their work, seeing what was occurring.

"Who's that?" Jak asked.

Krysty shook her head, feeling her hair tighten to her as she did. "I don't know, but I've got a feeling it's going to be nothing but trouble."

MILDRED, DOC AND J.B. had no idea of what was taking place on the edge of the clearing as they were ensconced in the center of the activities taking place where the Pilatans were preparing to leave. They were helping to load the livestock with their packs when Sineta and Markos approached them.

"Leave that for a second," the baron said, "we have something we wish to discuss with you."

"Ah, joy, surely you wish to inform us of your impending nuptials," Doc announced happily.

Markos furrowed his brow and gazed at Doc, not sure if the older man was being humorous.

"May I ask just what you mean by that?" the sec boss requested gravely.

"Don't you take any notice of the old coot. He's just having one of his crazy moments," Mildred said hurriedly, not wishing Doc or the sec boss to derail the conversation before it had begun in earnest. "What is it?" she added to Sineta.

"We have been discussing seriously the future of our community and we would wish for you to travel forth with us in perpetuity," Sineta said.

Mildred whistled. "That's something I wouldn't

have expected. I wouldn't have thought you would have wanted us hanging around forever."

"Especially as we're not part of you," J.B. added. "There's still a lot of people here who think we're outsiders and should stay that way."

"But that is precisely the point," Sineta interjected. "We do not wish you to travel with us as outsiders. We want you to become part of Pilatu and to join with our community."

"I think you may find that quite a sizable proportion of your people may find this hard to come to terms with," Doc pointed out. "There is still—at the very least—a residual resentment against us."

"I know this, and I also acknowledge that you are aware of it, too," Sineta said, speaking with great care and thought, "but if this is ever to change, then we will have to start teaching these recidivists at some point."

"So we're to be instruments in a lesson?" Mildred queried, amused at the manner in which Sineta had put her point.

"Not quite like that," the baron replied, acknowledging her clumsiness with an embarrassed smile. "You have much to offer us in terms of knowledge and understanding, and we want to learn from that…most of us. The others will realize in time, as we have. In return, we can offer you a kind of security. Something, perhaps, that you have been searching for, a kind of peace and belonging. Is that not true? I could see it in you when we were on the island," Sineta implored to Mildred.

Mildred felt uncomfortable for a moment. She had to pick her words carefully when she replied. "There

is a certain degree of truth in what you say, but I have
my own commitments and belonging. Maybe I'll tell
you about them later, when we're not in the middle of
packing to move on."

She had hoped to stall indefinitely, unwilling to have
to explain herself, but Markos's words cut short any
hopes.

"This is good. We will all discuss this matter—ourselves and the rest of your people—when we pitch
camp tonight."

"That wasn't exactly what we had in mind," Mildred
said to the Armorer as they finished loading the cattle
and moved out.

"Yeah, well, mebbe there are things that are going
to make having to explain that unnecessary," he said
slowly.

Mildred followed his gaze to where Dean was walking with Sharona, Ryan and Krysty some distance behind.

"Hmm. I'd like to know what that's all about, and
who that woman is," Mildred mused.

"She looks vaguely familiar," the Armorer said.
"This could be trouble."

THE PILATAN CARAVAN moved out of the clearing and
away through the woods. They took a route that carried
a direction contrary to the direction of the ville from
which the war party had arrived earlier in the day. They
had no wish to encounter more raiders and indeed desired
to put as much distance between the ville and themselves
as possible. Wherever their fate lay in the search for land
to build a new Pilatu, it certainly wasn't in that direction.

By the time they had packed and begun to move, it was already into the late afternoon. The baron and the sec boss made a conscious decision to carry on marching through most of the night to put distance between themselves and any war parties bent on revenge. But by the middle of the night, it became apparent that the exhausted Pilatans would need to rest. Scouting sec parties that had been sent ahead, and also to track back to warn of any approaches from the rear, had nothing to report. There was even a lack of predatory wildlife in this part of the plain and woodland. Stretches of flat, open land had been punctuated by sudden bursts of woodland, which the Pilatan caravan had skirted around rather than risk becoming entangled. It was in the shelter around the edges of one such outcrop that Sineta and Markos brought the caravan to a halt, to allow the exhausted people to take some rest.

As the caravan settled to rest for the remainder of the night, Markos and Sineta once again broached the subject they had raised earlier with Mildred, Doc and J.B.

Having posted sec sentries for the night, the sec boss came over to where the companions had settled with Sharona. Ryan was about to tackle the matter of who this woman was, and why she had seemingly arrived out of nowhere when believed chilled, when the sec boss requested that he and the baron talk with them.

In truth, Ryan was relieved for the distraction. He hadn't been looking forward to tackling the subject and had had no idea where to begin. Come to that, he still had no idea of where Sharona had been or how she had landed in the same place as the companions—and he had absolutely no idea what her intentions were with regard to her son and to the rest of the traveling party. She had been reticent on the matter during the day's march, refusing to be drawn on her own life and instead pumping Dean for details of what had occurred to him during the time that they had been parted.

While the rest of the companions were waiting for Ryan to explain, they were stunned when he told Markos that it would be fine to talk to the sec boss and the baron.

"What the hell did you do that for?" Krysty asked angrily. "We're owed an explanation, aren't we?"

"And I'm sure we'll get it—in time," Ryan said pointedly, staring at Sharona. "But first let's hear what Sineta and Markos have to say."

"I think we know some of it," J.B. ventured.

Ryan frowned. "So we've all been keeping secrets. Fireblast, this had not become a habit."

Any argument was cut short by the arrival of the baron and the sec boss, who outlined the proposition put to half of the companions earlier in the day.

Ryan whistled. "There's a lot of your people that could make it rough for us, if we agreed," he said.

Markos nodded. "That much is true, and I acknowledge that we are not asking you to undertake that which is easy, but I feel that we could learn so much from you. Speaking personally, I know that I have learned much."

Ryan grinned. "I told you about that. You learn about tactics as you go along, and you'll learn about the mainland as you go along. Anything that we say or do right now is no substitute for actually living it and learning from experience."

"This much I have gathered," Markos said with due consideration. "But that is not the only thing I have learned, and in many ways, it is the least of my concerns." He continued in a halting tone, stopping to consider every word. "My brother—in the days when I believed him to be a man of honor and integrity—taught me that the black man and the white man were completely separate and that never the twain could meet. That is something that was deeply ingrained in me, perhaps even more than I was fully aware. But I do not feel that way anymore. We are different, but we are equal. That feels so strange, even now, for those words to pass my lips and to be more than just hollow.

"It is strange to consider that just a few short weeks ago, when I first encountered you in the Pilatan woods that I shall see no more in this life, I thought of you as little more than scum who were trying to oppress, if not chill, Mildred. And I did not believe that it was possible for you and she to exist within the same group without a hierarchy of some manner to intrude. But I was wrong. I have learned, more than anything, that it is not your origin—in either a racial or geographic sense—that matters, but rather the manner in which you act and conduct yourself that is important. It is not where you consider yourself to be in terms of origins, but rather how you consider yourself and conduct yourself…how you act toward yourself and others as we all try to survive and make a life in what can be an extremely prejudiced and hostile environment.

"And that, my friends, which I am proud to call you now, is why I feel it important that you become part of Pilatu and travel with us not just as yourselves but as a part of our community. There are still those who feel as I once did. Still those who would have us stay separate from the other races—whatever they may be. Perhaps they have learned something from our encounter with the sec force last night. But then again, some attitudes are hardily ingrained. Only a long-term process can help that."

There was a silence after the sec boss had finished. It had been a difficult speech for him to make, as he was a proud man who was admitting to mistakes. But it had been undoubtedly heartfelt.

Sineta added her voice to his before any of the companions had a chance to reply.

"It is not just for this reason that we wish you to become part of us. In the time since I have known Mildred I have come to look upon her as the sister with which I was never blessed, and I value her opinions and counsel. With her greater experience of the world in which we have entered, I would be a fool to wish you a speedy parting. She is of great value to me as baron of Pilatu and also as a person I love deeply."

Mildred embraced Sineta. "I think of you in the same way, but I don't know if it would work. We're not ready to settle down, any of us. We don't belong anywhere yet."

"But why not belong here?" Sineta queried, noticing the manner in which Dean looked at the new arrival as Mildred spoke. For a moment the baron was distracted with the feeling of foreboding that the boy's glance gave her. She wondered if any of the companions had noticed as she continued. "You told me when we on the island that it was the first time you had felt as though you had a sense of belonging for a great amount of time."

Mildred smiled wryly. "Greater than you'll ever know. But I was wrong. Part of the belonging was only in my mind. In the real world, in day-to-day terms, this is where I belong…" Mildred looked into the distance, seeing something that no one else could, before continuing in a wistful tone of voice. "You see, the island, and the way you had lived for so many generations, was like a chasm of time, a gap into which you had fallen, where so much had stayed still for so long. You'd been in this chasm, and had preserved so much of the way you had always been, never really changing or having to change. But there does always have to be change, and that was brought home to me when you had to leave the island. There's so much that you've had to face up to and assimilate already since leaving Pilatu, and there'll be so much more.

"And it wasn't just the island and the people that were part of that chasm. I had it in me, too. There was something in me that had been cast into that pit so long ago, before I even knew it myself. I had to lose something of myself to fit in, hide some part of my identity to operate in the world as it was. That chasm was a real thing, as well. I lost so many years, lost the world that I used to know, and maybe I lost even more of myself. Then I came to Pilatu and found a part of myself that I didn't even know was there anymore, and I felt like I'd gone from being blind to being able to see with the clearest, most incredible vision that I'd ever known.

"But it wasn't focused. I've come to realize that the

parts of me that I thought were lost were there all the time, but they just weren't so simply proscribed anymore. They were values that hadn't been lost, but had been more universally applied. I did belong, I'd just never had time to think about it. I had a family, a tribe, and I don't know if it's at all possible for us to fit in with anyone else."

Sineta reached out and took Mildred's hand. "I shall miss you—miss all of you—if you depart. But I shall understand."

Markos grunted. "I'm not sure that I can say the same. I will abide by any decision, but I feel a little lost."

Ryan slapped the sec boss on the back. "You know what? I kind of feel the same. Sometimes people use a lot of unnecessary words to explain simple things. At the end of the day, anyone has to live their own way and learn their own lessons. And the problem is, I think ours are just different to yours. We're looking for something—a place we can call home, a place that seems right for us. What we need isn't what you need. Pilatu needs a plot of land where it can build a ville, start to farm and start to trade. Somehow, I think that just isn't for us."

"Then what is?" Markos asked.

The one-eyed man shrugged. "I don't know, but I'll let you know when we find it, because I'm sure we'll all know when we do."

Markos and Sineta rose to leave the companions, both seeming to accept that their allies wouldn't join permanently to them.

"Travel with us a little longer," Markos said by way

of parting. "We would welcome your company until you feel the need to strike out on your own."

"Wouldn't have it any other way," Ryan said simply.

The companions sat in silence, watching Markos and Sineta leave them. Then Ryan turned and fixed Sharona with a monocular stare in the flickering firelight.

"And it strikes me that Mildred isn't the only one around here with a story to tell," he said softly.

"I DON'T REALLY KNOW where to begin," Sharona said hesitantly, "because it all seems so strange, and in a lot of ways as though it happened to somebody else, which it kind of did. I'm not the same as I was back when I last saw you," she added to Dean.

"You look…different," her son replied. "I knew it was you straight away, though. What happened, Rona? You were buying the farm. It was rad sickness. That's why you sent me away, because you didn't have long left. So how come…?"

"I wish I could answer that," she replied. "I truly wish I could, because then I could begin to understand what I've been through in the past few years and I could account for how I ended up here, right now. But I can't. All I can tell you is that I was deathly ill. I thought it was rad sickness and it wouldn't be long before I was finally chilled. That was truly why I sent you away," she said to Dean, "because I didn't want to see you at the end—didn't want you to see me. I thought it would be long and painful, and I had to make sure that you were looked after in some way and that you'd be all right when I was gone. And let's face it, we didn't have much of a life near the end anyway, with me having to work in a gaudy to earn some jack."

Dean winced at the memories. Now he had his mother back, he didn't want to remember those days and what she had been through so that they could survive. "Don't, please," he said softly.

Sharona ruffled his hair. "I've got to, sweetheart, if I'm going to explain in some way what happened to me. You see, after you'd gone, I started to waste away more and more. I became so thin that even the cheapest gaudy slut had more meat on her bones than I did. I couldn't even earn a living with my body anymore—sure, I'd pick up the odd trick, but not enough to keep alive. And even though I knew the end was near, there was still a part of me that wanted to keep alive...you know, that spark that won't let you give up, even when you feel like there's no hope.

"So there was nothing left for me there—you were gone, and I couldn't earn a living in any way.

"But there was a convoy coming through, a trader called Nyland. Evil, nasty piece of work, but with some surprising edges. Can't remember ever seeing a woman trader before, especially one that was so small. She must have just been five feet, if she was that. But I've never seen anyone, man or woman, who could take so much jolt or drink so much and still stay on her feet. And that was when her temper got worse. I once saw her take on a man twice her size and beat him in a fight by crushing his balls with her teeth while he tried to break her neck. He let her loose in sheer pain and she chilled him by beating him with a table.

"And yet she took pity on me. She found me when

I was trying desperately to turn a trick. I was willing to take on two of her crew for the price of one because I hadn't eaten for days. But when I stripped naked they laughed, and one of them wanted to satisfy himself by beating me first. Guess I must have screamed louder than I thought, because she found me. She had this number two called Dimitri, a fat guy with glasses who liked boys. He had a temper almost as bad as hers. The two of them ripped the shit out of these guys and left them chilled. Only thing she moaned about was how the hell was she gonna find replacements at such short notice, and she argued with Dimitri that they should have just beaten them up a little. I swear, I thought they were gonna rip the shit out of each other next.

"Anyway, they noticed I was there eventually, and I guess she remembered why they'd gone in so hard in the first place. She asked me why I was turning tricks when I looked so bad, and I told her. That's when she offered me the chance to join her convoy. With these guys chilled, she needed someone to act as quarter-master as to cook and clean.

"I figured she must be a little crazy—I was buying the farm— But it was a better offer than anything else I'd had for a long time, so I went with it. Once I was in her convoy, I saw a few people like myself…the lame and the useless, and I figured that it was her hobby. But at least I didn't have to screw anyone for jack anymore and she was okay if you kept on the right side of her. She had a healer from the bayous by the name of Mama Celeste. She fussed over me for weeks on end, saying that I had something called tuberculosis and a bad thyroid problem. She had a store of medicine she kept in an old footlocker, and she doctored me as if I were her own child. I got better. It wasn't rad sickness after all. I was going to live.

"Mama Celeste was my savior, and I got strong really quickly, although I never put much weight on again and I looked different from when you knew me," she said to Dean. "My skin's still shitty and breaks out sometimes, and I look older than I am, but inside I got a whole lot stronger…stronger than I was before and sure as hell a whole lot stronger than I look, which came in useful sometimes.

"I stayed with the convoy, and I started to do more. And we were a good little outfit. We became the tightest little outfit working this side of the coast, and we were such a stupe-looking bunch that no one figured we'd ever be the trouble we could be. Nyland became the trader that no one ever wanted to cross. Mebbe even more so than Trader," she said to Ryan.

"Anyway, this went on for some time. I didn't think much about my old life. Not because I'd forgotten you," she said to Dean, "but because I figured that wherever you were, you were probably doing better there than you ever would with me, and that's okay. I just put it out of my mind whenever it came back to me. But then it started to change.

"The people you fought back there were from a ville called Broadmead, and they're not bad people. They were always fair to us when we traded with them, and we came back to them a few times. But when we were on our way back this time, I couldn't stop thinking about my son."

Sharona looked up into the night sky, finding it hard now to express what was inside.

"Dean was always on my mind, and I used to dream about him all the time. I hadn't done that since the days when the sickness was really bad. I figured that mebbe it was welling up again…but after a few nights I knew it wasn't about that. I knew that the most stupe, impossible thing was happening. That somehow, in a way I couldn't explain even if I wanted to, I knew that Dean was coming near to me and that if I followed my instincts, then I would find him."

"Hot pipe!" Dean exclaimed. "That's what it was." He explained, when faced with questioning glances, "Since we did the last jump, I've had dreams about Rona, and all the while we were on Pilatu, I kind of envied Mildred that thing about family and belonging that she was getting. It was like there was something that I was missing and it wasn't anything I'd thought about, but it was just there."

Sharona nodded. "I stayed behind the last time we hit Broadmead. I knew that I had to, that if I just waited long enough you'd be brought to me. All I had to do was have patience and wait till it got really strong. And I could see you, I knew you were near. Then when the sec patrol got ambushed, and they wanted a raiding party, I volunteered to go on it. They didn't want me, but they were always too scared of Nyland's crew to say no to us. And the rest…" Sharona trailed off with a shrug. There was nothing more to say.

But plenty for them to think about.

THE PILATAN CARAVAN spent the next two days journeying across the plain until they came upon the remains of an old highway that stretched, in jagged and broken line, into the distance. The growth of vegetation around the highway was considerably less than farther back through the plains they had just traversed, making their progress easier. There were little signs of any villes nearby, and after some consultation with the companions, who had traveled these kind of routes many times before, Sineta and Markos decided to strike out ahead. They had put a considerable distance between themselves and the ville of Broadmead. Whoever they encountered now would find them willing to take matters on different terms.

During the long trek, Sharona took the chance to be with her son as much as possible, and Dean was also eager to spend time with his mother. The rest of the companions, knowing that they had spent so much time apart, and that the youth was still in shock at the sudden and unexpected reappearance of his mother, let them be. Krysty couldn't shake the notion at the back of her mind that there was something amiss with Sharona, and this wasn't to be a glorious reunion. Was this some kind of residual jealousy because Ryan's ex-lover had reappeared? Was it because she had, almost without realizing, slipped into the role of being a surrogate mother to Dean when he needed it? She didn't know and didn't feel inclined to delve too deeply in case she didn't like what she may find.

But the alarm bells didn't stop ringing.

Sharona made the most of the time she had with Dean to catch up on what he had been doing since she had last seen him, but when he talked of what they would be doing in the future, he noticed that she seemed uneasy and gave him pat answers that suggested she wasn't comfortable with the idea of traveling with them. He broached the matter with his customary lack of subtlety as they rested by the side of the blacktop one late afternoon.

"Rona, why don't you want to come with us? Are you going to sneak off and leave me again?"

Sharona leveled him with a stare, pausing to pick her words before answering. There were things about the question that hurt. She said, "I never left you willingly, you know that. And I came looking for you, waited to find you, so I don't think it's likely that I'm going to turn around and sneak off, as you put it—"

"I'm sorry," Dean cut in with a small voice. "I didn't mean…"

Sharona sighed. "I don't blame you, Dean. You were young, and you wanted to stay, and I wouldn't let you. And I'm not going to let you go this time."

"Then why do you sound so distant when I start to talk about the others and where we'll be going or what we'll be doing next?"

Sharona paused. "Because I don't know if it'll be the right thing for me to go with them…or you, either."

At first Dean could say nothing. He was too shocked by what Sharona had said. The companions were his life and now that his mother was back, he wanted her to be part of that, so he could have that sense of family that he had spent his time on Pilatu yearning for. Why didn't she want that?

Sharona looked at him with a sad smile, as though she had read his mind. "They're your people, not mine," she whispered. "I don't know them and I don't see how I can fit in."

"But they're really good—been really good to me. I mean. I know Doc's a bit crazy, but he's got courage. Jak takes a long time to know, but he's the best hunter you'll ever see, and an amazing fighter. I've learned so much from him. Mildred is great, and J.B.'s so cool with all the shit he knows, and Krysty has been like a mom to me, and then there's Dad…" Dean suddenly trailed off, as it began to make more sense to him. Something clicked in his head.

"Yeah, exactly," Sharona answered. "Your dad is really thrown by me turning up. I can tell because he's said nothing to me about it since that night when I tried to explain it all. And Krysty can't be too happy about me being here, either. Can't say that I blame her. So it'll be hard for us all to get along. But why do we have to?"

"I don't follow," Dean said, although he had the nastiest feeling that he knew what was coming.

Sharona grabbed him by the shoulders and her deep-set eyes lit up as she said, "Why don't we just go off by ourselves? Mebbe we could try to find Nyland's convoy again, or find a ville where we could settle and make a life for ourselves. Somewhere that we won't have to face shitloads of danger every day, where we can just live in peace and get back the time we've lost."

"Why do we have to do that?"

Tears filled her eyes, trickling down her cheeks. "Because I don't want to share you with anyone. Why should I? I've lost so much time with you. I sent you away thinking I was about to buy the farm! I can't see myself sharing you and risking you every day in some insane search for…for what?"

Dean shook his head. "I don't know. I don't know if I can leave them all behind. Please don't make me."

Sharona could see the real hurt in his face and she looked away.

"I truly don't know if I can do that, Dean. But I'll think about it. It's all I can promise you."

# Chapter Fifteen

The Pilatan caravan traveled across the new lands for several days, covering a rapidly changing terrain. Some sections were arid, the land scorched and barren, where others were lushly vegetated with overhanging woodlands that provided cover for the shrubs and grasses to propagate. There was little wildlife to bother the caravan. Most of the mammals were small and the birds weren't of a predatory variety.

There was, however, one moment when the Pilatans came face-to-face with a facet of mainland life with which the companions were all too familiar.

It was on the third day, as they crossed a stretch of land that was so sunblasted and rad damaged that little could grow. The only thing that linked this to any of the other areas they had passed was the ubiquitous two-lane blacktop that still wove its broken-backed way across the land. A scout party reported that they had located a source of water. The Pilatans were plentifully supplied with food as Jak had taught them supplementary hunting skills that they had practiced with great aplomb on the small mammals and birds. But water was always a problem. They only had a certain amount of water that they could store as they journeyed, so the search for water was always of paramount importance.

The scouting party had reported that they had found a spring about three miles to the northeast. Markos led the caravan in that direction. It was on the way that Krysty turned to Ryan.

"Something bad's about to happen, lover. I'm not sure what, but it doesn't feel good," she commented.

Ryan looked at her. Her hair was waving in the breeze, curling around her head. It wasn't tight and defensive, but it was alarmed. He turned to the other companions.

"Triple-red—keep your blasters ready."

"Shouldn't we tell the others?" Sharona asked, readying her own Vortak precision pistol, which she had kept hidden about her person.

Ryan shook his head. "They've got to learn these things the hard way. Besides, what am I going to tell them? They don't really know much about Krysty being able to sense trouble."

Sharona shrugged. "Have it your own way, Ryan."

The one-eyed man shot her a glance. "I will," he said harshly.

Dean was about to respond when they were distracted by a shout from the front of the caravan.

"Water ahead—and what the hell is that?"

Looking to where the spring lay, the companions could see a mass of naked people…no, not people, for there was something animalistic about the group, who acted more like a pack of wild dogs.

"Stickies!" J.B. exclaimed.

Markos turned. "What are stickies?"

Ryan shook his head. "Time for explanations later. Just know that they're vicious and they need chilling!"

His words came not a moment too soon, as the pack by the spring sighted the caravan and turned to charge toward them. From the manner in which they had been greedily consuming from the spring, they had probably not seen water for some time…by which token, they had probably not seen food for as long. And the Pilatans would look like good food to them.

"Don't let them get near. Just blast the bastards!" Ryan yelled.

He mentally weighed the odds. At a rough glance, it seemed as though there were as many stickies as there were Pilatans, and the caravan was armed. Against that, many of the Pilatans were children, or old, and none of them had experience of what a stickie was capable of. With their sharp teeth, their bloodlust frenzy, and the flattened, rubbery suckers on their fingers that could grip and crush a victim, it would be a close-run thing. And which way it would run, he didn't want to predict.

The companions, under Ryan's direction stepped away from the main body of the caravan and began to fire on the stickies. There was still enough distance between the blasters and the intended victims for a lot of the shooting to be random rather than aimed, but several of the creatures went down either chilled or fatally wounded as the slugs from the handblasters and the charges from Doc's LeMat percussion pistol, J.B.'s M-4000 and Ryan's SIG-Sauer ripped through them. J.B.'s load of barbed metal fléchettes were particularly effective, as the spiked and white-hot metal ripped through the mass of flesh that was the crowd of charging stickies, mangling bone and filling the air with a fine mist of blood.

However, even though some of their number hit the dirt, the promise of food and the fear caused by the carnage among them spurred the stickies on even more and they continued their charge toward the Pilatan caravan.

"What manner of creatures are these?" Sineta whispered in awe. As most of the Pilatans, she hadn't yet started to fire, frozen in surprise and horror as she watched the mutie horde cover the distance between the spring and the caravan with a deceptively fast, loping strides. They were gaining ground quickly—too quickly for Markos, one of the only Pilatans with the presence of mind to fire on the approaching danger, and he turned and yelled at his people.

"They're dangerous and deadly if you don't start firing," Mildred screamed in the baron's ear as she ran to her side, still snapping off shots from her ZKR, and reloading on the run. "Now start shooting, for God's sakes, and aim for their heads!"

Galvanized into action by Mildred and Markos, the baron and the rest of the Pilatans began to fire. But some of the stickies had made enough ground to now be on top of the caravan. One grabbed at a sec man, frozen in fear, and wrestled him to the ground, the suckers tearing the flesh on his face as the sharp rows of teeth made to rip at his throat and shoulder. His scream was high, built on fear and pain.

Mildred moved across swiftly and placed her ZKR on the side of the creature's head, firing and blowing its skull open, splattering the terrified sec man with brain and bone. The chilled stickie fell from him, but where the skull had been cracked like an eggshell, the teeth from the bottom jaw stayed imbedded in his face.

Another scream from behind made Mildred whirl, cursing herself for leaving Sineta's side. A stickie had made it as far as the baron and had jumped her, dragging her to the ground. They were rolling wildly in the dust, the baron vainly fighting to throw the mutie off her, just holding its head away from her face by keeping the heel of her hand firmly under the creature's chin, pushing it up. But the stickie's strong arms—a deceptive strength given the seemingly pale flabbiness of the creature's flesh—were pulling her arms down, the suckers biting into the skin through her clothes, deadening the muscles as the iron grip cut off the blood supply.

Mildred tried to take aim, but they were moving too much. She stood too much risk of hitting Sineta if she fired.

Jak saw what was happening and before Mildred even had a chance to register what he was doing, the albino hunter had sped past her toward the struggling couple. Holstering his .357 Magnum Colt Python and palming one of his razor-sharp, leaf-bladed knives, he took the stickie at a run, a swift arm movement slicing across the front of the creature's head, opening up its face from the top lip to the forehead, slicing through the nose and puncturing one eyeball along the way. As the creature's fetid breath mixed with the blood and eyeball mucus that dripped onto her face, Sineta found herself gagging, fighting to hold down the bile that rose in her throat and would choke her if she gave in to the urge to vomit while she was still pinned down.

The stickie screamed in a high, keening voice, loosening its grip as it registered pain. Sineta responded immediately, throwing the mutie off her. Even before it had landed, Jak followed up to finish the job, pinning it down and slicing across its throat with one swift, efficient motion, cutting through the neck to the spinal column at the rear.

Sineta didn't have a chance to thank him. Instead, she showed her appreciation by blasting the stickie that was making for Jak's exposed back.

Gradually, as the firepower of the caravan decimated the stickie horde and thinned it out, the stunned Pilatans began to gain the upper hand, forcing the remaining stickies to run in fear and terror. When the retreating muties were out of range, and the Pilatans were safe, Markos turned to Ryan, having assessed that the caravan had sustained only minimal casualties.

"Now are you going to tell me all about those creatures, and any other hazards we may need warning about?" He grinned, flushed from the success of battle.

Ryan returned the smile. "When we've cleaned up."

WITH REPLENISHED STOCKS, the caravan once more went on its way. Ryan and the other companions had outlined some of the dangers that the Pilatans may face from the likes of stickies, but despite the increased vigilance of the sec patrols, there was nothing more to report as they made their way out of the rad-infected section of country.

As the land became more verdant once more, they found themselves climbing an incline. The land around was rolling plains and they seemed to be taking one of these on the ascent as they followed the blacktop. It was a shallow incline, but a long one—at least a day's march—and it would finally take them away from the old predark route they had been following for the blacktop curved away from the incline and came to a sudden halt where a chasm had been cut into the land by an earth movement. A sec party including Ryan and Markos had made its way along the remnants of the road until it came to the sudden dip of the chasm. It was about sixty feet wide and stretched like a scar on the land as far as they could see in either direction. Looking down, the chasm seemed to be at least a hundred feet deep, with trees and shrubs growing down sides that were too steep to countenance a descent.

"It would appear, friend Ryan, that this is the end of the road, if you'll excuse the appalling word play," Markos said ruefully. "From our discussions, I gather that many villes and trade routes are built along these old roads and that would have been our surest chance of hitting something approaching civilization."

"Yeah, apart from the fact that civilization is just a word that I've seen in some old predark books," Ryan said quietly.

"Point taken, my friend. Let us just say that it would bring us into contact with other people. But now…"

"Well, it's not that great a disaster. There's more than one old blacktop left across the land. If we keep going, we'll come to something sooner or later—some place where you can settle."

"But not you?"

Ryan smiled wryly. "I doubt it."

The sec party returned to the main body of the caravan and reported their findings before carrying on with the trek up the long incline.

It was an easy trek after the past few days. There was a plentiful supply of animals, fruits for food and water in streams that flowed down and across the downs at strange angles. It was such a peaceful procession, that actually reaching the peak of the plain was somewhat of a surprise. The pinnacle stretched out before them for a hundred yards, before beginning the descent into a valley below.

"Wow, just look at that," Dean whispered softly as the caravan came to a halt and they all surveyed the territory in front of them. The far side of the valley was a much shallower incline, leading on to lands beyond. They could see the remains of old roads in the distance and the marked-out remnants of arable fields and pasture. At one time, before the nukecaust, this land had been prime farming acreage and had road contacts to villes that may lay beyond, which were still possibly extant and served by trade convoys.

"Now that looks good to me," Mildred said to Sineta. "What do you think?"

"I think that it may be what we are looking for," the baron said on reflection. "It has farming possibilities and the space to build a new settlement. Moreover, it is not at present populated, so we will not be intruding on another ville's space and sparking conflict that we can ill afford while still settling."

"All in all, sounds perfect," Mildred mused.

"Perhaps it will be," the baron said softly. "Perhaps for all of us?"

"That I couldn't say," Mildred replied in as non-committal a tone as possible, for she had just noticed that J.B. and Ryan were conferring about something they had seen down in the valley.

The caravan began its descent down the soft slope toward the floor of the long valley, and the perfect settling lands that lay there. Ryan beckoned to Mildred to join them. As she did, he indicated a small crevice in the land that lay about three miles to their left, at the join of the incline to the valley floor. Casting her eyes over it, Mildred could see that it had all the recognizable hallmarks of a hidden redoubt. To most eyes, it would look like nothing more than a small rock indent in the land, but the trained observer would be able to tell the camouflage around a redoubt entrance. Some may have been stripped of this after skydark, but this one still retained its disguise.

"We'll tell them tonight when we rest and then strike out for it tomorrow," Ryan told her. "We've got a few things we need to sort out among ourselves," he continued with a meaningful glance at Sharona and Dean, before adding, "That's if you want to come with us."

Mildred smiled wryly. "I've made my choice, Ryan."

The caravan continued until the twilight, when they established camp for the night. After they had eaten, Ryan joined Markos, Sineta and Mildred.

"I've got something to tell you," he began. "Come first light, we'll be moving on."

"But where to?" Markos answered, bewildered. "I

can see nothing around here that could distract you from our shared path."

"There's something. Something to do with following the dream, I suppose." Ryan smiled when he saw the sec boss's uncomprehending expression. "It's something we have to do. Besides, we have our own problems to contend with and we need to be able to concentrate on those."

Sineta nodded. "It must be difficult, with the boy's mother appearing as if from nowhere. But we will miss you—all of you," she added pointedly, looking at Mildred.

"You mean you will be going with them?" Markos asked Mildred. When Mildred nodded, he said, "I wish you would reconsider…all of you." With which he stood and walked away from them.

"I didn't figure we were that important," a mystified Ryan said, half joking.

"I think it may be more than that," Sineta replied perceptively, indicating that Mildred should go after him.

Mildred got to her feet and walked after the sec boss, who stood on the verge of the camp, looking out into the night. He turned as he saw her approach.

"I don't think there is anything more that can be said really, is there?" he asked.

"Maybe." Mildred shrugged. "But maybe you should know that this is the hardest decision I've ever had to make. And if you had the slightest idea of how weird and strange my life has been next to yours, you'd know how deep that cuts."

"Then why are you going?"

"Because I have to. I know we both pulled back from each other, but maybe something could have happened if I stayed."

"So why don't you?" There was pain and anger mixed in his tone.

"Because I have other loyalties that cut me deeper still. Not just to J.B., but to all of them. We've got bonds and ties that were forged in fire, and you can't walk away from those."

"And, in truth, I would not expect you to," he said softly before walking away from her.

WHEN THE MORNING CAME, the companions prepared to leave and the entire tribe rose to wish them well. As they made to leave, Sineta approached them.

"Words are so easy and seem so pointless at a time like this," she began, "but nonetheless, I feel it is important that I say this. Without you, we would still have had to leave Pilatu and begin again, but it would have been a harder, more costly experience. We owe you much, and we will never forget you." The baron embraced Mildred, her eyes filled with tears of regret. The companions parted company with Pilatu. In the end, it was as simple as walking in a different direction to the caravan, which began to move off and down into the valley, searching for a spot to begin building.

Markos didn't watch the companions leave and Mildred didn't look for him.

After they had walked some distance, they stopped to rest. The redoubt could still be reached before nightfall. Mildred turned to look back to see the Pilatan caravan stretching out across the valley floor. J.B. came up to her, standing behind and resting his hands lightly on her shoulders.

"They'll be fine. Good people with good leaders," he said at length. When Mildred didn't reply, he said after a pause, "Millie, tell me honestly, did you really want to go with them? I mean, are you with us because of the past and not the future? I mean—"

She turned and silenced him by putting her fingers to his lips.

"John," she said softly, "when have you ever known me to do anything that I didn't feel was the right thing? The right thing for me, and for those who I want around me," she added, stressing the last half of the sentence.

The Armorer started to answer, but before he could speak she shook her head.

"Never," she whispered. "And that still stands."

THEY MADE THE REDOUBT by nightfall. The recessed entrance was shut tight. Without an exterior trigger it was a problem as to how they would gain entry. But not a problem that hadn't been considered.

"Jak, you remember we've been to redoubts that had vents for their air-conditioning and cleaning systems?" Ryan asked. When the albino youth nodded, the one-eyed man continued, "Do you reckon these vents would have maintenance and service hatches?"

"Remember climbing down one," Jak replied. "Just need find it."

Without another word, Ryan followed Jak as the albino scaled the shallow wall of rock around the recessed entrance. The two men scoured the top of the small plateau formed in the side of the valley by the redoubt entrance, moving out of sight of the rest of the companions.

"What the hell are they doing?" Sharona complained.

"Trying to get us in," Krysty snapped in a tone that would brook no argument, causing Mildred and J.B. to exchange glances.

Meanwhile, on top of the plateau, Ryan and Jak were searching in the fading light for signs of a venting system.

"Usually hidden by rock pile," Jak indicated. "And has narrow channel into service tunnel."

"You think you'll have any trouble getting past the rad shielding?" Ryan queried, knowing from past experience that the maintenance shafts were gated by lead-lined, airtight doors.

Jak shook his head. "Never locked, just tight stop air. Not trust stupe sec with codes and keys." He grinned. "Most seals rubber and rotted—" He broke off as he found the vent. "Here."

Ryan joined the albino youth and helped him move the rock pile that had been carefully placed more than a hundred years previously to cover the vent outlet. The movement of the earth after skydark had only helped to camouflage the vent, as more rocks had moved onto the pile. It was almost completely dark as they finished removing the obstruction. Below, the rest of the companions waited patiently—with the exception of Sharona—for word from above.

Jak looked up at the night sky. It was clear, with a crescent moon that cast a wan light over the land.

"Go back, Ryan. Tell others what's happening. See

you soon," he added with a grin that split his white, scarred face as he slid down into the vent.

The one-eyed man watched him go, then carefully descended to the entrance below. While he outlined the situation, Jak wormed his way through the vent.

It was tight and pitch-dark. It was only the albino's wiry frame and the fact that his pigmentless eyes could adapt to almost zero levels of light that enabled him to make progress and marked him as the only one of the companions who could have fulfilled this task. He squirmed and wriggled down the narrow vent, the heat soon building up around him despite the constant up-rush of expelled air from the conditioner, making him sweat heavily, a sweat that was dried by the rushing air before it reached his eyes, the eyeballs gritty and sore in the constant flow of arid air.

As he made progress, his fingers sought the telltale impress of the service hatches. The panic of enclosure was beginning to prick at the edges of his mind—how could he go backward in this tight, downward vent if he didn't find a way into the service hatches—as his fingers found that for which he sought. Prizing the hatch open, so that it fell down across the vent, tem-porarily blocking the flow, he found that he had been right about the rubber seals. Wasting no time, lest the open hatch door caused a blow-back in the condition-ing system, he pulled himself into the service tunnel and reached down to pull the door shut.

The maintenance tunnel was lit by a low-level red strip and had a larger circumference than the vent. Jak was able to relax and breathe more easily for a second before beginning the long haul into the redoubt. It was easier, but finding his way around the maze of service tunnels would take time. It was almost impossible to get totally lost, as he would emerge somewhere in the redoubt, but he wanted to come as near to the surface level as possible. There was no way of knowing if the redoubt was inhabited in any way, and he was keen to adopt any measure that would reduce risk.

In a short time, Jak dropped back into the air-conditioning system so that he could wriggle to a vent and make a recce. It was important that he find out where he was and if he could see any signs of life. The vent showed him he was in an upper level, near old admin offices.

He stilled himself as much as possible and listened carefully. There was nothing. Sniffing the air, Jak found it was stale. Every instinct told him the redoubt was empty. But he still refused to take chances. Moving back into the maintenance tunnels, he found an exit on the same level and cautiously emerged into the body of the redoubt, his Colt Python ready to hand.

He was more relaxed by the time he had traveled from the service hatch to the main redoubt door. There were no signs of life and no signs that the redoubt had been occupied since predark times. He keyed in the sec code to open the door and greeted the companions with a rare smile.

"All ours."

RYAN OPTED to wait a few days before they made a mattrans jump. Rather than keep traveling across open country for who knew how long, he figured that they could take their chances with the random setting of the mat-trans, and find out where it took them. But first he wanted them to rest. As the redoubt was still well-stocked and in good working order, it would be an opportunity to rest and recuperate before taking their chances with fate once more. Showering, changing and finding the dorms in good order, they rested, leaving everything to the morrow.

And there was something left that had to be tackled soon. Sharona had been distancing herself from the rest of the companions while they traveled with the Pilatans, only really associating with Dean. If she was going to travel with them, then it was important that this rift be healed. And if not...

But there would be time to deal with that the following day, the one-eyed man thought as he lay awake, trying to figure out what the shocking return of Dean's mother meant.

The next day brought no solutions. Ryan awakened to find the others had already risen. After showering, he walked to the kitchen where he found Mildred, Krysty, Doc and Jak.

"Where are the others?" he asked as he prepared his breakfast from an array of self-heats.

"John's gone to check out the armory," Mildred said with an indulgent expression crossing her face. "You know what he's like."

Ryan returned the expression. "Yeah, he must've been worn out last night, because he didn't go straight to it." Then, after a pause, he added, "What about Dean and Sharona?"

Krysty grimaced. "I don't know—anyone else?" she queried, but was met with blank looks from Mildred, Jak and Doc. "They were up before either of us, but where they are…"

Ryan rubbed his chin thoughtfully. "I suppose she can't be doing any harm."

Doc was bemused. "My dear boy, why would the woman want to do harm? She thought she would perish and sent her son away. Then, when she recovered, he was gone from her. Is it not natural that she should want to spend time with the boy? And, vice versa, as it were? That is, that he should wish to spend time with her," he added by way of explanation when he saw that the old Latin term meant nothing to Krysty, Jak or Ryan.

"That's a fair enough point, but it's not so much the time…" Ryan began, petering out with a shrug as he found he couldn't exactly explain what he meant.

Krysty finished for him, "It's more a matter of her attitude about things."

Mildred looked at Krysty closely. "You sure it's her that's the problem? I mean, are you certain that you don't just feel a little put out because she's suddenly appeared?"

Krysty frowned and looked at Mildred. The question could almost be insulting, if not for the depth of expression in the black woman's brown eyes, eyes that showed her understanding.

"Yeah, mebbe a little," Krysty admitted. "But I've thought about that, and there's more."

"Get bad feeling," Jak chipped in, breaking his silence. "Pulling Dean away from us. His choice, but not good when we fight or stand together."

"Exactly," Ryan agreed. "Before we leave here, we

have to sort out what's going on between us all. We have to pull in the same direction or else—"

"Or else all strength is dissipated," Doc said sadly.

Oblivious to all this, Dean and Sharona were on a lower level of the redoubt. The woman had awakened her son early and, after making him breakfast—a rare treat for Dean, who had to fend for himself along with the other companions—had asked him to show her around the redoubt and had listened carefully while he told her all he knew about them.

"It's incredible to believe that there are so many of these old predark places across the land, and that despite that so few have found them," she said to him.

"Yeah, but most of them are so well hidden or disguised that you have to know that they're there," Dean told her, pleased to see his mother attentive to his every word. "The only reason we're using them is that Doc, Dad and J.B. found one. And unlike most people who ever found them, they don't just loot them. They're interested in working out how to use the mat-trans."

"The what?"

Dean smiled. "That's the really great part. The mat-trans is how we travel. It's an old comp system that kind of breaks you up into little bits, then shoots you across Deathlands to another chamber where you get put back together again. Of course, it's a bit more complex than that."

Sharona shook her head. "Those whitecoats before the nukecaust sure were sick bastards."

"I don't know," Dean said, his face falling. "It's not so bad."

Seeing how her son was crestfallen, Sharona added

quickly, "Well, I guess it depends how you use it. I mean, if you can use it to go where you want…"

Dean grimaced. "I didn't exactly say that." And when she gave him a questioning gaze, he continued. "The thing is, it's kind of random. We know how to trigger it, but there aren't any manuals or instructions for how to get past the sec codes in the comps to programme a destination, and they have this random setting where every time you trigger the chamber, it'll send you a different place. If I could work out the sec fail-safe, then we'd really be able to use it for wherever we want. But now it's kind of wherever it sends us."

"So you don't actually know where you're going."

"No," he admitted.

"And you couldn't replicate a jump from here?"

"No," he said, a little puzzled. "But why would you want to?"

"I didn't say you would. I was just pointing out that mebbe you need to do a little more work on this old tech. And mebbe your dad doesn't really give you that time."

"What do you mean?" Dean queried.

Sharona shrugged. "Well, it seems like he's always keen to move on all the time. Mebbe it wouldn't hurt just to stand still for a while. That's what I'd like—a chance to stay and just get to know you again."

"But you'll get to know me the longer you stay with us," Dean said in a tone of voice that indicated he thought it was obvious.

Sharona grimaced. "I really don't know if I can travel with you."

Dean was shocked. "But you said—"

"I know what I said, but the truth of the matter is that I just can't see me getting on with your father or with Krysty. They're suspicious of me, and mebbe they're right to be. After all, they've been looking after you for one hell of a time, and where have I been?"

"But that wasn't your fault!"

"Doesn't matter. It's not a question of fault. It's just a fact that they've been there and I haven't. Which means that I resent them for that, even though it's not something they did on purpose, and they resent me for suddenly appearing, even though I didn't plan it this way. That's just the way it is."

"Yeah, I guess so," Dean said softly. "I just figured everyone would be as pleased as I was."

"Never mind." Sharona ruffled his hair. "Sometimes things just don't go as you planned them. You should know that by now!"

"Guess not. So what do you want to see next?" he added in a bright voice, trying to change the subject.

"I don't know. You decide," his mother replied.

Dean took Sharona by the hand and led her out of the mat-trans control room, not noticing the way she looked back over her shoulder with a thoughtful expression.

"IT DOESN'T MATTER what you say, we have to move sooner or later," Ryan said in an exasperated voice. "Fireblast and fuck it, haven't you listened to a thing anyone has said?"

"Yeah, I've listened, and it doesn't make a whole lot of sense, if you ask me," Sharona snapped. "For someone who's a leader, you don't have much in the way of ideas, do you?"

The companions and Sharona were gathered in one of the old briefing rooms. By J.B. and Ryan's chrons as well as those in the redoubt, it was midafternoon, but in the disorienting environment of the redoubt, where light was controlled by the flick of a switch, it could have been any time. And it felt like any time as once again Ryan's attempts to marshal forces and move on were being interrupted by Sharona.

The redoubt had been thoroughly investigated, and although the air conditioning and electrical plant were in good order, and would keep going indefinitely, there was little doubt that the supplies were limited. Food and self-heats were in sufficient quantity to sustain the companions for a couple of weeks and then leave nothing to carry away with them, or they could be used as traveling supplies if the companions began their journey immediately. The med bay had been stripped of anything useful by Mildred and deposited in a satchel she had found, and the armory used by J.B. to replenish their supplies of ammo, plas ex and grens. Beyond that, there was nothing left in the redoubt that was of much use. Old vid machines could have taught them something about the redoubt base and the surrounding area, if not for the fact that all the tapes remaining were sec camera recordings, showing nothing but an empty base.

So it wasn't just the pressing matter of the supplies that prompted Ryan to suggest a move from the redoubt—boredom was also a factor. And, if he was truly honest with himself, he didn't feel comfortable about how much Dean was sticking to Sharona. It felt as if he were losing his son again, and the longer they rested in the redoubt, the more of the boy she could steal. At least if they were on the move, they would be operating as a unit.

But when he had called them together and suggested the move, Sharona had been immediately divisive. Of course there was no plan beyond making a jump; how could there be? Everyone knew that you couldn't plan for what you didn't know, simply from experience. But Sharona wouldn't allow for that.

The thing Ryan couldn't decide was whether she was doing it to be deliberately destructive or whether she just didn't understand. He looked around at the others, hoping someone else would take up his argument, so that it wouldn't seem to be a mother-father divide to Dean, which he suspected was part of her point.

His glance around the room spurred Mildred to speak.

"I think it's really unfair of you to say that about Ryan's abilities as leader," she began, picking her words carefully so as not to appear hostile. "There can never be an advanced plan when making a mat-trans jump, and the proof of a leader is in the ability to marshal forces and think on your feet when problems arise. And I guess the proof of Ryan's ability to do that is that we're all still here, aren't we?"

There was a murmur of agreement.

"But why do we have to put ourselves in that situation?" Sharona continued. "Why didn't we just go along with the Pilatans?"

"Because we have to follow our star, somewhere

over the rainbow," Doc said sagely, giving a glimmer of meaning to words that had Sharona looking puzzled. He continued. "Until we find our dream, that is."

"Crazy words, but right," Jak agreed. "Look for something never find with Pilatans."

"But there must be a better way of doing it than risking our lives every time you use that damn machine," Sharona said in exasperation.

"How?" J.B. asked reasonably. "How else can we cover such distances with such speed?"

"Well, who says you have to cover the distances at all, especially when you don't know where you're going. And it's not just your lives you're risking, it's my son's," she added, storming out of the room.

Dean shot an accusatory glance at the rest of them as he followed, to calm his mother.

Krysty screwed up her face. "Well, that went well. You know, I really don't think she wants to get along with us."

Mildred shook her head. "I'd figure it's more definite than that—and we should keep an eye on the bitch."

"DEAN, WAKE UP. Quickly."

The words were urgently whispered and accompanied by a shake on the shoulder that jolted the youth from slumber. Blearily he looked up and saw his mother standing over him and looking scared.

"Wha...what's the matter?" he asked in a sleep-slurred voice as he sat upright.

"I think we've got a problem," she whispered urgently by way of reply. "I don't think you're the only ones who've managed to work out how to use the mat-trans. I was down there, and I heard it in operation."

"Hot pipe! I know we've come across others who can, but what were you doing down there?" he asked suddenly, realizing the strangeness of the situation.

"I couldn't sleep. I was just wandering. I think I went down there because I could feel there was something wrong, I don't know."

Thoughts raced through Dean's mind. Maybe she did go down there because she could feel something. And there were others, as they well knew, who could use the mat-trans. The odds against two sets of travelers ending up in the same redoubt were huge, but not impossible. So if that had happened, then he'd better get the others.

Dean struggled out of bed, flung on his clothes and checked his Browning Hi-Power.

"Come on, hurry up," Sharona whispered from the doorway.

"Better wake up the others," Dean said, still not completely awake—otherwise he would have wondered why his mother was whispering when she could have awakened the others with a shout. They were on another level to the mat-trans and there was little chance of alerting any intruders to their presence from here.

"Do you really need them?" Sharona asked. "By the time we've roused them all it could be too late. Besides, I'm sure you don't need them. We've got the element of surprise."

Dean furrowed his brow. That was true, he guessed. They should be able to outfight any opposing forces if they got them trapped in the mat-trans chamber.

And it would give him a chance to prove himself to his mother.

Dean followed Sharona to the elevator, waiting beside her in silence until it reached the level of the mattrans chamber. He could think of nothing to say, still trying to clear his head of sleep.

They came out of the elevator and made their way to the comp room swiftly, using the buttresses on the corridor walls for cover. Dean could hear nothing that would indicate any intruders, but he just figured that whoever they were, they had not, as yet, left the anteroom. If they were anything like the companions, they would be taking this slowly.

That would mean time for Sharona and himself to mount an attack.

They reached the door to the comp room, which was open. Sharona made to move forward and recce the room, but was stayed by a gesture from Dean.

"I'll check—cover me," he mouthed.

Heart thumping as the adrenaline kicked into his system, Dean moved across to the doorway and risked a look inside the room. It was quiet and seemingly empty—but he could see through to the anteroom and noted the door of the chamber was ajar. It was possible that the intruders were still in the chamber itself.

He backed away so that he could speak to Sharona. He took command, and was glad to do so, as it was a way of showing his mother how much he had developed since they were last together.

"There's no one visible in the comp room or anteroom—they must still be in the chamber. We'll move in, me first, and use the comp consoles for cover. Make our way around so that we flank the chamber. Then you cover me while I take it."

"You sure about this?" Sharona asked.

Dean wasn't sure how to answer. He could see a mixture of emotions in her eyes. On the one hand, she didn't want him to risk his life, but on the other she was proud of the man, and the warrior, that he had become.

"Yeah, I'm sure. Let's do it," he said firmly.

Dean entered the room first, using a comp terminal to shield himself while his mother covered him from the door. Then she entered, covered by the Browning Hi-Power. In this way, they made their way toward the chamber and its open door.

Now flanking the chamber, Dean looked across at his mother, nodding curtly as he made the last move. While she covered him, he kicked the door fully open, so that the backswing would immobilize anyone behind the door, and entered the chamber, finger poised on the trigger.

The chamber was empty.

"There's no one—" he began, turning as Sharona entered the chamber.

She swung the door shut before he had a chance to register what was going on. The lock clicked softly, triggering the mat-trans process. The disks on the floor began to glow and a mist rose in vaporous streamers around them.

"What are you—" he began, but was cut short by Sharona.

"I'm sorry, baby. It's the only way I can do this," she said, shaking her head, tears rolling down her cheeks. "Forgive me. It'll be for the best, you'll see."

Dean didn't have time to fully assimilate what was happening before the rapidly accelerating mat-trans process made him feel light-headed and sick.

His last thought as he began to black out was that there had to have been another way.

"RYAN!" KRYSTY YELLED as she jolted awake. Her dreams had become nightmares and she had a sense of foreboding.

The one-eyed man sat bolt upright, and looked at her.

"What?" he snapped, concerned.

Krysty looked at him. "It's Dean. And it's something bad," she said quickly. "I don't know what, but—"

"Nothing would surprise me about Sharona," Ryan said curtly as he got out of bed and pulled on his clothes. "I'm going to check on them."

Krysty was dressed by the time he returned and his expression did little to allay her sense of dread.

"They're not in their room. I'll wake the others."

Ryan roused the rest of the companions and, in varying states of wakefulness, they turned out from their dorms. He explained briefly, as Krysty emerged into the corridor, and was about to split them into pairs for a search, when the woman broke into his instructions.

"No need. I think I know."

In truth, Ryan had already guessed but didn't want to admit it to himself as the companions followed Krysty to the gateway.

The mat-trans chamber itself was still glowing slightly.

"Dark night, why would she do that?" J.B. asked. "And why would Dean go with her?"

Mildred shrugged. "She might have tricked him."

"Or perhaps the boy had made a decision to go with his mother," Doc said sadly.

Jak shook his head. "Not without telling us."

Krysty agreed. "Whatever Dean had decided, if it was entirely his choice, he would have talked to us about it. It just doesn't feel right, not this way."

"It doesn't matter," Ryan croaked in a harsh, broken tone. "Whatever happened, Dean must have told her about the last-destination button and the time restriction.

"The bitch knows we can't follow her. I've lost him."

Stony Man is deployed against an armed
invasion on American soil...

# ROLLING THUNDER

The Basque Liberation Movement, a militant splinter cell of
Spain's notorious ETA terrorist group, has seized a state-of-the-
art new supertank equipped with nuclear firing capabilities. The
BLM has planned a devastating show of force at a NATO
conference in Barcelona. As Stony Man's cybernetics team
works feverishly to track the terrorists, the commandos of Able
Team and Phoenix Force hit the ground running. But a clever,
resourceful enemy remains one step ahead, in a race against
the odds getting worse by the minute....

# STONY MAN®

*Available
August 2004
at your favorite
retail outlet.*

Or order your copy now by sending your name, address, zip or postal code, along with
a check or money order (please do not send cash) for $6.50 for each book ordered
($7.99 in Canada), plus 75¢ postage and handling ($1.00 in Canada), payable to Gold
Eagle Books, to:

| **In the U.S.** | **In Canada** |
|---|---|
| Gold Eagle Books | Gold Eagle Books |
| 3010 Walden Avenue | P.O. Box 636 |
| P.O. Box 9077 | Fort Erie, Ontario |
| Buffalo, NY 14269-9077 | L2A 5X3 |

Please specify book title with your order.
Canadian residents add applicable federal and provincial taxes.

GOLD
EAGLE®

GSM72

# TAKE 'EM FREE

## 2 action-packed novels plus a mystery bonus

## NO RISK

### NO OBLIGATION TO BUY

# James Axler
# Outlanders®

## MASK OF THE SPHINX

Harnessing the secrets of selective mutation, the psionic abilities of its nobility and benevolent rule of a fair queen, the city-kingdom of Aten remains insular, but safe. Now, Aten faces a desperate fight for survival—a battle that will lure Kane and his companions into the conflict, where a deadly alliance with the Imperator to hunt out the dark forces of treason could put the Cerberus warriors one step closer to their goal of saving humanity...or damn them, and their dreams, to the desert dust.

*Available August 2004 at your favorite retail outlet.*